Three Fat Singletons

J M Bartholomew

Dear Susie

I have loved spending
time with you. looking
forward to getting to
know you better ".

With much love

Joe

ACKNOWLEDGEMENTS

Maria; without your support 12 years ago I would never have continued writing. You picked me up when I most needed it and gave me the idea to write a comedy. I hope you enjoy it! Thank you xx

Glenys; through it all you have been there, good, bad and downright ugly. I will always cherish our friendship.

David; without you in my life there would be no sun. Thank you for all your encouragement and for putting up with me! Without your support I would not have been able to have the freedom and space required to finish this book. Your faith in me is really something to behold. You are a blessing to me and your children.

Faith; you are my joy. I will love you for all eternity.

CHAPTER 1

Jesse lunged for the phone in the hope it might stop the ringing in her head.

'Yeah,' she answered sleepily.

'Hi babe, it's me! You said give you a call and I didn't want to wait. What're you up to this afternoon?' Jesse found herself distracted by Chloe, her three year old Rottweiler, who was happily chewing the solid dry skin off Dotty's feet. It was nauseating, but it made for strangely compelling viewing.

Babe? She pulled at her memory – who was this chirpy guy who had the audacity to call her *babe*? She opted for honesty.

'I have a hangover.'

'How about I come and pick you up at two o'clock and we go out?'

She was getting a vague memory of a nice-looking bloke with blond hair who had been talking to her in the nightclub. She couldn't remember much but found an excitement building in the pit of her stomach which could only mean he was worth a second visit. Trying to sound a bit more energised, Jesse said 'Sounds good, let me give you the address.'

'You told me last night, Worple Road, I know where it is. See you at two, babe,' he said then hung up. Although she could remember he was good-looking, a PE instructor or something similar, therefore presumably with a good body, she was irritated by the babe remarks. Still, she could put a stop to that at two o'clock; she was a lot of things, but she was no man's *babe*.

'Dotty, do you have to let Chloe do that? It really turns my stomach. You really should go to a chiropodist and get your feet sorted, they're disgusting.'

With a look of pure pleasure on her face Dotty replied, 'My feet are too bad to go to a chiropodist. I'd have to sort them out myself first and I haven't actually seen my feet since 1986!'

Jesse giggled. 'You may not be able to see your feet but it doesn't stop you picking your manky toenails and flicking them on my bloody carpet. Chloe! Stop that now!'

Dotty pouted. 'Spoilsport. Make us a cup of Earl Grey, love.'

'On the provision that you tell me what you remember about that bloke I was with last night,' moaned Jesse. While Jesse was in the kitchen searching for a cup that wasn't chipped - Dotty was particular about some things - Dotty told her that her date's name was Richard and he was indeed a good catch - funny, good-looking, athletic, had lots of money and a great car.

Jesse was in high spirits as she sunk into her bath of Radox and Bergamot oil, sipping her tea followed by an aspirin chaser and a Berkeley Menthol cigarette. Dotty on the other hand was downstairs watching *Hollyoaks* with a look of pure glee on her face, not just because Chloe had returned to her feet and was now licking in between her toes, but because of the web of little white lies she had woven to Jesse.

'God forgive me,' she prayed under her breath while rolling a Cadbury Creme Egg around her lips, getting ready to dig her tongue into the delicious yellow and white goo. Had Jesse seen the smug look on Dotty's face she would have realised there was going to be a problem with her date.

Unfortunately, she hadn't.

****

Dotty raced into the kitchen when the doorbell rang at five to two, as she would never have been able to control herself if she'd seen the look on Jesse's face when she answered the door to Richard. Jesse had been sitting on the bed in her bedroom for ten minutes waiting for Richard to arrive. She wouldn't have it look as if she was ready and waiting for a man if he came calling, so she came skipping down the stairs at the sound of the bell, shouting 'Hang on!' She grabbed her leather jacket from behind the door and swung the front door open to reveal a rather chubby-looking, short, ginger-haired boy with a childish grin on his face. She took in his fluffy chin, lifeless eyes, wonky teeth, big ears and too-large gold necklace and still managed to smile politely and say, 'Hi Richard.' The door closed heavily behind her, and she left her good spirits inside as she walked to his battered Suzuki Vitara jeep. When he got straight into the driver's seat, instead of opening her door for her, Jesse erased the first of his performance brownie points from her mental checklist. Putting on her seatbelt, she asked, 'Where are we going, then?'

'I don't know. Where do you want to go?'

A look of irritation flicked across her face as she said, 'You were the one who asked me out. I thought you might've thought where you were going to take me before picking me up.'

Sensing her irritation Richard said 'Let's see where the car takes us!' If Richard thought this act of spontaneity was going to impress her, he was wrong and she erased a couple more brownie points from her list. When he got on the M25, Jesse was curious - until he went only one junction and arrived on a road that led to Windsor. Jesse noted that he could have chopped ten minutes off the time if he'd gone through Staines Town Centre and across the bridge, but decided to keep quiet; she wasn't sure whether she was grumpy because of his inability to be original or because of her hangover.

It was a truly beautiful day. The air was crisp and the blue sky was clear of clouds, and being a Sunday there was little traffic on the roads. She was not at all surprised when Richard swung the jeep into the Harvester - it was the most unimaginative place he could possibly have taken her, and on a Sunday the place would be full of children. She ordered a Diet Coke and didn't offer to split the bill.

Richard guided her to a table at the back of the restaurant. Jesse decided she would sit near the wall on a bench, thinking Richard would sit opposite.

He didn't. As he snuggled in next to her she could smell garlic on his breath and she tried to turn her grimace into a smile.

'So, tell me about yourself, Richard.' Jesse hadn't been on a date for eighteen months and had no idea of dating etiquette, so she decided to let him bore her about his cricket, the pupils to whom he taught PE, the rugby club of which he was a member and his golf handicap. She managed to look interested while tuning out completely and saying, 'Oh really, mmm, uh hu, right' whenever he paused for garlic breath. Jesse was wishing she had never answered the phone that morning and imagined herself now curled up on the sofa with Dotty eating HobNobs and watching *Hollyoaks* instead of being tortured with boredom by Tricky Dicky. He had been saying something about how close he was to his family, his father especially, when Jesse tuned back in.

'What about your mum and dad?' Richard asked - his first question to her since sitting down. She seized her moment to frighten him off.

'My mum and dad have been divorced for five years, actually. Dad's a drug smuggler and is serving year two of a six-year stretch. He was caught in Spain with two million pounds' worth of cocaine. Can you believe that? My dad! Anyway, obviously Mum left him. She's out of hospital now but still has to go to AA meetings every week. I've been taking rage counselling ever since but I've nearly got it under control now.'

Richard looked shocked and his next question was to be expected.

'So, what do you do for a living?' A complete change of subject.

'Actually I'm a singer.' This wasn't exactly the truth. It was what she hoped she could earn a living doing whenever her CD fell into the lap of an A&R man who actually had some vision. 'I've just cut my demo CD and am in the process of sending it out.' This did get a reaction.

'Wow, that's great! Bloody hell, you make me feel really boring compared to you.'

'Mmm,' was all Jesse could manage.

'So you're going to be famous, then. Wow!'

'Hopefully. Who knows?'

'I'll have a famous girlfriend, then, wow!'

You wish, you bloody bore, fuck off and die. Jesse smiled sweetly and kept her lips tightly closed.

'What do you want to do now, then?'

Jesse wanted to go straight home, but felt it wasn't fair. She couldn't have lived with herself if she'd made him feel bad. They had been out for less than an hour so she said 'Fancy a quick walk down the river?'

'Sounds romantic!' said Richard with a rather toothy leer, downing his Coke in one mouthful he said, 'I'll be back in a minute, I need to use the shitter,' and got up, leaving Jesse choking on her lemon. As they crossed the road to the riverbank, Jesse realised she had made a mistake in suggesting a walk, not only because he had grabbed her hand and was swinging it wildly backwards and forwards but also because there were very few people around and lots of bushes. Jesse didn't pause for breath for a full fifteen minutes, striding purposefully down the riverbank, hoping the chat would distract him from his quest, which was very obviously trying to find a quiet moment for a quick snog. Every time someone walked past and got a decent distance behind them, Richard would stop and look both ways as if checking the coast was clear. One thing Jesse made transparent as soon as they reached the riverbank was she absolutely hated public shows of affection. Every time he stopped, Jesse would exclaim, 'Oh, look at that swan...boat....flower...' while violently removing her hand from his and striding on at speed. Jesse was quite pleased with herself for managing the whole half hour round trip with only having to hold his hand, and was pleasantly surprised when Richard came to her door first rather than his own when they returned to the jeep.

As he opened her door with one hand, he

grabbed her breast with the other and lunged at her face, his tongue visibly protruding out before making contact with Jesse's clenched lips. Pushing him away with disgust, she ranted.

'I'm sorry Richard, I don't know what kind of tart you think I am but I'm not the sort of woman that goes in for kissing on a first date!' This of course was a lie - had he been anywhere near good-looking she would have been incredibly disappointed had they not ended the afternoon with a passionate grope.

'God! I'm really sorry babe, I didn't mean to overstep the mark. After last night I didn't think you'd mind me kissing you.'

'Last night I was pissed as a fart, as I'm sure you were aware. I'm not like that normally, really. I'm sorry to have shouted but you took me by surprise and I like to take things slowly. All right?'

'No problem.'

'Good. Shall we go, then?'

'Sure.'

Jesse flashed him an innocent smile before turning around and stepping up into the jeep. As much as she couldn't stand the guy, it was not possible for her to be openly rude to him. Apart from the fact that she hated any kind of confrontation, she was at least five miles from home in the middle of nowhere and needed the lift - she tried her utmost never to walk anywhere. They drove back to Jesse's two-bedroomed semi in silence. He walked her to her door, gave her a peck on the cheek and said he'd call in the morning.

That was the last Richard ever saw of Jesse.

CHAPTER 2

Eighteen months!

Jesse had been sitting in her car trying to get over Staines Bridge for nearly twenty minutes, contemplating her love life. Or rather, the great gaping void where her love life should have been. She had been single for coming up to two years and it had been over eight months since that riverside disaster.

Unbelievable. I have not had sex in over eighteen months! What the hell is going on here?

Wanting to share her distress, she punched Dotty's telephone number into her mobile phone and as soon as Dotty answered, she said,

'It's been eighteen months since I've had sex! What's that all about, Dotty? I can't believe it. I knew it'd been a while but eighteen months! What am I going to do?'

'Darling, I haven't had sex for seven *years*, so I'm not in a position to dish out much sympathy here.'

'It's not the same, though,' Jesse whinged.

'Why, might I ask, is it not the same?'

Jesse suddenly had to think fast - she realised she'd hit a sore point and needed to be tactful with her friend.

'You don't believe in sex before marriage, Dotty. That's why *you* haven't had sex.' Jesse let out a silent breath, pleased with her own quick thinking.

'You're right of course, but if I *did* believe in sex before marriage, I still wouldn't have had any opportunity in the last seven years.'

'That's only because God knows that's your decision and He... erm... isn't giving you temptation. If you were happy to have sex before marriage, you'd be presented with lots of opportunities, I'm sure.' Jesse felt uncomfortable saying the word God out loud, but it sometimes got her out of sticky situations with Dotty. She had no idea how it worked with God and temptation but had to divert attention away from Dotty and back onto her own desperate situation.

'Anyway, what about me? Me! Me! Me! I'm going to seal up if I'm not careful!'

'For heaven's sake, just get yourself a vibrator like everybody else.'

'Oh, I've got one, but I don't use it very often. Angie bought me it for my thirtieth last year but it's supposed to be a G-Spot one and it has this kind of... weird... hook thing on the end of it, so if it turns inside you it feels like it's coming out of your arse.'

'Oh, yuk!' Jesse could visualise Dotty's look of distaste and it brought a smile.

'Have you seen *Sex In The City*?' asked Dotty, recovering quickly.

Or changing the subject, thought Jesse.

'What does that have to do with anything?' she said, slightly distracted by the business of looking in the window of every passing car in case there was a breathing man in it that looked half decent.

'They're forever talking about this vibrator called *The Rabbit.* It has a really long willy and little balls in the bottom that turn around and it has a thumb for... well, you know.'

'No, what do you mean?' Jesse giggled. Dotty could talk intimately about boobs and fannies but could not even say the word 'bottom' without pulling a funny face.

'Jesse! You know what it's for! Anyway, I got one a few weeks ago and it's great.'

'You got a vibrator? Really? I don't believe it. Where from?'

'A sex shop in Soho.'

'You went into a sex shop?' Jesse's mouth hung open in shock. She knew Dotty had never had sex, so the idea that she might actually have a libido that needed exercising came as a complete surprise.

'Yeah. So?'

'I'm just surprised, that's all.'

'Actually I did say I was looking for a present for a hen night.'

'Aha! Great excuse.'

'I thought so.'

'So why didn't you get me one, might I ask?'

'I think I might've been pushing my alibi if I'd asked for two, don't you?'

Dotty was glad she wasn't having this conversation in person as she could feel her cheeks getting warm.

'Oh Dotty, please get me one. Please.'

'No way.'

'Pleeeease.'

'No. You can always ring up and order one and get it delivered.'

'Yeah, right! I actually speak to my postman on a daily basis, you know. You can guarantee it's got *vibrator* in great big letters all over the very obvious brown paper packaging. I'd never be able to look him in the eye again!'

'Don't be so bloody dramatic. It's probably wrapped in cellophane so you can see it clear enough that it doesn't need to be announced in writing!'

'Hardy har. Look, Dotty, gotta go, I'm in danger of getting into third gear. I'll call you later.' Without waiting for a response, Jesse hung up and sneaked past the traffic lights, which had just turned from amber to red. Making her way steadily home, she spent the next ten minutes trying to figure out how to get hold of The Rabbit without causing herself any embarrassment.

She popped home to walk Chloe, then got back in the car for the drive over to Mary's house in Feltham for their traditional Saturday afternoon chat over coffee and digestives.

As Jesse pulled off the A30 heading towards Feltham, she had a moment of inspiration. She would indeed order The Rabbit - but she'd order one for Mary too. Jesse bit her lower lip, giggling to herself, visualising Mary opening the unexpected package.

She could clearly imagine the horror on Mary's face once she realised what she held in her hands and Jesse wrangled with her conscience for a little while before concluding she had no choice but to order one for Mary too. Jesse and Mary were tired of their zero sex life so it was the act of a good and true friend to relieve their frustration, if not their situations.

Knowing Mary would probably be scrubbing her hands for several minutes after opening her gift did nothing to change Jesse's decision.

***

Dotty listened to the distant wail of a siren as she dunked her Dairy Milk into a mug of hot chocolate and pondered her recent visit to Soho.

Dotty never once entertained the idea of sex outside of marriage but she was prepared to push those boundaries as far as she could. She'd found herself wanting *more* recently, and was getting more and more frustrated, physically and emotionally. She passed the Easy Rider sex shop every morning on her way to work but had never really paid much attention; until she discovered *Sex In The City*. The cartoon bubble announcing they sold The Rabbit didn't mean they were now selling bunnies after all. Today the sign took on a whole new meaning and she was intrigued, and sorely tempted. As the day wore on, she found she couldn't think of much else so at lunchtime, rather than head to Dunkin' Donuts for her usual box of mini doughnuts she headed to the Easy Rider.

Dotty walked past the entrance three times before mustering the courage to walk into the shop. The red strips of plastic dangling from the doorway obscured the view and she was terrified of what might lay inside the shop. She had read the odd Mills & Boon story and knew that there was more to sex than the missionary position, but her imagination now conjured up pictures of dominatrices and bondage and she was half expecting someone in a black mask with a zipper mouth to be at the counter.

Furtively checking over her shoulder to ensure no work colleagues were near, she forced herself to enter and stepped over the threshold. Her senses were assaulted with the strong sweet smell of vanilla, not what she was expecting at all. She spotted the saleswoman behind the counter and was relieved to see she was wearing a black jumper rather than a mask and showed no interest in stopping the conversation she was having on the phone, simply nodding to Dotty as she entered.

This was definitely the strangest place Dotty had ever found herself. The lingerie section at the front of the store was delicate and seductive, and Dotty only wished they had her size. Dotty knew not to even touch any of the hangers as nowhere other than a specialist shop sold bras big enough to wrap around Dotty's huge frame. She gave a wistful sigh as she passed the satin and silk knickers and couldn't resist running her fingers along a lacy balconette bra.

As she made her way further into the store the silk and satin changed to black and red lace and eventually crotch and nipple-less items were on display. Feeling a little embarrassed but determined she wasn't going to leave empty-handed, she made her way to the back of the store where she had spotted the word *Toys* lit in pink neon.

Dotty inadvertently knocked a whip off a display stand with her backside as she squeezed herself past two rails of clothing. Holding the whip now in her hand, not sure where it had fallen from, she caught her reflection in the mirror behind the shelf and was mortified at what she saw. She could only see half her body reflected, but her face was pink, lit with neon and her beige bra stood out clearly through her white blouse, which was slightly dishevelled from wading past the narrow rails of bras. The image of herself holding the black whip in her hand, its leather strips dangling across her hand and reaching the floor next to her green sandals, was intriguing. Would a day come where she would ever brandish a whip with her husband? She bloomin' well hoped so.

Making a space for the whip among the many gadgets on display, she found her hand resting on The Rabbit. Heat flooded her face immediately and without reading or discovering what she was about to buy, she hurried it to the counter and dropped it in front of the sales assistant as if it carried the plague. Dotty repeatedly checked her handbag on her journey back to work, paranoid that anyone would know what she had just bought. She couldn't resist going straight to the toilets to read the details of her new toy. She wasn't sure about the smaller rubber pointy thing but the coloured beads were a nice touch she thought - useless probably, but pretty.

Later that night she found out that the red, white and blue beads did indeed have a purpose - and a jolly nice one too.

***

CHAPTER 3

For Mary, this was no ordinary Saturday. Rick Astley was in town. He was drop-dead gorgeous and she just had to see him. She crept out of the house while her mother was preparing dinner and ran down the street, got on a bus and then onto a tube and joined the masses in Leicester Square screaming for her idol until her throat hurt. She did manage to see his hand waving in the air but never managed to get a glimpse of his beautiful face. Still, it had been worth it. She'd been in the presence of her beloved and she had enjoyed every squashed and sweaty hour spent among his throng of fans. All the way home she'd daydreamed about being in his arms, calling him Rickie and cooking him homemade lasagne, right until she entered the two-bedroomed maisonette shared by her family of five.

She turned to shut the front door when she felt the sting of the wooden spoon hit the back of her left thigh.

'Mama!' She didn't need to see who was brandishing the weapon. Her father would be upstairs in the bedroom, praying for her safe arrival. Mary bitterly regretted borrowing her sister's white miniskirt -

she been in her usual jeans she would hardly have felt the continuous sting of the spoon. Her mother screamed in Italian until her face turned almost blue. When she ran out of steam she let Mary retreat to her bedroom, where she cried standing up, hugging the wall where Rick Astley looked out from one of her many posters.

She was lying on her stomach still gently crying, more from humiliation than pain now, when her father knocked and entered her room. Coming across to the bed, he perched on the edge and told her how she had been a naughty girl and she should never worry her mother like that again, but he was sorry she was hit with the spoon. Then he handed her a Mars Bar and left. After nibbling the chocolate from around the edge she started to suck the toffee and decided to never upset her mother or father again.

She kept her word.

Her parents had left England to retire to their home town of Naples three years ago now, but still Mary missed them. She spent three weeks with them each Christmas. They would eat two three or four-course meals every day and sleep every afternoon between four and six to recharge their bodies for the evening session. Her father would still sneak her a chocolate bar from time to time and Mary found this very endearing, although her mother clucked her tongue in disapproval. Her parents had grown old very gently but they now both looked like cute grandparents, as opposed to her parents, and this brought out Mary's protective nature. She missed looking after them as much as they missed nurturing their unmarried daughter. They worried about her constantly and this brought its own kind of guilt.

They hated the fact that their youngest daughter, now thirty-six years old, lived alone in a large three-bedroomed house with no man to look after her. Mary was an independent woman with a good job. She was in business travel and travelled all over the world, but they still wanted her to get married and give them at least one grandchild before they died. Every Saturday her mother called her at six pm to catch up on the gossip and every time she would ask if Mary had met anybody yet and time and again Mary had to respond, 'No, Mama.'

It wasn't that she didn't want a man in her life, she just didn't want *any* old man. She wanted to find the love of her life and anything less wasn't worth the hassle, as far as she was concerned.

There had been a time, over ten years ago now, when Mary had believed she might have found *the one*. She had been visiting Greece with her friend Heidi when she met Grigor. He owned a small bar in Kardamena, near Kos. Their chemistry was electric on first glimpse. Grigor's stare was intense and Mary could feel his eyes burning into her body all evening. Heidi was oblivious to Mary's shaking hand as she worked her way through a packet of twenty Marlboro Lights in only two hours, trying to concentrate on her friend's conversation but really wanting to grab Grigor and take him to the nearest hotel and devour him. It had taken four nights of being propped up at the end of Grigor's bar before she got her wish.

By this time Heidi was more than aware of her friend's feelings for the dark rugged Greek. In fact, Heidi was so fed up of hearing his name that she began tuning out of most of their conversations, as somehow or other it would end up getting back to 'Grigor this' and 'Grigor that.' Heidi was bored with the bar and, quite frankly, the giggling company of Grigor and Mary, so she had decided to get an early night.

Mary never touched a drop of alcohol at home, but something about Greece, or maybe Grigor, had made her drink far too many vodkas and she was seeing double. She thought nothing of Grigor shutting the bar and escorting her to the nearest hotel and booking them into a room.

The next few hours went by in a pleasurable blur. Mary was drunk but she was also very happy to have Grigor kissing her all over. He spoke her name over and over again while touching her in places she had never dreamed would bring so much pleasure. She awoke a few hours later, alone. She had a raging headache and felt sore all over and although she couldn't remember quite what had happened that night, she knew she had enjoyed it. Walking through the hotel reception at six am was not quite as easy as when she had walked in the previous evening. She felt all the staff glaring at her and was sure she had heard the receptionist say 'Tart' as she passed by. By the time she reached her apartment she was in tears.

Heidi was sleeping when Mary barged into the apartment and purposefully slammed the door.

'Mary, what on earth is the matter? What happened?' said Heidi, rubbing her eyes and reaching for her glasses.

'How could you leave me with him, Heidi? He could have been a murderer or something. He just left me in the hotel room on my own. He just had sex with me and then left. God! It was so embarrassing. Everyone looked at me as if I'd booked into the room for sex or something. It was so degrading...and I don't know why but my back is really bloody sore.' Mary lifted off the shirt that she had woken up in and turned her back to Heidi.

'Holy cow! What the hell did you get up to last night, girl? Your back! Your bloody back!'

'What? What?!' screamed Mary in panic as she ran to the bathroom to get a look at herself. Looking over her shoulder into the mirror, she was horrified but also rather proud of the wild sexy side of her personality that had allowed herself to be bitten all over. She had large purple-black love bites on her arms, back and bum, and plenty of them.

'Did it hurt?' asked Heidi.

'It can't have done or surely I wouldn't have

allowed it,' said Mary, sounding not at all sure.

'You don't remember?'

'Of course I do! Well, not specific details but I know it was good.'

'So good he left you there this morning?' Mary wanted to rip Heidi's arched eyebrow right off her face.

Sitting on the toilet five minutes later, she was horrified to realise Grigor had very obviously not used a condom. She didn't know anything about the man with whom she'd spent the night. What if he was one of these blokes who had a new girl every two weeks?

'Heidi! Heidi!' Mary staggered out of the bathroom with a look of horror on her face that truly frightened her friend.

'What?!' shrieked Heidi, bouncing off the bed.

'What if he's given me something? What if I've caught something from him? What if he's given me VD or crabs or AIDS! AIDS! My mum will kill me... oh God, my mum will really kill me, Heidi.' Mary slumped on the edge of the bed and started crying again.

'Oh come on Mary, what are the chances of you catching AIDS?'

'Bloody a lot, I'm sure!' wailed Mary.

'Look, Mary, in terms of percentages it really is unlikely. You're far more likely to have caught crabs or VD or Chlamydia or Herpes or...'

'All right, all right, you don't need to spell it out, I get the picture. I'll have to go to the doctor as soon as we get back. How bloody embarrassing. Why me?'

'Why not you? All you've done is what thousands of desperate women do each year - shag a local while on holiday. It happens all the time. You're not the only one, you know?' Heidi was apparently trying to make Mary feel better, but the desperate comment hadn't gone unnoticed.

The rest of the day dragged for Mary. She was far too embarrassed to show her proofs of passion by wearing her bikini to the pool. So instead she sat on her pool-facing balcony trying to read a trashy novel all day while occasionally hearing Heidi's laughter over the sound of the pop music blaring from the small poolside bar. She watched the hands on her watch tick slowly until they reached seven pm - opening time at Grigor's.

'Are you sure you don't want me to come with you?'

'No thanks. I want to see what he's got to say for himself and if you're there he might not want to speak to me. Do I look all right?'

'You look fine. I'm not sure about the toothpaste around your neck, though, Mary. Why don't you just leave them visible? I think they look a tad more noticeable now.'

'Are you sure you never packed a scarf?'

'Er... *quite* sure, darling, it's 90 degrees out there!'

'Yeah, me neither. Never mind.' Mary tipped her nose to the sky and said, 'Okay, I won't be long,' and strode purposefully out of the room, giving Heidi a chance to get to the mirror and preen herself.

When Mary walked into the bar, she couldn't see Grigor.

'Hi Costa, vodka and tonic please. No Grigor yet?' She managed to sound nonchalant.

'Not yet. He always spend Sunday with his wife and children. He don't get here until around eight.'

Mary hid the impact of his words well.

'I didn't realise Grigor was married. He never said anything,' she said, trying to control the acid simmering in her stomach.

'Yes, with two little boys. Loves his boys. Very special to him.' Mary got the message loud and clear, not by what he said but the way he looked apologetic and didn't look her in the eyes. Mary had not anticipated drinking alone. She had wanted a showdown so she drank her vodka quickly, said she'd be back, and went to get Heidi.

After much discussion, Mary decided it best to forget Grigor and spend her last two evenings in Greece giving Heidi her full attention. They ate in a lively taverna to the right of their hotel, had a brandy in the hotel lobby and had an early night.

Monday was their last full day so they spent it on the beach rather than poolside. Mary wasn't sure whether Grigor would come looking for her or not, and she could not decide whether she wanted him to, but she had decided she would be found far easier at the pool than the beach.

After a lazy day of sunbathing they went to the local nightspot for their last evening. They took their time getting their hair and make-up done. Heidi needed some help as she hadn't yet invested in a pair of contact lenses and her blue eye shadow was reminiscent of a Sindy doll until Mary came to her aid. They both wore black dresses with strappy heels and handbags barely big enough to fit their cigarettes in. Both women carried their lipsticks tucked into their bras for emergency use and both applied *Romance* by Ralph Lauren a little too liberally. They entered the hotel lobby looking rather sexy with broad smiles on their faces, which were instantly wiped off when they saw Grigor sitting at the lobby bar, obviously waiting for Mary.

'Heidi, why don't you take a seat here and I'll get us some drinks,' said Mary, leading her friend to two comfortable sofas within earshot of where Grigor was sitting at the bar. 'Vodka and tonic?' She turned her back to Grigor and mouthed the word 'fuck!' to Heidi, then placed a smile on her face and walked towards the bar.

'Hi Grigor, how are you? Two vodka and tonics, please.' Mary watched the barman pour their drinks as if he was the most interesting thing she had ever seen, while Grigor looked on in silence. After she'd paid she said, 'Thank you. See you later Grigor,' and returned to Heidi. As their table was so close to the bar, Mary and Heidi communicated via arched eyebrows, rolling of eyes and discreet hand movements. In less than a minute, Heidi conveyed to Mary via a nod that Grigor was looking directly at the back of her head and Mary indicated with a gentle shake of her wrist with her thumb and middle finger pressed together in her lap that Grigor was a wanker. It took all of two minutes for Heidi to finish her vodka.

'Do you fancy another drink here or shall we go straight to the club?' said Heidi, already standing with her empty glass in her hand.

'I don't mind, actually. Do you fancy another drink here?' said Mary casually while flicking her eyes from Heidi to her glass indicating that she definitely wanted another drink here.

'Might as well have one more here,' smiled Heidi. As Heidi approached the bar, Grigor left his seat and made his way to where Mary was waiting.

'Hello Mary. Have you enjoyed your time in Greece?' asked Grigor, pulling a chair close to where Mary was seated.

'Most of it,' smiled Mary. Grigor looked uncomfortable. 'I was hoping to spend some more time with you before you left but I think maybe I have upset you.'

'Upset me? Why on earth would I be upset?'

'Costa told you about my children. I should have told you myself.'

'Costa told me about your children and he also told me about your wife.' Mary had dropped the smile and was now glaring at the man sitting opposite her.

'Yes, I am married but it is not what you think.' He reached for her hand but Mary snatched it away and folded her arms across her chest defensively.

'Oh, let me guess, your wife doesn't understand you, you only stay with her for the sake of the children and you sleep in different rooms?'

'Yes. You are right. I stay because I love my children. My children are very happy now. Why would I want to upset them by leaving their mother?'

'Look, it's none of my business,' said Mary, gathering her cigarettes and lighter and standing up, 'All I'm saying is you should have told me you were married because I would never have slept with you - ever.'

'This is why I did not tell you,' said Grigor with a shrug of his shoulders. Mary's eyes widened in disbelief.

'You bastard!' She turned but had taken only two paces towards the bar when Grigor grabbed the top of her arm and swung her around to face him. His face was contorted in anger and Mary thought he was going to shout at her, but instead he pulled her onto her toes and kissed her forcefully. She had never been kissed like that in her life. He kissed her with such passion that she completely forgot where she was and had it lasted a moment longer, she might have cried with emotion. He gently released his hold of her arms and kissed her softly on the lips one more time.

'Mary, please stay with me tonight. You are

very, very special to me.' He paused for a moment before whispering, 'I have fallen in love with you.' Even though she felt consumed by passion, Mary had always been ruled by her head and not her heart. So she took a moment to catch her breath before responding.

'Sorry, Grigor. I don't sleep with married men. Goodbye.' As she ran out of the hotel towards the street, she could hear him calling after her, 'Mary! Mary! Please, Mary!' He caught Heidi by the arm as she rushed to follow her friend and without looking at him she shook herself free and shouted, 'Fuck off!' before leaving the lobby.

Mary spent the entire evening crying. Heidi spent it trying to get both of them really drunk in a half-empty bar they found at the end of the strip.

'Oh Heidi, he said he loved me!' Mary wailed for the umpteenth time since entering the bar.

'That's what men do when they want to get laid,' Heidi said bitterly.

'But he sounded genuine. What if he meant it?'

'What if he did? What can you do about it? He's married, Mary. Married. With kids, and you're going home tomorrow. There's nothing you can do about it.'

Mary was quiet for a while before she said, 'I could stay.'

'What?'

'I could stay. I could get a job out here.'

'Doing what, for heaven's sake?' Heidi looked at

her friend in disbelief.

'I'm a travel exec, I speak two languages. I could get work in a hotel.'

'You speak Italian, not Greek, and anyway you can't give up your job in England to become a receptionist in some piss-pot town in Greece. It's ridiculous!'

'It's not ridiculous, Heidi. I think I love him.'

'Right, you're drunk. Let's go back to the hotel.' Heidi sounded angry now.

'I'm not drunk! Okay, I am drunk, but I'm being serious. I think I love him.'

'You think you love him? You've known him all of one week. You've spent one night together, to say nothing about the fact he conveniently forgot to mention he has a wife and two kids. Mary, wake up to yourself. You don't even know the man. You're not in love. You just had sex for the first time in bloody ages and you're in lust!'

'But I've never felt this way before. The way he kissed me, it was so beautiful. I've never, ever, been kissed like that before in my life. I felt like he really wanted me, Heidi.'

'I'm sure he did. He wanted to have sex with you before waving you off at the airport!'

'Do you really think so?' Mary looked pleadingly at Heidi for answers. Heidi held her friend's hand and softened her tone. 'I really don't know, sweetie. But I think you would be silly to give up everything you have at home just to be a mistress to some Greek you've only just met. He's already told you he has no intention of leaving his wife so what can he possibly offer you?'

'Well, we spent nearly the entire week with him and saw him every night. It was only Sunday that he was with her.'

'You honestly think you'd be happy sharing a man with another woman? You know you'd be miserable, Mary.'

'It might work.'.

'Look, I don't want to be mean or anything but he said he wanted to spend the night with you. He didn't say he wanted to spend the rest of his life with you. He didn't even mention having a relationship with you.'

'I didn't give him much of a chance though, did I?' Mary lit a cigarette from the one she was smoking and exhaled loudly.

'Look, Mary, it's nearly one o'clock, we've got six hours until we get on the coach and we haven't even packed. I think we should go back to the hotel and get some sleep.'

'You go back. I'm going to go to the bar and see if I can speak to Grigor. I'll never know if I don't at least speak to him.'

'Oh for heaven's sake, Mary, you really are a pain. Come on, I'll walk with you.' Heidi downed her drink and helped Mary out of her seat, and they started a slow walk down the strip.

The air was warm and a faint breeze touched their bare shoulders as they walked arm in arm. Even in the distance they could see the neon lights were not flashing and the windows were black. But still they continued until they stood facing the locked doors of the bar.

They sat down on the sandy pavement and Heidi lit them both a cigarette. They sat in silence forming smoke rings in the air until Mary whispered, 'Let's go home.'

***

Ten years on, sitting alone in her three-bed semi in Feltham, Mary found herself thinking about Grigor again. The fact that Grigor was married was what had ended their brief romance. However, since that time Mary had had affairs with a travel agent called John, a minister called Saeed and a booking agent called Justin - all of whom had been married and whom she'd *known* were married before getting involved. She had not loved any of them and even the sex had been just about average.

Mary returned to the fridge for the third time in almost an hour. She knew she shouldn't have bought the Nutella at Tesco that afternoon. But she was hormonal, and when nearing her period she didn't deny herself anything, which allowed her to feel supremely guilty for the rest of the following week and therefore justify her severe mood swings.

She was far too comfy on her cream sofa with

matching blanket tucked under her size four feet to be getting up every ten minutes to raid the fridge. She got a silver teaspoon, the now half-empty jar of Nutella and some Italian Morello cherry chocolates that her mother had given her at Christmas, and continued to watch *You've Got Mail* for the third time that month on Sky, while spooning the spread direct from the jar. Just before Tom Hanks finally kissed Meg Ryan she turned off the television. She emptied the bin, which only contained the jar of Nutella and an empty chocolate box, wiped and then polished the draining board and fluffed up the sofa cushions before retiring to her bedroom.

She put her bedroom television on timer and curled up in bed waiting for sleep.

A typical Saturday night.

CHAPTER 4

After parking her brand new Volkswagen Beetle
directly outside the living room window of Mary's
house, Jesse beeped her horn to alert Mary to open the
front door. As the door opened, she jumped out of the
car and sprinted to her friend's house, holding her
laptop above her head as shelter from the storm.

'Hi honey, how're you doing?'

'Fine thanks. It's bloody freezing out there.'
Jesse gave Mary a kiss on both cheeks before handing
her the laptop and taking off her boots in the hallway.
Jesse had known Mary for seven years now and didn't
need to be reminded to take her shoes off when
entering her home. Showing off her clean white socks,
Jesse stepped from the plastic runner in the hallway to
the lush green carpet in the lounge. As usual, the
lounge smelled of potpourri - citrus today - and was
immaculate.

Jesse headed straight to her usual position on
the dining room chair nearest the patio window. Jesse
liked this seat as it was directly opposite the kitchen,
which was always gleaming and a pleasure to look at,
and because she couldn't bear to watch Mary fluff up

her sofa after she had sat on it. Today there was another reason for sitting at the table - Jesse had bought a chocolate cake which she intended to finish off with several cups of coffee and she couldn't trust herself not to get chocolate bits on the cream sofa.

'Coffee?'

'Does the Pope wear a silly hat?'

'Canderel or sugar?'

'Canderel, please. Do you want to bother getting plates for this cake?'

'You didn't intend to eat it all in one go, did you?' Mary's left eyebrow was raised in anticipation.

'I suppose not.'

'I'll get some plates, then. What did you get up to yesterday?' asked Mary.

'The usual. Actually, tell a lie, I went to Annie's.'

'Oh right, how is she?' Mary had already separated the large cake into four equal pieces and was finding it hard to speak with her mouth full.

'She's fine. I got the usual lecture about not getting out enough.'

'What did she recommend this time?' Mary couldn't help but smile. Annie was a long-standing friend of Jesse's and was most concerned by the fact she had been single for so long. She was well-meaning but as she'd been married for many years, she'd forgotten how hard it was to meet people, especially when you had the added complication of being large.

Jesse had introduced Annie to her future husband and Annie was the only one Jesse confided in. Annie had never told a soul about Jesse's affair with the company director or her affair with the fifty year old IT guy, or the fact that she was cheating on both men with the chief barman in her parents' pub.

When Jesse worked in the city she'd had lots of colleagues and acquaintances and was the life and soul of the party, but since she'd started working from home she had remained friends only with Annie.

Annie was always giving suggestions to Jesse on how to get out of the house and sometimes Jesse would take her ideas on board, but more often than not they ended in disaster. One idea had been to join a line-dancing class. As Jesse hardly did anything without Mary, they had both gone along on a Wednesday night to see what it was all about. Out of the fifty or so people who were there, only two were men, one was at least sixty years old and the other's Stetson was broader than his shoulders. They had enjoyed the music but it soon became obvious that Mary had two left feet and absolutely no coordination or rhythm whatsoever. After only two dances, Jesse's face was so red with exertion that she got several worrying glances from other dancers.

Mary fared far better in the Spanish evening classes, although once Jesse realised there was homework involved, she never returned after lesson two, leaving Mary no choice but to give up as Jesse had provided the ride. They both enjoyed the pottery class but as there were no men present, the fact that it clashed with EastEnders was enough of an excuse to give up. 'Actually she gave me the number of some club called Entertaining London. Apparently it's a club for single people but is aimed at going out and having fun rather than finding a man.'

'Mmm, sounds interesting. Are you going to join up?'

'Only if you do.'

'Oh Jesse, you know I can't.'

'Why not? You never leave this bloody house.'

'That's because I haven't got any money. How much is it?'

'It's £90 but you can pay £30 to go along to one event first before joining, so you've got nothing to lose. Dotty said she'd come along if we could organise it for a Friday night.' Jesse took a bite of her cake before adding, 'You can't say no because I've already bought us tickets.'

'What!'

'I knew you'd say no so I got the tickets already, so if you don't come along you'll have wasted £30.'

'Jesse, you know I can't afford £30 just to piss up the wall.'

'But I can. It'll be my treat. I've paid for all of us to go so there can be no arguing. We can all jump a cab together, I'll put it on my business account and we'll buy our own drinks when we get there. Diet Coke can only cost three quid, Mary, hardly expensive!' Jesse was being a bit bullish and she knew it, but when she wanted something she normally made sure she got it.

'I can't go. I've got nothing to wear.'

'Bullshit. You've got loads of clothes.'

'They're all for travelling. I've got nothing to go to a club in.'

'What about that pale blue shift dress with the long jacket, that's beautiful?'

'That's also too small to get over my thighs!'

'You only got that last summer, you haven't gained that much weight.'

'Oh yes I have. I'm nearly twelve stone now.' Mary sounded miserable.

'You really can't get it on?'

'Nope.' Mary started on her second piece of cake.

'What about that short red jacket and skirt, that's nice?'

'The skirt's too short and it shows all my cellulite.'

'Can't you wear the jacket with a black pair of trousers?'

'I suppose I could,' Mary admitted. 'I just bought a new black jumper actually that might be thin enough to go under the jacket.' Jesse was about to pull her up about the fact that she shouldn't be spending money on clothes if she was in so much debt but decided against it. 'There you go. No excuse now!

Friday it is.'

Mary had been defeated and could only smile at the way Jesse always managed to manipulate her so easily. She was in the kitchen making Jesse another coffee when she asked over her shoulder, 'Any news on the CD yet?'

'No. I got a few more rejection letters this week but I'm used to that now. I'm still sending out fourteen a day, every day, but I'm getting nothing back. I'm almost thinking of giving up on this singing lark.' Jesse's tone was upbeat but Mary knew her well enough to know she was feeling dejected.

'Don't be silly. It only takes one person to like it. I think it's great.'

'You're biased.'

'Obviously I'm biased but I wouldn't tell you it was good if it wasn't, would I?' They both knew this was a lie but Jesse said, 'I know you wouldn't. Thanks.' After finishing the cake, they both lit up cigarettes and listened to Westlife playing in the background. After a few minutes of quiet contemplation Jesse asked, 'I don't suppose you fancy going on holiday, do you?'

'I'm not sure. When were you thinking of?'

'I don't know. I was just thinking, neither of us ever leaves our houses or goes anywhere interesting and yet when we're on holiday we always have a really good laugh. I don't know about you but I could really do with a laugh right now.'

'Yeah, me too. Where were you thinking?'

'Greece, of course.' Ever since Jesse had got off a plane in Heraklion Airport at the age of twenty two she had never been to another country on holiday. She never went to the same resort twice but she insisted on Greece every time, no arguments. 'Do you think you could get us another cheap deal from work?'

'Probably, but it depends on when you wanted to go. I've got a lot of trips to do this year.'

'How about the second or third week in April. Are you around then?'

'I'll have a look.' Mary retrieved her calendar from the kitchen wall and sat back down. 'I'm doing China in March for three weeks, I've got a short hop to Amsterdam returning on 6th April and then South Africa on 22nd April so we could only do the 12th as we fly on a Thursday.'

'I haven't even printed off my work schedule yet so I'm sure I could do that. Do you fancy it?'

'If I can get it cheap enough, yes. It'll be a nice break between work trips. Is Dotty free?'

'I haven't asked her. I only just thought about it! We'll be giving her plenty of notice. So long as it doesn't cost more than three hundred I'm sure she'll be fine.'

'But she'll need spending money, though.'

'True, but you know what Dotty's like - she won't realise that until a week before she goes. She always manages to find the money somehow.'

'She's worse than I am when it comes to getting

in debt.'

'That's because Dotty lives in denial. She believes if she prays enough she'll win the lottery. I'm sure that's why she's so blasé about her debt. At least you try to pay your credit cards off. Dotty just keeps on spending.'

'Shall we call her and see if she wants to come?' Mary asked as she reached for her phone. Jesse could see the time on the oven clock from where she was sitting, 'Don't bother yet, she's at church until seven tonight.'

'Seven? But it's only three o'clock now.'

'You know what she's like. She does the morning stint and then she does that prayer group until the evening thingy.'

'I thought she did the prayer group in the week.'

'She does. That one's at her house, though. This one's at Rosie's house.'

'Who's Rosie?'

'Some other born-again she knows.' Jesse raised her eyebrows as Mary rolled her eyes. 'Actually,' said Jesse with a grin on her face, 'She's praying for me and you this week, all three of us in fact.' Mary looked horrified, 'What for?!'

'To help us lose our weight.'

Mary's expression slowly changed from one of horror to one of contemplation. 'I guess it can't harm. I could do with all the help I can get on that front.'

'You and me both, sweetie. You and me both.'

Jesse watched as Mary examined her diary intently. 'So how many weeks have we got and how much weight can we lose?' Mary looked up in surprise and smiled. 'You know me so well.'

CHAPTER 5

For Dotty this was no ordinary Sunday. She woke as usual to her flatmate screaming up the stairs.

'Dotty, I'm not going to tell you again. It's half past nine. You've got fifteen minutes to get yourself ready or I'm going without you!'

Dotty rolled off her mattress onto her knees and paused for breath. She had long given up on beds as they were far too difficult to get out of. So she opted for a mattress on the floor, which didn't look very appealing but was practical. Holding her hand against the wall for support she heaved herself off the floor and was relieved to find she had no back pain. She'd been going to an osteopath for nearly a year now but when push came to shove she knew she would never get relief unless she lost some of her weight.

Dotty's bedroom was a hideous mess. Clothes, make-up, music, shoes and chocolate wrappers were strewn across the floor. Although she was embarrassed enough to hang a sign on her door saying, 'If you enter you are dead', she never seemed to have the energy to actually clean up. After spending five minutes in the bathroom applying make-up and fixing her hair, she returned to her room and chose her outfit for the day: orange ankle-length dress printed with large yellow sunflowers, navy leggings underneath to stop her thighs from chaffing, red socks with fishes on, black Jesus sandals and an orange cardigan.

As she made her way down the stairs she saw Shelley stood by the open door - with a face like thunder. 'Morning, Shelley. Do I have time for a quick cuppa?'

'No! We're going to be late. Get your coat and let's go.'

Dotty hurried into her anorak while trotting down the hallway to the kitchen.

'What are you doing, Dotty?!' Shelley shouted.

'Keep your knickers on, I'm just grabbing some breakfast.' Dotty and Shelley shared the fridge but the top two shelves were Dotty's - one shelf for actual food and one for goodies. Without stopping to think, she grabbed a Mars Bar and a Double Decker, shut the fridge door and hurried back up the hallway where Shelly had her back to Dotty and was making her way out of the house. Keeping an eye on her flatmate's back, Dotty took a small amount of pleasure from sticking her fingers up several times while poking out her tongue.

It took Dotty fifteen minutes to get to church. As usual, she had timed it to perfection and managed to find a seat before the vicar took to the pulpit. She'd been suffering from a sore throat for a few days and had cancelled her regular solo piece, which enabled her to simply sit and enjoy the service instead of worrying until it was time for her set.

Dotty was a classically-trained opera singer and had travelled the world. She had set herself big ambitions with regards to her career and when the English National Opera had turned her down two years in a row, she had simply quit. She had loved singing but never imagined her weight would ever factor against her. She was a size twenty-six when she first joined Trinity College of Music at the age of twenty. Since the age of eight she had consistently gained at least one stone a year and moved up a dress size to accommodate.

It wasn't until she'd auditioned for the English National Opera that it was obvious there was going to be a problem. In order to be a solo performer she would need many costume changes and each of her outfits would have to be specially made as she was now a size thirty-two. An extremely thin man in his early fifties took Dotty aside and said if she lost two stones in weight he would take her on next year if she came back to audition.

A year later, exactly one month before her audition, Dotty went on a liquid diet and lost two stones. Unfortunately, the gentleman concerned considered two stones a lot and had obviously anticipated Dotty being a size eighteen when she returned - she was not.

The rejection had been too much for Dotty to shoulder.

Her parents had put her on a pedestal from a young child and when she fell off it this time, they disowned her. Dotty was constantly reminded of how much it cost to put her through Trinity College - how much they had *wasted* on her education. How disappointed they were that she had wasted all her opportunities. She was ashamed of her size and more so, her inability to do anything about it.

It was at this time she turned to Christianity, which she believed saved both her life and her sanity. It had taken two years of counselling for her to accept that she did have a great talent and that people could benefit from her gift and so she had offered to sing one Sunday morning at her church.

Dotty had practiced on the Saturday with the organist who, after practically falling over himself to congratulate Dotty, was sworn to silence. She had opted for the German version of *Ave Maria* and she'd sung it to perfection. Nearly everyone in the congregation had cried with the depth of emotion portrayed in her singing, and Dotty had felt happy to be alive for the first time in years. Since that Sunday she'd been voted in as head of the church music group and performed nearly every Sunday. But not today.

Today she sat and enjoyed the service before accompanying the vicar to the vicarage, where they enjoyed a traditional Sunday roast. She then met with the prayer group at Rosie's house, where they enjoyed three hours of praying followed by tea and biscuits, before walking back to the church for evensong. She arrived home at seven, made pasta and garlic bread for herself and Shelley. When Shelley left at eight pm to go visit her mother, Dotty made herself a pot of Earl Grey, arranged a saucer of ginger biscuits and seated herself comfortably on the lounge sofa before reaching for the phone.

She had placed an advert in the Talking Hearts section of the local newspaper and it had appeared in Wednesday's edition. She had not told a soul and had purposely waited until today to call for the replies, knowing this was the only day she would get the house to herself.

She let out a gasp of excitement when the recorded voice announced, 'You have four new messages.' She grabbed her pen and paper and prepared to write down all the names and numbers, stopping pen in air when she heard a deep Arab-sounding voice say, 'Hi, me name is Meck, I am very romantik and I love fat ladies... '. She pressed two to skip and move on. The second male had a strong Italian accent and sounded very phlegmy. 'My name is Ronaldo. I'm thirty four and am in London most weekends. I am Italian and I have Italian blood and looks. I am very romantic and would love for you to come to my flat...' She pressed two to skip. Message three: 'Hi. My name is Frank. I am six foot four so you should be at least five foot eight. I hope you are Rubenesque rather than rotund and I like a large hip and juicy inner thigh...' Skip.

By the time she got to the fourth message she was deflated. It took a moment for her to realise the fourth voice didn't sound like he headed the charts for Ten Most Wanted, then she actually warmed to his soft Scottish accent. 'Hi there. My name is Ron. I loved your advert. I thought it was very funny. Body of Dawn French, voice of an angel - that conjures up a lovely image. On your voice message you mentioned that you were a Christian, which is another reason why I had to respond. I used to be a vicar. I'm a journalist and broadcaster now but I have a degree in Divinity and it's still a large part of my life. Maybe we could have a cappuccino some time and have a wee chat about it. You did mention that you wanted someone aged between thirty and forty. I'm a little bit older than that, I'm afraid - I'm forty eight. Also, I wasn't sure whether you were joking when you said you wanted to meet a Brad Pitt lookalike but I'm hoping you were as I'm more reminiscent of Saint Nicholas! As you might've guessed, I'm from Scotland but I frequently come to London for work and would be honoured if you would meet with me. Please give me a call and we can have a wee chat. Thanks for listening. God be with you.' Dotty took down his number and listened to the message again to make sure she had got it right. 'Well! A vicar! How more Christian can you get?' she declared aloud while heading to the fridge for a slice of cheesecake.

After leaving a message on Ron's answerphone, Dotty put on an exercise video. Jesse had recommended Vanessa Feltz's video called *If I Can, You Can,* so she sat eating her cheesecake while watching Vanessa get sweaty and tried to gauge how much of it she might be able to manage. When her phone rang at half past nine she took a deep breath and said 'hello' in a deep, sexy voice.

'Oh, can I speak to Dotty please?' asked a confused Mary.

'Hi Mary. It's me.'

'Oh sorry, Dot, I didn't recognise you. Have you got a cold or something?'

'Er... yes, a bit of a sore throat, actually. What's up?' Dotty was in no mood to talk to Mary. She had no call waiting and Ron could be trying to get through.

'Nothing. Jesse was here earlier and we've decided to go to Greece again in April. Do you fancy it?'

'Er, yes, sounds great, e-mail me the details.' Dotty sounded impatient.

'Well, we don't know where we're going yet. I thought I'd pick up some brochures from work and we could choose a resort. Do you fancy coming over some time this week and we'll go through them?'

'Why don't you bring them with you to the club on Friday and I'll look at them over the weekend?' She had no intention of travelling on British Rail for two hours just to go through some brochures when she knew Jesse would end up choosing the resort anyway.

'Oh yeah, I forgot about Friday. I really don't fancy going to a singles club. It's not really me, is it? Did you know about it?'

'Not before Jesse had already bought the tickets. She didn't even ring to see if I was free.'

'Well, you know what she's like.'

'Yes, I know *exactly* what she's like. If Jesse wants, Jesse gets. She just clicks her fingers and expects us to drop everything and come running.'

'Oh come on, Dotty, she's not that bad.' Mary hated being critical of anyone and felt uncomfortable with the way the conversation was going. 'Anyway, a night in town might be fun. I haven't had a dance in ages.'

'I haven't been dancing since I split my skirt up to my waist doing the conga in Ritzy.' Wincing at the memory, she added 'And as if that wasn't mortifying enough, I had a hole in my pink waisty knickers.' Dotty was giggling at the memory, although it had taken her a long time to find it amusing. Mary on the other hand had no problem seeing the funny side and was laughing loudly down the earpiece.

'Blimey, that was so funny! Do you remember Jesse and I were rolling about on the seats laughing and you had no idea, you just carried on until the end of the song! Afterwards when you realised your bum was hanging out, you ran to the ladies so fast you fell over and those two bouncers had to help you up. Oh, it was so funny! I wish someone had taken a photo!'

'Well, as you know, I'm always happy to provide your entertainment, Mary.' Dotty was irritated that Mary was still laughing. 'Look Mary, sorry to cut you short but I'm expecting an important phone call so I have to go.'

Mary instantly stopped laughing and grew serious. 'I haven't upset you, have I, Dotty?'

'Don't be silly, I just need to get this call I'm expecting. I'm not upset.'

'Are you sure?'

'Positive.'

'Really?'

'Mary. I'm fine. Please. Forget it.'

'Only I couldn't bear it if I'd upset you.' Mary was on the verge of wailing now.

'Mary! I'm not upset. Honestly. Now bugger off and let me take this call. Okay?'

'Okay, if you're sure.'

'I'll call you in the week to arrange where to meet Friday.'

Having agreed their schedule, and with Dotty having assured Mary another twice that she was fine, she hung up and stared at the phone, willing it to ring again immediately.

***

She had waited by the phone until midnight in the hope that Ron would call, but he hadn't. The disappointment weighed heavy in her chest as she began to lock up the house ready for bed. She was embarrassed to have placed an ad looking for love but she had been without a partner for so many years the loneliness was sometimes overwhelming. She was the life and soul of any party, always first to laugh at herself, but recently she'd been feeling there wasn't much to laugh about. She was sick of being fat, miserable and lonely. Only Jesse understood the sadness she hid underneath her façade; many a night she had spent crying on the phone to her friend.

At exactly twelve o'clock she took a mug of Horlicks and a bar of Dairy Milk to her bedroom. As was her routine, she got herself settled on the mattress, lay on her back and put her hands together to pray. Her nightly prayers took her a long time as she couldn't bear to miss anyone out. She asked for good health for her mum, forgiveness for her dad, love for Mary and Jesse and support for anyone mentioned in her prayer group that week. She always ended her session with the Lord's Prayer, and not until she was convinced she had covered everyone would she whisper, 'Amen.'

Dotty spent a further five minutes dunking her Dairy Milk into her Horlicks before settling down on her stomach to fantasise about Ron. She had conveniently forgotten that he had mentioned Saint Nicholas in his ad and she imagined a famous, devastatingly good-looking anchorman for the Scottish nightly news. He was tall and dark with impressively white teeth, good skin and shoulder-length hair (she had developed a thing for long hair on men after watching *Robin of Sherwood* in her teens). He wore an expensive dark grey suit and crisp white shirt as he pulled up beside her in his black Jaguar. After handing her a red rose he scooped her up into his arms and carried her into her house, heading towards her bedroom where the four-poster bed was waiting for them. Dotty enjoyed her dreams more than her waking life sometimes; she dreamt in colour and they were vivid and she nearly always remembered them in the morning. She had a beautiful face anyway but in her dreams she had a beautiful face with a beautiful body to match and could seduce any man alive. In reality, however, the only things Dotty seduced were the English muffins she intended to scoff for her breakfast every morning. Those she could coax out of their cellophane wrappers practically with a come-hither look and a crook of the finger.

Before heading off to work she changed her answerphone message to include both her mobile and work numbers - just in case Handsome rang.

CHAPTER 6

No matter how hard she tried, Jesse had never managed to be on time for anything. If it had anything to do with business she was on the button - personal life, useless. It wasn't because she didn't try hard enough, it was because she tried too hard. It was such a rare occasion for Jesse to get out of the house that she always prepared her outfit and work schedule and bath times the day before so all she had to do was bathe and step into her clothes. Still she was late. She had pre-booked her cab the night before and taken the controller's advice about leaving a full hour before she had to arrive at Waterloo. Normally it took her just over one hour to get ready so she allowed herself two full hours so she could take her time applying her make-up.

She had just received her new Bobbi Brown pink glitter eye shadow via the post from Selfridges and was looking forward to trying it out. She wore her usual black bootleg trousers and boots with a low-cut black top, but the pièce de résistance was the pure silk overcoat she'd had made, which had arrived only that week. It was floor length with long sleeves and a very

59

large hood, which was trimmed in purple feathers. It started from the shoulders as a deep navy and ended in red at the bottom. The entire lining was painted vivid yellow and red and looked glorious when she walked and kicked the coat out with her legs. Jesse didn't even ask how much it was before deciding to have the dress and bag made to match.

By five o'clock her hair was fluffed, make-up applied, the dog had been fed and her handbag filled with powder, lipstick and condoms.

Ten minutes later the taxi was stuck in traffic on the way to Waterloo. She sent a text message to Dotty and Mary saying she would be fifteen minutes late and told them to change their destination from the clock at Waterloo to Costa Coffee. It was six thirty before she arrived at Waterloo to rapturous applause from Dotty and Mary, who were sipping cappuccinos on the concourse outside the coffee house.

'Hi guys, sorry I'm late. The traffic was bloody dreadful. Would you believe I left the house at five!'

'No!' they both echoed.

'I did! I promise.' Jesse grinned and gave them both a kiss on the cheek.

'Darling, you'll be late for your own funeral' smiled Dotty.

'Amen to that,' Jesse said kicking her bag under the small chrome table and pulling up a chair. 'Mary, you're wearing make-up. Your skin looks lovely, it really suits you.'

'Well, my spots are so bad now I needed something to cover it up. I'm sure it's those vitamin B capsules I'm taking but it's either bad skin or back to taking sedatives on the plane.'

'You're the only person I know who could actually choose a career as a travel exec and yet be terrified of flying! You are funny, Mary. Who do you have to shag to get a drink around here?!' Jesse yelled.

'Jesse!' Dotty hissed, 'It's self-service.'

'Well, I'm not drinking here again, then. Anyone want a top up?'

'No.'

'No thanks.'

'Fair enough, back in a min'.' Jesse got herself a large cappuccino and three chocolate brownie cookies before returning to the girls.

Dotty rubbed her hand up and down the arm of Jesse's new velvet coat. 'This is lovely, Jesse, where on earth did you get it?'

'Actually I only got it this week. I had it made specially. It looks like velvet but apparently it's made from pure silk. The underneath looks like silk, sure enough, but the outside, I'm not sure myself.'

'How much did that set you back?' Dotty asked with a raised eyebrow.

'Well, it did come with a matching silk dress and little dolly bag, so really it wasn't that expensive when you think about it. What about you? That's a lovely shirt you're wearing.'

'Thank you. How much was it, Jesse?!' Both Dotty and Mary knew it had to be expensive for Jesse to be evading the question.

'All right, it was just over five hundred quid. But I think it's worth it, don't you?'

'Well, it does look nice.' Actually it had cost over seven hundred pounds but Jesse couldn't admit to spending seven hundred on a summer coat that she would probably only ever wear once or twice, especially as both of her companions had serious money troubles.

'Have you not noticed Dotty's nails, Jesse?' Jesse turned her head to find Dotty proudly waving her fingers in front of her face.

'Blimey, Dotty! What are they?'

'Don't you like them?'

'Oh no, they're lovely. Just unusual, that's all.' Jesse looked at Mary for help but she appeared to be finding the bottom of her empty mug fascinating. 'I guess I'm surprised you'd paint them such a dramatic colour... especially when you haven't even got any nails.' Mary started to choke on her coffee and excused herself to the public toilets.

'Do you think they look awful?' Dotty was about to get in a strop.

'Honestly? Yes. They're dreadful. But hey, who gives a shit? Once they see you coming, your nails will be the last thing anyone cares about.'

'Meaning I'm such a fat bastard that there's no point in trying to make myself look good because no one will see past the fat?' Dotty raged.

'I didn't say that. I was going to say you are so bloody pretty that no one would care what your nails looked like. Jeez, Dotty, don't be so flaming sensitive.'

'I'm not being sensitive, I just thought that was what you were going to say,' said Dotty. Now it was Jesse's turn to get angry.

'Don't confuse me with a wanker, Dotty, I would never say something like that and you damn well know it. You really piss me off sometimes.' Jesse crossed her arms and pouted.

'Sorry, I didn't mean to overreact.' Dotty paused before sheepishly asking, 'Do you really think I'm pretty?'

'Oh dear, what's going on here?' asked Mary as she returned from the loo.

'For what it's worth, yes I do, and nothing is going on here so let's go.' And with that, Jesse was up and moving.

'What's the matter with her?' Mary asked, reaching for her briefcase. 'Don't worry about it, give her ten minutes and she'll be fine.'

'If she's not, I'm going home.'

'Yep, me too.' They arrived at the taxi rank just as Jesse was stepping into a black cab. 'The King's Head pub, Ludgate Circus, please.'

'Is that where we're going?' asked Mary.

'No, I just thought we'd see a couple of the sights first. Of course that's where we're going! We might be a bit late, though. It says seven o'clock on the tickets.'

'We don't have to do any of this sitting-around-a-table thing and then swapping partners, do we?' Mary whinged.

'Well, if we do we'll leave immediately and I'm not playing any stupid party games either.'

'I'm with you on that one, honey,' agreed Dotty.

'In fact, let's make a pact. Anything that doesn't involve food, drink or sex and we're gone.'

'I'm with you on the food and drink, but if they're having sex in there, I'm off,' added Dotty with a serious look on her face.

'If they're having sex in there I'm becoming a Gold Member!' laughed Jesse.

'How long should we give it until we leave?' asked Mary.

'For heaven's sake, Mary, we haven't even got there yet. Let's try and be positive here. You never know, you might actually enjoy yourself. Now there's a thought.'

'I was only asking,' said Mary defensively.

'All right, ladies, here we are, the King's Head,' said the driver.

After paying for the cab, the women stood on the busy pavement debating whether to go in. It looked innocent enough. Just like a normal pub, in fact. They huddled in a circle to block out the bitter wind and Jesse asked,

'What do we think, girls? Shall we go in or not?'

'Of course!' shouted Dotty above the sound of the traffic. 'I haven't had a boogie in ages. Come on, let's go and get a drink.'

It wasn't that strange, really. The only noticeable difference was a ridiculously bubbly, thin oriental lady at the door checking tickets and adding everyone that entered onto their mailing list. Most people must have come straight from work because the place was packed to capacity. As it took nearly ten minutes before they got served, they all ordered doubles and stood at the bar looking uncomfortable. Dotty and Jesse were great people watchers and took in the atmosphere around them. Mary was one of the most unobservant people either of them had ever met and had no idea she was already attracting attention from the opposite sex.

Mary was petite at five foot nothing with a straight brown shoulder-length bob and dark brown eyes to match. Even though she was a little bottom heavy, she had a fragile look about her that men loved. She had decided on the black trousers, red suede jacket and new black jumper with flat pumps. She had worn make-up for the first time in over a year and a thin silver choker adorned her neck. If it wasn't for the leather briefcase, you would have no idea she was a career woman.

Dotty had opted for a more casual look. She normally favoured Jesus sandals but tonight she had chosen a pair of men's black patent shoes that looked reasonably smart with her fake leather black pants. She wore a leopard print twin set with a black chiffon scarf tied neatly around her neck. Two pink glittery hair slides lifted her hair to reveal long drops of sparkly gems.

The three made an odd looking group. Mary was stylish, Dotty was slightly outrageous and Jesse looked a tad Gothic. They felt conspicuous standing by the bar but the vacant seats that were available didn't look strong enough to hold Dotty's weight.

Jesse paid for the next two rounds of doubles simply because she believed Mary didn't realise what she was drinking and wanted to get the girl tipsy. It was working. Mary was useless at holding her drink and when it came to the third drink she needed to sit down. Jesse did a scout around the pub and found a few tables with sturdy wooden seats around them and formed a plan. As soon as the food was unwrapped, they would make their way against the flow of people to the back of the pub where a table would be vacated. As it was Jesse's plan, and it worked, Dotty and Mary then had to fill up her plate while she saved the seats with a look of triumph on her face. She had a great vantage point of the whole pub. They were sitting next to the dance floor, but could see the entire length of the bar from where they were positioned.

By the time the two ladies arrived back with the food, Jesse had already decided there was no talent in the place whatsoever.

'What, none?' asked Dotty, craning her neck, searching the throngs of bodies for a looker.

'Not that I've seen. In fact, it's exactly as I imagined. No wonder they're all single, they all look like right sad bastards. I mean look at him, I wouldn't want to meet him in a dark alley, and that one there looks like he's stuck a whole packet of Rice Krispies on his face,' moaned Jesse.

'So what do you want to do, then?' Mary asked.

'Stuff our faces, get drunk and have a boogie.'

'Sounds good to me.'

CHAPTER 7

Mary was at first intrigued, then confused and horrified when she realised what she was looking at. She fumbled with the packaging to make sure there was no branding on the box and then sat down, relieved to find there was no advertising the fact that she had just had delivered not one but two vibrators. She double-checked the label. Yes, it was her exact address including postcode, and her surname had been spelled correctly. One of these monstrosities she could understand to be a prank, but why two? She was not surprise when the name Jesse popped into her head.

'Of course. Who else would it be? Very bloody funny. Ha bloody ha.' She took the unwanted package and put it on the coffee table, then examined the contents thoroughly while she raged at Jesse on the telephone.

'Jesse, it's Mary. I don't suppose you'd know anything about my receiving two vibrators this morning, would you?' Mary's tone was uncharacteristically fierce.

'Gosh, they took a long time to arrive, I ordered them weeks ago. Are they any good?'

'Are they any good? What the hell are you talking about? How should I know if they're any good or not?'

'You mean you haven't tried it out yet?'

'Of course not! I'm not going to either. Anyway why, might I ask, didn't you get it delivered to your house rather than mine?' Sarcasm was thick in Mary's voice but Jesse ignored it.

'I thought it would be nice for you to receive a gift in the post rather than me bringing it to you. I thought it would make it more special, that's all.' Jesse actually sounded sincere.

'Well, I don't want it. You'll have to give it to someone else.'

'Why don't you want it? You haven't even tried it out, for heaven's sake!'

'Look, it's bright pink with bobbles all over it and two willies. What am I supposed to do with the small one....' Jesse could almost hear the flash of recognition in Mary's head. 'Oh, I see. Blimey, that must be really painful. Have you actually tried this out, Jesse?' Mary's tone had gone down an octave.

'Actually no, but Dotty has. Dotty told me I should get one. She thinks they're great.'

'No! I don't believe it. Dotty? Are you sure?' Mary was gobsmacked and her jaw hung open waiting for Jesse's confirmation that their darling Dotty had used a ghastly vibrator.

'I'm telling you, Mary, she told me to get one.

Mary, are you still there?'

'Yes.' Mary sounded distracted.

'Look, why don't I leave it with you for a few days and see what you think? I'll pop over on Saturday to take you to Tesco if you like and I'll pick mine up then. If you don't want yours we'll just send it back.'

'There's no *we* in this, Jesse. You got it, you'll take it back.'

'Have it a few days and we'll see, okay?'

'I suppose so.' Mary sounded distracted and Jesse grinned, knowing Mary was likely to try out The Rabbit very soon. That brought a graphic image to her mind, making Jesse's cheeks burn with embarrassment. Shaking the image out of her head she said, 'All right, Mary. Gotta go. See you Saturday. Bye.'

CHAPTER 8

Jesse was forced awake by Chloe, who had jumped on her abdomen while getting onto the king size bed with her dirty rag of a sock held in her mouth, obviously wanting to play. Jesse kept her eyes closed and pulled the sock around for thirty seconds, mumbling encouraging sounds to Chloe, then turned on her side and tried to go back to sleep. Chloe was having none of it. After jumping around her side of the bed for a few minutes, tossing the sock into the air, she got bored and sat whimpering at the bedroom door, her way of announcing, 'You'd better get up because I need a wee'. When Jesse did nothing Chloe added a hint of a yowl, which translated roughly as 'Well all right, but don't blame me when your slippers are soggy'.

Jesse was ordinarily a very impatient person but astounded everyone with the patience she showed her dog. Obediently she got out of bed, put on her leopard print nightgown and headed downstairs to let Chloe out into the back garden. Putting the kettle on, she held her breath as she prepared Chloe's breakfast; low-fat biscuits with Chunky dog food. Today's flavour was rabbit and pasta and it turned Jesse's stomach. She took the red throw off the sofa, put it in the washing machine and replaced it with her pale green throw. Chloe had a hormone imbalance that meant she moulted every single day of the year. Jesse didn't mind, anything was acceptable when it came to her beautiful Rottweiler.

She made herself a cup of tea and sat on her white leather reclining chair (the only piece of furniture Chloe didn't share) debating whether to have a Slim-Fast milkshake or toast for breakfast. She opted for two slices of toast covered in smooth peanut butter with a banana in the middle, sprinkled with sugar, and a fresh cup of tea. By 8 am, she'd made herself another two slices of toast, this time with butter and honey spread, and then tried to distract herself by running a bath as the fridge was still wanting her attention. Their holiday was fast approaching and, as usual, Jesse had not managed to lose a single pound in weight. She had joined a gym before Christmas, but unfortunately, working out always left her famished, so in fact she'd put on half a stone. She'd left the gym pretty quickly – she couldn't afford to put weight on like that, not with the holiday coming up.

The previous night Jesse had gone through her wardrobe and put all the clothes she hadn't worn in over six months into two black plastic bags and left them outside to be picked up by the British Heart Foundation. She was now thoroughly fed up. There was only one item of clothing in her wardrobe that was under a size twenty, which was a floor-length black riding skirt in a size ten. And that was over ten years old now. Holding the skirt up to herself, the waist looked impossibly thin. She guessed it might do up around her inner thigh but decided not to try it just in case it didn't - there was only so much a girl could take.

This wardrobe-culling had become a six-monthly ritual. Jesse was not a shopaholic - she could go months without buying herself anything, but she had a habit of buying ill-fitting clothes out of desperation. Most of the clothes she had bagged for charity the day before had been last year's summer wardrobe, nearly her entire summer wardrobe, to be exact. She had bought several sleeveless tops which made her extremely self-conscious when she wore them. She had two pink T-shirts where the round collar almost choked her, along with two white muscle tops that made her look like a butch lesbian. She gave away three long tent-like dresses, none of which did her any favours, and a pair of white hipster jeans which, when she sat down, revealed her size twenty knickers. Her swimming costume was threadbare due to her mother putting it in the tumble drier when she'd visited earlier in the year and she couldn't find the bottom to her bikini, which was the only part of the bikini she actually wore because, fat or not, she lived with the hope that at some stage she might actually get undressed in front of a man and didn't want her rather large breasts showing ivory white triangles.

She did a tally of what she did have that was suitable for the holiday: two pairs of denim shorts; two black vests; two pairs of gingham capri pants; a pink blouse and a pair of flip flops. She could shop alone or call Mary; neither proposition thrilled her. When she shopped alone she bought disastrous items that she would never wear. When she shopped with Mary it meant trudging around all the shops that Jesse couldn't buy clothes in, such as Next and Principles, which made her feel like a fat frump. After five minutes' deliberation she called Mary - at least with Mary she would come away having bought something that might actually look nice.

When Mary heard Jesse's car horn she came skipping out of her house with her burglar alarm sounding behind her, dressed in her usual navy tracksuit and trainers. She always wore this outfit when she was in the mood for shopping. Jesse was wearing her leather boots with a four-inch heel and groaned at her own stupidity. She was going to be soaking her feet by the end of the day.

By four o'clock Jesse was feeling a mixture of resentment towards Mary's ability to shop in the best stores, guilt for the amount of money she had spent, in pain due to her boots and as attractive as a warthog.

Back at Mary's house, Mary made the coffee while Jesse got the receipts together. 'How come you always manage to get far more clothes than me and spend less?' accused Jesse.

'I didn't buy that much more,' said an apologetic Mary.

'No, just two pairs of trousers, one blouse and a pair of shoes.'

'But the shoes only cost me ten quid. How much were your sandals?'

'I don't know.' Jesse started flicking through the receipts. 'Oh well, there you go, my sandals were £50 and those sequined shoes were £80.'

'What about the ones from M&S?'

'I didn't buy....oh yes, I forgot about them. Er, £50 for the high-heeled ones with the black rose on and £65 for the strappy sandals. I'll have to send one of them back. I'm not spending that much money on bloody shoes. I didn't even need shoes. I still haven't got anywhere near enough clothes for Greece.'

'We've got nearly a month to go. The sales will be over soon and then you'll find something decent, you always do. If not, you can always go to Dawn French's shop up town.'

'Not after the last time. I don't mind spending money on clothes but £400 for a plain white blouse was ridiculous and I never wear it because it cost so much. How stupid is that?'

'You could have got a car for that,' said Mary, placing a packet of ginger nut biscuits on the table.

'No, *you* might have got a car for that. It's just not fair. Evans and Ann Harvey have the monopoly because they're the only ones that do bigger sizes so they can charge a fortune. They're all geared towards forty five to sixty five year olds....apart from the Seven range, but that is so outrageous...what's that look for?'

'You! You always get on your soapbox when you've been shopping.'

'Okay. Let's change the subject, then. Have you spoken to Dotty this week?'

'I spoke to her last Thursday. She wasn't very happy, actually.'

'Why? What's wrong?' Mary had Jesse's full attention. Jesse was fiercely protective of Dotty and if anyone upset her they would have Jesse to deal with.

'Oh, nothing's happened. It's just she's concerned that she's going to have a bad plane journey again. Apparently she looked in her diary from last year's holiday and she's gained ten pounds since.'

'Well, in that case I'm not sitting next to her this time. No friggin' way. If she can't get a grip on herself then I'm not going to pay for it. Last year was ridiculous. I was in agony for the whole flight. The lining in my jeans left an imprint on my legs for over two days. The fact that I had to sit with my elbow on her shoulder did me no favours either. She's known this holiday was coming and she knew how pissed off I was last year with it. Well, I tell you, no way, no bloody way.'

'I'll sit next to her, then.'

'Be my guest. I tell you another thing. If she's gained ten pounds since then she might not even fit in the seat.'

'I must admit,' Mary said sheepishly, 'she did mention she was concerned about that.'

'Well, I tell you, if we have to leave her stood on the tarmac then I'll do it.'

'Jesse, there's no need to be like that,' Mary scolded.

'Wait until you've done the journey and then tell me how I should and shouldn't be. You'll change your tune, I'll put my mortgage on it!'

They sat in silence for a while, dunking their biscuits into their tea. Jesse was obviously angry at the thought of another horrific plane journey, but Jesse also had a habit of snapping out of her moods very quickly. Mary waited to see if this was one of those days.

'So have you tried The Rabbit yet?' Jesse tried unsuccessfully to suppress a grin.

'No.'

'No?' Jesse's eyebrows were arched and gave Mary a look that said, 'I know you're lying now, come on, tell me all about it.'

'I haven't had time.'

'You've had weeks!' Jesse took a sip of her coffee and waited to see if Mary would respond. When Mary said nothing, Jesse admitted, 'I tried mine out'. Mary still said nothing. 'I thought it was quite good, actually. Far better than that G-Spot one.'

'How about we change the subject?' Mary gave Jesse a pointed look. Jesse took another mouthful of coffee and pondered Mary's lounge. 'What's missing in here? Have you moved things around?'

'No. The running machine has gone.'

'Where to?'

'I've dismantled it and put it in the garage. One of my workmates is going to come and collect it next week.'

'Oh, Mary! How many times did you actually use the bloody thing?' Jesse was incredulous that Mary had spent over £300 on a treadmill and in less than two months was giving it away.

'I only used it once or twice and it makes the lounge look untidy. You know what I'm like.'

'It's that bloody Biding TV. Please don't watch that thing anymore. You're always getting suckered into buying something and you know it's all crap.'

'Actually,' Mary said rather defensively, 'I bought a pair of sapphire earrings last week and they're lovely.'

'Let's have a look, then.'

Mary had a loving look on her face when she opened the soft grey pouch and produced a pair of fake sapphire and diamante earrings.

'They're not that bad really, are they?' Jesse was trying to be tactful, as she thought they were horrific and didn't feel the need to be brutally honest to Mary, who looked really pleased with them.

'I like them,' Mary said smugly, gently putting them back in their pouch where they would doubtless stay for a few years before she finally got around to giving them to one of her aunties as a Christmas present.

'Have you had a chance to look through the brochures I gave you on Greece?' Mary asked while making fresh coffee.

'Yes actually, I was thinking I quite liked the sound of Rethmynon in Crete. I've got it in my bag, actually.' Jesse fumbled around in her leather bag, pulling out empty Snickers and Flyte wrappers until she found the single page of the brochure she'd ripped out.

'Here it is. I liked the look of the Maria Apartments. They've got a two-bedroomed apartment with a pool and bar and it's an adult-only hotel.'

'That'll be a relief to Dotty.'

They both fell into silence for a moment, remembering their last holiday where Dotty was constantly heckled by the under-tens saying things like, 'Mummy, why is that lady so fat?' and, 'Mummy, look at that lady's feet.'

Unfortunately for Dotty she also got hassle from adults, both male and female, and it saddened their hearts to remember it.

They had become quite well-known by the poolside as they were constantly laughing and getting drunk and basically made for unusual viewing. One afternoon in particular was burned into Jesse's memory. They'd decided to head for the hills to walk among the olive groves to get a bit of exercise before arriving back to the apartment to join in the pre-arranged Barbeque Night. It was easily eighty degrees and the trek had taken over two hours to complete. All three returned huffing and puffing and sweating profusely. Walking past the pool bar en-route to their apartment, one of the Newcastle Wankers (a name the girls had given a group of three Geordie men who sat at the bar from 10 am and never had their football shirts off their backs) shouted, 'Don't worry if you smell bacon! It's only Dotty!'

None of the girls broke step and continued into their apartments as if nothing had been said. Before Mary had closed the door behind them, Dotty was reaching in the fridge for the Dairy Milk with tears already on her face. It only took five minutes of counselling, 'They're just wankers... abused children... shit for brains... ugly buggers... et cetera,' before Dotty stopped feeling sorry for herself and became violent.

Standing on the balcony overlooking the pool, Dotty stood with her hands on her hips and shouted at the top of her voice, 'Oi! Yes you, you ignorant shits, next time you've got something to say, say it to God first as He's the only one who can remove my fist from your fucking arsehole!' The entire area came to a hushed silence and several of the mothers around the pool looked astounded by her language. The bartender paled visibly and the Geordies stood in silence, not finding anything to say to the lunatic on the balcony.

Dotty turned triumphantly on her heel, strode

off the balcony and went straight to bed. The rest of the afternoon had been unbearably tense until a scream came from the bathroom where Dotty had been in quiet contemplation for over half an hour. Mary and Jesse had come running to investigate, throwing the toilet door open only to find the plastic toilet seat split in two on the floor and Dotty rubbing the side of her arse where the seat had pinched her bum after she'd shattered it.

The three girls looked at each other in sombre silence until Jesse let out a volcanic scream of laughter that broke the atmosphere. All three girls laughed uncontrollably - Mary's a silent open-mouthed tonsil display, Dotty a top-C scale and Jesse's intermittent donkey-like screams between breaths. Jesse was holding her crotch to stop herself from pissing her knickers while using the other hand to rummage through the beach bags to grab the camera for a photo opportunity that couldn't be wasted.

To date, that was the worst moment Jesse had experienced with Dotty and she tried wherever possible to foresee unnecessary pitfalls, hence the deliberate choice of an adult-only hotel.

'So what do you think? I thought it looked quite nice,' Jesse commented.

'Well, it's adult-only, has a bar, has a pool and it's a place we've never been before. I'll have a look in work tomorrow and see what I can do about the price and give you a call. Are you getting a new swimsuit this year?'

'If I can find one that fits, yes. I think I'm going to have to go uptown in the week and try the bigger shops. I'll see if Dotty can meet me for lunch or something. I haven't been shopping with Dotty for ages.'

Mary gave Jesse a rueful smile, 'Just remember to wear clean knickers and flat shoes.'

'Yes mum!'

CHAPTER 9

Jesse signed for her cab and entered All Bar One in Islington High Street at exactly one o'clock. The bar was packed to capacity and, after waiting for nearly five minutes to get served, she had to shout over the din to order her glass of Pinot Grigio. She had decided not to take Mary's advice on her choice of footwear and was already regretting having to stand on her black leather three-inch heels for what seemed like forever. There were no tables available so she propped herself up against a pillar in the centre of the room and tried not to look conspicuous. She reached into her suit jacket to get her mobile just as Dotty came bursting through the doors looking radiant.

'Hi darling, you're looking mighty fine.' Kissing Jesse on the cheek, she took in her nearly-empty glass and said, 'Ready for another one?'

'You'd better make it two. It'll take ages to get served,' Jesse grumbled, pissed off to have been kept waiting.

As soon as Dotty reached the bar she was greeted by a smiling bartender who took her order, recommending a bottle rather than two large glasses.

He swiftly put the wine into a cooler box and walked it to a free table that had become vacant only seconds before. Jesse was impressed by the personal service and Dotty looked most pleased with the attention. Raising her glass to Jesse, Dotty said, 'Cheers,' and took a gentle sip of the wine.

'Got any gossip,' Dotty enquired.

'Nope. You?' said Jesse, shaking her head.

Dotty spread her hands across her belly in a cat-who's-got-the-cream kind of manner and said, 'Well, seeing as you asked, yes I have, actually.'

'Don't say a word until I've lit my fag,' said Jesse excitedly, grabbing her rather expensive flip-top lighter. She hadn't seen Dotty this pleased with herself in ages and it was obvious a juicy tale was about to ensue.

Taking a sip of wine and a deep drag on her fag, Jesse nodded that she was ready.

'It's a long story so don't interrupt, okay?'

'Of course I won't. Get on with it,' beamed Jesse.

'Okay, you know I placed that ad in *Talking Hearts*? I got a response! He left a message on my answerphone last week and he sounded lovely. His name is Ron and he's Scottish.'

'Scottish? Oh bloody hell, Dotty, you'll never be able to understand him and they're all tight-arses and...'

'You said you wouldn't interrupt!'

Hands in the air, Jesse raised her eyebrows and made a zipping gesture over her lips.

'Okay. Like I said. He's Scottish. He has a degree in Divinity and...'

'Divinity! Oh, sorry. I'll shut up.'

'A degree in Divinity, he's a journalist and he sounds bloody fantastic. Anyway, I rang him back and left a message on his answerphone and he called me last night! Oh Jesse, we had a really long chat and he sounds lovely. He's coming to London next week and wants to meet me. This is the one, I can just feel it.' Dotty looked at Jesse, who was still sat in silence. 'Okay, you can talk now.'

'What does he look like?'

'He said he's quite tall, brown hair and nice teeth - and you know how important teeth are to me.'

'Yes I do, and I also know how important a six pack and drop-dead good looks are to you, too. I hope you're not expecting too much, Dotty.'

'Not really. He does have a really nice personality.'

'So did the last guy, but you didn't care a toss about that once you met him.'

'Oh come on, Jesse, that was different, he was bloody ugly.'

'From what I remember, you said he was an extremely intelligent guy who was a mountain tracker guide, loved children, wasn't a Christian but was open-minded about it and loved big women.'

'That's right,' Dotty said, knowing what was coming.

'I seem to remember you saying, "this could be the one" just a few hours before you met him.' Jesse was purposefully dragging out the detail of the event to make her point. 'He gave you flowers at the tube station. He even wore the yellow rose you insisted on so you could recognise him. He paid for dinner and escorted you home. Now, what was it you said about him?'

'Ugly fucker, I think.'

'Yup, I think that was it! So before you start building your hopes up again, Dotty, I recommend you take this Scottish guy off the pedestal you've put him on and try and be positive about things other than his looks.'

'I'm not only concerned about his looks, you know. He is really funny as well and that's important, right?'

'What did he say that was funny, then?' Jesse enquired.

'Well, I can't remember now, but I know I was laughing a lot. Anyway, I've agreed to meet him at Waterloo this Friday. He thought it was so funny when I said to him I'll be wearing a pea green jacket with a banana on my head!' Dotty started laughing so hard with the memory that she was attracting glances from the other tables.

'A banana on your head?'

'Well, I just said it for effect. Anyway it was funny. So what do you think I should do with him?'

Jesse gave Dotty a knowing smirk.

'You know what I mean! Should I offer to take him to dinner?'

'Absolutely not!' Jesse was outraged by her innocence. 'He's Scottish, for Christ sake! You have to find out if he's the stereotypical tight-arse and if you offer to pay for dinner, you'll never find out. No Dotty, don't even hint at paying for anything and see if he coughs up. You don't earn enough money to be supporting a scrounger, never mind a Scottish one that no-one will be able to understand.'

'I was thinking of suggesting the cinema...'

'Bad idea. If he's coming all the way down from Scotland, the least you can do is get to know him. You've got to make sure he can make conversation... plus you don't want to go groping in the back row until you know he's *the one.*'

Dotty detected the element of sarcasm in her friend's voice and smirked her own sarcastic response back. 'Well, I've decided, whether he's the one or not, I'm not placing any more ads.'

'I don't blame you, Dotty. I don't know how you do it. I couldn't for the life of me stand outside a tube station waiting for a complete stranger to come up to me and say, 'Hey babe.' You've got guts, I'll give you that.' Jesse genuinely didn't think that personal ads were the way to go but secretly envied Dotty's courage in meeting all these strangers. Jesse had placed her own ad just last week out of desperation, but hadn't even rung in for messages as she knew she'd never meet them through fear of rejection, and that she might meet the boogieman. Dotty had no sense of personal security and Jesse envied that, too.

'You'll have to text me as soon as you've met him and then call me as soon as he leaves.'

'Of course, darling, you'll be the first to know.' Dotty finished her wine and said, 'I don't know about you but I'm ready to shop! I've got to get a new bra for Friday, the one I've got is falling apart. I'm thinking black and red.' Dotty looked to Jesse for encouragement.

'Black and red sounds great, Dotty, but I'll be surprised if Evans do anything that sexy. Still, we'll have a look. I have to get a swimming costume and some T-shirts. No shoes, though. Please don't let me buy any more shoes.'

'You help me with the bra, I'll keep you from the shoes,' Dotty said, while struggling to get out of her seat.

'Deal!' said Jesse, waiting for Dotty to complete her ensemble by putting on the pink fluffy gloves to match her pink scarf and, to Jesse's horror, earmuffs.

CHAPTER 10

It was five minute past six when Jesse received her first text from Dotty, who had just met Ron underneath the Waterloo clock. The message read: 'He looks like Les flippin' Dawson, I shit u not. Gonna be a long night. I'll call u when I've got rid of him.' Although the description brought a smile to her face, Jesse felt disappointed for Dotty. She had been so obviously excited about meeting this guy and Jesse knew how desperate she was for him to be perfect. Les Dawson, my God. Did that mean fat or ugly - or both? Jesse forwarded the text message to Mary to keep her in the loop. Less than a minute later, Mary was on the phone.

'Ah, it doesn't sound good, does it?'

'Nope, poor cow.'

'I think we'd best meet up over the weekend and build her confidence back up, although I don't know quite what to say to her, really. I mean, how many has she met now?' asked Mary.

'Too many, as far as I'm concerned. It's not doing her ego any good and they're all butt ugly, according to Dotty. But buggered if I know where she can meet men, or should I say where *we* can meet men.'

'It's just a thought but a friend of one of my workmates is a bunny girl for a place called Big Ladies Paradise.'

'Big Ladies Paradise, what's that?' Jesse sounded dubious.

'It's a club for big ladies and men who only like big women. Apparently it's really positive and is packed with loads of members. They go to different bars each month so you'd have to ring up to find out when the next one is. You don't have to be a member and it's five pounds on the door. Why don't you mention it to Dotty?'

'I'm not sure. We'd have to go with her though.'

'Count me out, that last one was enough for me. I can't be bothered anymore. I'm going to wait for the holiday. I'll just make do with ogling Angelo on Saturday when he cuts my hair!' Mary'd been going to see Angelo for nearly two years and had developed a lingering infatuation, which was no great surprise as he really was gorgeous. They had been flirting outrageously for nearly six months now and it had become the highlight of Mary's month.

'Maybe you should let him know you're all on your lonesome this weekend. You never know, Mary, he might take the bait!' Jesse knew what was coming.

'Oh Jesse, you know he's married,' Mary whined.

'And?'

'And? And I'm sure he's not really interested in me anyway. I'm sure he's like that with all his customers, although I must admit, I think I'm the only one he kisses on the lips. I've only ever seen him kiss his other clients on the cheeks.' Mary sounded wistful and it made Jesse smile.

'I wouldn't mind kissing him on the cheeks either!'

'Oh Jesse, what are you like!'

'Desperate! Anyway, getting back to Dotty, don't mention this Paradise place. Let me investigate it first and then I'll see if it's suitable for us or not.'

'Okay. By the way, I can get the holiday for just under £300 when I take my discount off.'

'Excellent!' exclaimed Jesse. 'Book it.'

'I already have, honey. Call me later when you hear from Dotty, all right?'

'All right, take care.'

Jesse kept herself busy while waiting for the call by consulting her *Feng Shui Guide for Beginners*. By the time Dotty rang, Jesse had removed her bedside lamps and replaced them with red candles, put all the books from her shelf into her office, tidied up her junk cupboard, put her new red sheets on the bed and flowers in a jug. Sitting pride of place on her bedside table was a Chinese wishing bowl.

The previous week, her friend Gill had thrown a Balinese furniture party, which basically meant she filled her house with furniture and incense and gave everyone a glass of wine in the hope they would spend lots of money - and they did. Jesse'd bought a Balinese CD tower and the Chinese wishing bowl. Gill assured her that if she wrote on a piece of paper the one thing that she wanted most in the world and put it in the wishing bowl, it would come true. She had spent ages looking at her yellow Post-it note before simply writing *love*. As an added touch she gave the piece of paper a kiss before folding it gently and putting the lid on the bowl. She cleansed the entire house by walking from room to room using incense nuggets and playing loud music with all the windows open. She had been wanting to do this for two days but the book insisted it must not be even attempted unless it was a fine day - and today it was, at least in terms of the weather. As far as Jesse's mood was concerned, it was not fine at all.

For a moment after speaking to Mary, she had been looking forward to the holiday and then all the old memories came flooding back - the travel sickness, the diarrhoea, seating on the plane, the flight, inevitable cold sores, the bikini, the hangovers, finding clothes to fit and, worst of all, the possibility of not getting laid. For two years now Jesse had not had any action and it was getting her down. Jesse had become so fixated on the fact she was getting no sex that six months previous she'd thrown her old bed away, convinced it was jinxed. Since buying her new bed, specifically selected for the rails on the top and bottom of the headboards that would suit handcuffs perfectly, she had tried the personals, clubs, and now Feng Shui. Jesse was becoming embarrassed by her desperation to find a man, but could do nothing to stop herself. She had been living alone far longer than she'd ever anticipated and, as much as she hated to admit it, she was lonely and wanted someone to share her life with.

***

It was nearly eleven o'clock when Jesse's mobile went off.

'Hi Jesse, it's me!'

'Are you at home?' Jesse asked bluntly.

'Yes.'

'Right, give me fifteen seconds to get a fag and I'll call you back on the landline.' Jesse hung up and ran to the kitchen for the last dregs of her bottle of Pinot Grigio. She flicked the TV off, lit a menthol, took a sip of wine, curled up next to Chloe, who was gently snoring on the sofa, and dialled Dotty's number.

'Hello,' came the sombre voice of Dotty.

'Oh God, was he really that bad?' Jesse's tone was apologetic.

'Actually he was worse than bad, but that's not the problem.'

'Oh?'

'The problem is that, as repulsive as he was, and I mean he really was a Les Dawson lookalike, body as well as face, I ended up throwing myself at him.'

'What? Why? What are you talking about?' Jesse was incredulous. 'How the hell did you throw yourself at him if he looked like Les Dawson?'

'I know, I know! I don't know what came over me...'

'Desperation, obviously.' She snorted.

'Obviously. It was so strange, though, Jesse. I wanted to vomit, he was that disgusting to look at, and yet there was something about his voice that I found so sexy and he was so obviously chuffed to be with me.'

'I'm hardly surprised, Dotty. If he's that bad, imagine what he normally has on his arm.'

'But he made me feel great! He opened doors. He wasn't embarrassed to hold my hand...'

'Why should he be, for Christ's sake!'

'You know what it's like, Jesse. Most men are horrified to be seen with me, never mind seem pleased that they're with me. He was beaming. He kept saying how lucky he was and how God had looked down on him finally. He really was romantic.' There was a pregnant pause until Dotty filled it with a very quiet, 'We had a fondle in the back of a cab.'

'What! What do you mean fondle! In a cab? Dotty, are you mad? You need your head examining, darling. What were you thinking of?'

'I don't know, I really don't. I'm going to have to ask the prayer group to pray for me now. I do feel sick when I think about it, I really do. You know what the strange thing is? I'm desperate for him to call me.'

'Oh Dotty,' Jesse sighed, 'What are we going to do with you? I'm not sure whether to be happy that you're going for this man's personality rather than looks, which I might say would be a first, or whether to check you into a mental health clinic.'

'I feel really strange about it, though. I feel really excited when I think of him touching me, and like I want to vomit when I visualise his face. That's not right, is it, though? I mean, really Jesse, it's not right, is it?'

'Who am I to say what's right, Dotty? I've not been looked at twice in such a long time, I can't really comment about what's right or not. I guess just think of the positive things and don't beat yourself up about it all. If he calls, deal with it then. If not, move on.' Jesse paused before adding, 'Mary told me about a club called Big Ladies Paradise. I've not had a chance to investigate it yet but apparently it's a club just for big women and for men who like big women. Maybe that's something you might want to think about. If it's aimed at bigger women then you might have more choice than Ron.'

'That sounds interesting. Would you come with me?' Dotty knew the answer before it was said.

'Of course I will, if you want me to.' Jesse resigned herself to yet another night of humiliation in a bid to find her friend a man, and perhaps herself one in the bargain, although she was doubtful.

Jesse's spirits were low as she blew out the last of the candles and emptied the ashtrays before going upstairs to bed. She let Chloe settle herself down on the sofa before putting her arms around the black, very hairy dog for a cuddle. After giving Chloe a kiss on the snout, she looked deep into her eyes and said, 'Oh Chloe, am I going to find a man?' Jesse thought Chloe had no response and was about to stand up and retire to bed, only to find that after a few seconds' pause a putrid stench reached her nose. Chloe had replied in the negative.

CHAPTER 11

Jesse was eventually woken on Saturday morning by the answerphone's continuous bleep. It was unusual for Jesse not to spring to life instantly when the phone rang, but the final glass of wine the previous evening had sent her into a deep dream-filled sleep. She was grumbling to herself as she trundled into her office to listen to the message. It was Dotty.

'Just to let you know, I've thought about it all night and if he calls again I'm just going to say the distance is too much as I'm looking for a long-term relationship. I still can't believe what I did last night. I feel disgusted with myself. I'm off to church to repent, I'll call you later. Bye.'

Jesse reset the machine and went back to bed, where she stayed the afternoon. She felt so down she couldn't muster the energy to have a bath so she put her hair in pigtails and headed for the shops. Six hours later Jesse had cleaned the house, written a depressing song about not getting any, moaned to her mother on the phone and as soon as it got dark, lit the candles in her lounge, put on *Dirty Dancing* for the second time that month and opened a bottle of Sancerre.

She was half-cut when Mary rang at seven pm in hysterics.

'Jesse!' Mary screamed, 'You're not going to believe this! Angelo has just rung me and said he's on his way to me. Just like that! He's serious! I mean it, he's on his way over. What the hell am I supposed to do?!'

'Calm the fuck down, girl! Christ, you're not joking?' Jesse had stood up, she was in such shock. 'How did this happen?'

'I don't know!' Mary wailed, 'I went and had my hair cut as usual and did the usual flirty thing. I happened to mention that I was spending the night in front of a video - alone - but that was it. No hint of anything else. He gave me one of those smouldering looks but then he always does! Fucking hell, what am I going to do?'

'Get laid, by the sounds of it!' Jesse's voice was reaching fever pitch to match Mary's.

'No! I can't! He's married! Shit! I'd better go and change my knickers.'

'Shit, Mary! I can't believe this is happening. I'm so bloody jealous!'

'I can't believe it either, I'm crapping my pants! Please come over. Please.'

'What? Why?'

'Because I don't know what to do with him, that's why. Please come over.'

'No way, Jose. You haven't been laid for ages,

mate. I'm not about to come around and interfere. You just need to calm down, get on some nice underwear, have a glass of wine and prepare yourself.' Jesse was laughing now.

'It's not bloody funny, Jesse, I'm shitting myself. Oh no! That's him pulling up. Fuck. I'll call you when it's over,' Mary whispered.

'Good luck,' Jesse whispered back before the phone went dead.

'Well, bugger me, Chloe. Mary's gonna get laid. That deserves a toast.' Jesse raised her glass to the air, said a silent well done to Mary and downed half a glass of wine.

***

She hadn't finished her drink before the phone rang again.

'Jesse! Guess what? He rang!'

It was Dotty and she was obviously deliriously happy. Jesse took time for a deep sigh before saying, 'What did he have to say, then?'

'He said he had a fantastic time. He said he really enjoyed the taxi ride, I mean he actually said that! Then he said he'd told his mum all about me and he couldn't wait to see me again. God, this really is the one!'

'Reality check, Dotty, we're talking about Les Dawson here. What happened to, "I feel disgusted and

I'm going to finish it"?'

'Well,' said Dotty rather smugly, 'I'm going to take your advice and go on personality. I'm sure once I get used to his face it won't make me sick and he's made it very clear he wants to have sex as soon as possible.'

'What! Dotty, hang on a minute, girl. I know I'm not into all this God stuff but you've not had sex all these years and now you're contemplating having sex before marriage, with a gremlin!'

'Don't be so mean, Jesse. I mean, really, I would've thought you'd be happy for me.' Dotty was indignant.

'I would be happy for you if I thought it was right, but I don't think it is. Okay, your sights have been set far too high over the years but that's no reason to completely lose all your standards. I just think you need to take time to think about this properly. What happened to Brad Pitt?'

'He's dating Angelina Jolie darling. Time to move on, I think.'

'I think so, too, but don't be too hasty. I know you don't have to love someone to have sex with them but it helps if you actually fancy them, for heaven's sake, that's what separates us from the men, Dotty.'

'You know, you're starting to sound very bitter, Jesse, you need to watch that.'

'Am I? Well, if I'm wrong and overreacting then I'm sorry, but I'm not usually wrong when it comes to men, darling. Just don't commit yourself to sex. If you have to do the fondling thing then go ahead, but don't waste all these years of abstinence on Les Dawson.' Jesse was grimacing.

'Well, on that note I'm going to bed. I'll call you when I lose my virginity.'

'Har de har. I'll speak to you tomorrow. Good night.'

'Night night, Jesse.' And that was that. Jesse looked at Chloe incredulously, 'That's both of my mates getting some, and what am I doing? Getting pissed and having a conversation with my fucking dog.'

Opening the second bottle of wine, Jesse was feeling adequately sorry for herself to ring in to her *Talking Hearts* ad. Ordinarily she would never have done it, but under the influence of alcohol Jesse took on a different persona. There was only one message but it was a good one.

From the callers timbre Jesse sensed he was black. He had a lovely soft drawl and a calmness about his voice. He was the producer for a shopping channel - on Sky, not QVC - he said. He liked music and sport, had enjoyed listening to her voicemail and his name was Jerome. Even though Jesse was completely pissed, she still had a bout of diarrhoea before making the call. He answered on the second ring and she immediately informed him she was pissed. He seemed to find this amusing and they continued talking for a full twenty minutes before arranging to meet the next day in Pizza

Express in Staines. He said he would be there at one o'clock and she'd recognise him because he'd be wearing a hat. Thankfully, Jesse wrote all these details on a Post-it note, before going to bed on her hands and knees.

***

Jesse arrived early. She absolutely had to get there before him. She couldn't be seen to be walking into a restaurant scanning the place for a complete stranger. Oh the shame! She asked to be sat at the back of the restaurant so she had full view of the entrance. She had already clocked that there was no-one in the restaurant in a hat. She had berated herself all morning for ringing him up. She was trying to imagine what he would be like - Denzel Washington in a suit and trilby was the best she could come up with.

Twenty minutes later and Jesse was debating whether to just order a pizza, look as if she'd only ever meant to eat on her own and then leave, looking like a confident singleton. She was just about to call over the waiter when she saw a hat - not a trilby. The man striding towards her with a full set of ivories on display, was indeed wearing a hat - a black baseball cap which matched his muscle top, black jeans and huge black trainers with the laces undone.

Jesse was mortified but hid it well. She nearly head-butted him when she went for the second kiss on the cheek. She ordered wine and he ordered mineral water - a sure sign they weren't going to get on. The first thing he commented on was that he normally went out with thin models. Allegedly he'd been a model before and used to date only skinny women but had decided to try something different. He said all this while smiling gleefully at Jesse's horrified face. Apart from the fact they'd both done the blind date thing for a laugh, completely out of character, couldn't believe they'd gone through with it, they had zero in common. The fact they were both desperate to get laid hung unsaid in the air. Jesse could tell he was weighing up the pros and cons of shagging this fat bird sat in front of him, while she'd already come to the conclusion that she was going to be no man's experiment into the depths of fathood. No sir-ee! After the 'try something different' comment, Jesse decided even if he'd been the one-and-only Denzel Washington, she'd have told him she'd rather shag a rabbit than get down on him.

Having being bored shitless for nearly two hours, Jesse made her excuses and left after negotiating a more successful cheek kiss.

Any passer-by seeing Jesse striding towards her car would have thought, now, there goes a confident woman. Inwardly she was trying to remember whether Julie Andrews had enjoyed being a nun.

CHAPTER 12

Mary lay naked on crumpled white cotton sheets, feeling a mixture of sheer bliss and shame. Every time she thought of Angelo's strong hands tracing circles on her breasts, a warmth spread through her entire body and an excitement bubbled in the pit of her belly. A neon light followed each memory written in pink and blue and flashed on and off incessantly - he's married. A heaviness consumed her, drowning out the warmth.

Why did she always fall for the married men? Her last single boyfriend had been Paul, her childhood sweetheart, whom she very nearly married. They had dated for years and by the age of eighteen they were living together. He was a lovely lad but that was all he's been - a lad. Mary needed a man. By the time she was twenty one it dawned on her that marrying Paul would be a mistake. They were fantastic friends and she loved him very much. Unfortunately it was a brotherly love, rather than a sexual one.

They sailed through for over five years before Mary got a little too tipsy at a nightclub and kissed another man. It was only a kiss but it meant the end of the road for Mary and Paul. If she had been able to kiss another man then surely Paul wasn't the one for her, not to marry, not to spend the rest of her life with. If she could be unfaithful to him now then what about in ten years' time? She was raised a Catholic and divorce was out of the question, so the very next day she packed one suitcase, took her photo album and left Paul with everything except his fiancée.

Jesse and Mary had discussed her inability to fall for single men numerous times over the years and had come to the conclusion that her relationship with Paul and the guilt that followed was the reason why married men were attractive in her eyes - no commitment.

The irony was that Mary was desperate for commitment, desperate for a man to call her own, to be able to hug freely, walk down the street arm in arm and eat out with but yet again, another married man had left her bed less than an hour ago.

She got out of bed and went to get her caffeine fix, taking the evidence with her. She put both the sheets and duvet cover directly into the washing machine, but couldn't resist a quick smell of Angelo's scent on the pillowcase before stuffing it into the machine to join the other guilty parties.

It was Sunday morning and, judging by the stream of light coming through her patio doors, it would be an unusually nice day for March. With the coffee made and cigarette lit, she buried her face in her hands and groaned out loud. The groan became a wail, ending in a desperate, 'Oh mama,' before she suddenly laughed out loud and threw her hands to her cheeks.

She couldn't believe how outrageously confident she had been in bed with Angelo. Okay, she had insisted on closing both the curtains and the blinds to ensure he couldn't see her body while he seduced it, but she did sit on top of him at one point, which was a first for her. Mary was very simple in the bedroom department; absolutely no light, no funny business below, no talking, no faking orgasms and absolutely no messy nonsense anywhere near her nether regions.

She did recall Angelo telling her to shut up after her third, admittedly hysterical plea for him not to make a mess down there. But she gave him a hand job to make up for this distraction. She felt bathed in a glorious light when she repeated over and over in her head what he had said when she insisted on rushing to the bathroom in the dark to put her pyjamas on so he couldn't see her naked.

'Mary, please don't cover up. You know you have a lovely bum.' Her response had been the usual self-deprecating snort of, 'Yeah, but you haven't seen the ton of cellulite I've got hanging underneath it', but even so, for a moment she felt like Kate Moss. She tried not to dwell on the hollow feeling when he left her bed at six am to go home to his wife.

The temptation to text his mobile was extreme but one thing she had learned over the years was self-control when it came to the men she dated. She accepted the snatched moments, the whispered phone calls and the pornographic text messages as part of the deal. She was terrified that one day she would fall in love with one of these married men, but constantly tried to convince herself that she was too strong and detached for that. She only had to remember Grigor in Greece to realise the game she was playing was a dangerous one.

She was showered and dressed in a navy tracksuit by the time Jesse arrived at noon carrying daffodils and a broad smile.

'Don't say a word until you've made the coffee,' she demanded, after giving Mary a kiss on the cheek and handing her the daffodils, 'I want to enjoy every minute of the juicy gossip.'

Mary laughed nervously. 'What do you mean, juicy gossip? I'm not giving you graphic details, you know.'

'Ah, spoilsport! Okay, just the basics. What he said, what he did, what you said and what you did. I think that should cover it.'

Mary had boiled the kettle before Jesse arrived so poured the water over the granules and sat down opposite her friend with two fresh cups of coffee and a hunk of panettone.

'So? Tell me, tell me!' Jesse had a wicked grin on her face and was looking at Mary expectedly.

'There's nothing to tell, really.'

'Don't be so bloody coy. Details. Now!'

'Okay, well, he pulled up in the car. Like I said,

I didn't even have time to change my knickers, but that didn't seem to bother him. I opened the door to him and he simply took my hand in silence and walked me upstairs.'

'No! Not a word?'

Mary let out a large plume of smoke from her lungs before saying, 'Not a dickey bird. It was so lovely. He undressed me really slowly while telling me how he had thought about what he was going to do to me for the past six months.'

'Six months? I told you he fancied you! Go on.'

'That was it, really.'

'What do you mean that was it? What was he like? What did he say? Did you give him a BJ? How big was he?'

'Enough, Jesse! I'm not going to tell you all the details. But he was quite big, actually. In fact, it was a bit like a fat tongue - small and fat and a bit flat, weird, but very nice, I must say.' Mary had gone pink in the cheeks and the two girls started to giggle.

'Did you orgasm?'

'No,' she said matter-of-factly. 'Actually he was a bit upset about that. He actually said, 'Let me lick you.'

'What did you say?' probed Jesse, knowing full well what Mary had said.

'I said, "No fucking way," of course.'

'Mmm, shocker.'

'Don't look at me like that, Jesse. There's

absolutely no bloody way someone's shoving their head between my legs. It's disgusting.' Jesse knew better than to tell Mary that it was the best bloody bit as far as she was concerned.

'But it was nice, though?'

'Yes, it was lovely. He was really romantic... and he said he loved my bum.'

'That's nice.'

'I said to him he should see my cellulite, though.' Mary was smiling at the memory.

'Darling, I'm not being funny, but you do know that men don't find it sexy to have a woman point out all their bad bits? You're probably pointing out bits that he's never even noticed before, but by you pointing them out it'll give him something to focus on. Not good, Mary, not good at all. Next time he might not notice your bum, looking for the cellulite you were talking about.'

'There won't be a next time and even if there was, he wouldn't be able to see it in the dark anyway.'

'True. Good point. So you're not going to see him again, then?'

'No. I don't think so. I'm sure he won't call me.'

'Mary, you always say that and they always do.'

'No, it was a one-off. He's married.'

'As was the last. You know he'll call you, Mary. You just have to decide what you're going to say when he does.'

'What would you say?'

'To be honest, I don't know. He's absolutely bloody drop-dead gorgeous, but he's married. I'm afraid I really go in for the telephone calls and going out to dinner. I'm not sure I wouldn't feel a bit cheap if he just came over for sex.' Jesse wasn't sure if she had been a bit too blunt, but Mary didn't seem to take it personally.

'I must admit, I don't actually feel cheap, but I am visualising what kind of a life I'm going to have if I get into a routine with him.'

'Crap, that's what it'll be like, with some absolutely fantastic moments.' Jesse had been here before with Mary and knew the routine. She felt so sorry for her friend that every man she seemed to meet was not hers to have.

'Why does this keep happening to me?'

'Because you're too naive and don't see it coming, darling. I've seen you with married men. You assume because they're married they're safe. You let your guard down, you're far too friendly with them and, hey presto, before you know it you're snogging him. You're not like that with single men. With single men you make them work for it, you're dubious of them and wonder what they're after. Married man equals safe.'

'I know you're right. That last trip to China proved that. I had no idea he wanted anything other than friendship. Even when he got locked out of his hotel and asked to stay in my room, I just thought we were going to top-to-toe it.'

'Are you talking about the black guy?'

'Yes, Benjamin. Honestly, Jesse, when he started rubbing his hand down my back I was so shocked but by then it was too late. Suckered again.'

'Made the trip pass, though, didn't it?' Jesse smiled at her friend.

'Yup, sure did!'

'I don't know what I'm going to do now.'

'Get out more. Come with me to the singles clubs. Let's go to the pub more often.'

'But I don't drink.'

'You don't have to. You can have a Diet Coke and still have fun.' They sat in silence for a few moments contemplating Mary's love life then Jesse said, 'Let's just hope there's some single talent in Greece this year.'

'Oh, I'm not going to bother,' said Mary in a determined tone.

'Hang on a minute. You've shagged Angelo once and already you're cutting off any chance of meeting anyone else who might actually be available?'

'No, it's not that, it's not because of Angelo.'

'No?'

'No. I'm just off men at the moment.'

'At the moment? Just one hour before Angelo arrived on your doorstep, you'd have admitted to being as desperate for a man as I am. What if you meet a really nice single man on holiday? Are you gonna turn

111

him down?'

'I won't meet one. They don't exist.'

'Come off it, you read enough Danielle Steel to know that's not true. There are loads of good men out there, you just have to sift through the shit to find one.'

'When was the last time you had a boyfriend, Jesse?' Mary sounded depressed.

'It feels like fifteen bloody years ago, but even so, I've not given up hope. I'll tell you one thing, Mary, as long as I may have to wait I won't be settling. I won't be settling for something that I don't want. I won't be cutting off my options to stay with second best and I don't think you should either.'

'I'm not!'

'You're already preparing yourself to be hurt by Angelo, while stupidly staying loyal to him, which he obviously won't be doing to you. He has a wife at home to please. Don't tell me you're not cutting off your options.' The frustration was showing in Jesse's tone of voice so she lowered it. 'Bloody hell, it's so awful, Mary. I just wish you'd find a really nice guy and settle down and have four kids and be happy.'

'Fat chance.'

'Hang in there, darling, you never know, he might be the very next person to knock on the door.' The doorbell rang.

Both girls smirked at each other as Mary went to see what Mr Right looked like. Unfortunately for both of them, it was not Mr Right. In fact it wasn't even a Mr, it was the old biddy from down the road, Cath. Mary knew Jesse would be out of the house within two minutes if she let Cath in, but she had a plant in her hands and a gappy smile and Mary had no choice but to let her pass.

'Hello luv. Oh hello Jess, how are you? I've been down to visit my sister in hospital. She's had this thing up her nose, you know, had to cut it out. Oh, it was disgusting. All pussy and bloody. She had it in a container next to her bed, you know. Showed it to me, she did. Put the kettle on, luv, and I'll tell you all about it.' Cath plonked herself down next to Jesse, as Jesse reached for her handbag and said, 'Thanks for that, Mary, I really am running late now so I'll call you on Monday.'

Cath brought with her the subtle smell of old farts and Jesse found it hard not to gag when she accidentally brushed past her to leave the table. There was something about old people that she simply couldn't cope with. She couldn't put her finger on it. Maybe it was the way every breath sounded like the last, or the saliva that lived on the corners of their mouths, or the two or three teeth still embedded in their gums, the cataracts or the smell, or just rotting flesh. She couldn't define it but knew she couldn't cope with it.

Mary walked her to the door and smiled apologetically as she rolled her eyes, indicating there was nothing she could do.

'Call me later if you get any news. Keep your

chin up, darling'. Jesse turned on her heels, striding to her beloved Volkswagen Beetle, not noticing how much she was hurting her arm for trying to rub Cath off it.

CHAPTER 13

The month had been a long and lonely one for Jesse. She had an ache in her right shoulder where she had been on the phone for what felt like ten hours a day. She had taken to answering the phone, 'Agony Aunt for the sexually frustrated', as both Dotty and Mary had been on the phone after every text message or phone call from Angelo and Les. She hadn't seen either of her friends in two weeks. For Jesse, every evening had been spent listening to Sheryl Crow on the stereo while contemplating where she was in life. On the upside, she had a stable business, more than enough money for her lifestyle, a dog she adored, two excellent friends, a fab car and was still enjoying her singing. One downside - she was fat and single. Her two friends were still fatties but, for the time being at least, they considered themselves no longer single. Jesse could see the two men were evoking excitement but they both had huge flaws. Angelo was gorgeous but married - it was going to end in tears. Ron, although Jesse couldn't help but call him Les now, was butt ugly and desperate for a shag - also going to end in tears.

After much analysis, Jesse had come to realise that it wasn't a man she was desperate for - it was one worth having that was the problem. What could a man give her apart from grief? Love and companionship? Sure, but she got that from her dog. Sex? The Rabbit was still proving fruitful. Money? She had her own. Apart from someone to go out with, she couldn't think of any other good reasons why she had been pining for a bloke for so long. She was simply lonely.

Due to Mary and Dotty's financial situations, both of the girls were completely useless with money and therefore always completely skint. They hardly went out anymore together. Even Tesco on a Saturday with Mary had come to a halt since Angelo came on the scene. Mary had become a recluse and Dotty busied herself with the church. Most weekends Jesse was quite happy to sit in front of a video with a glass of wine and a box of choccies, but every now and again, especially if it happened to be a full moon, Jesse walked the walls.

This was not going to be one of those weekends. This was the weekend she was going with Dotty to Big Ladies Paradise. The fact it was being held in a pub in Liverpool Street on a Saturday gave her cause for concern as the area was like a ghost town after six pm on a Friday. That wasn't her only reservation though: she had spoken to a very jolly lady on the phone who tried to reassure Jesse that it was indeed a high-class establishment and all the members were wonderful and friendly. If she hadn't added that there would be Bunny Girls on roller skates, she might have believed her. Dotty on the other hand was overly excited about the night. Although it was only Thursday, she had already organised her choice of outfit and booked a Nail Art appointment for the Friday, timed perfectly to coincide with having her hair highlighted. Although Jesse was dreading the night, she was at least going to be out of the house on a Saturday night. She had been compiling a list of ways to get out of the house for two days now and just stared at it blankly. For the life of her, she couldn't add anything else to the list. The list read: pubs, dancing, evening classes. That was it, nothing else. She had already put a line through these three choices, though, as she wouldn't do any of them on her own - she needed Mary to hold her hand and Mary wasn't available.

It was only out of sheer boredom that Jesse decided to leaf through her copy of *The Stage* again, not looking only for opportunities with record companies, but actually reading all of the situations vacant. That was how she came across an advert for a backing singer to join an established band who rehearsed in Windsor on a Thursday. She sat looking at that advert for a full half an hour until she convinced herself to ring it. As usual with anything traumatic she spent a quick five minutes on the loo, before lighting a cigarette and dialling.

'Hello, I wonder if you can help me? I'm ringing with regards to the advert you placed in *The Stage* newspaper this week for a backing singer.'

'Oh yes, right, fab, great. What do you do, then?'

'I sing.' Jesse nearly added *obviously* but bit her tongue in time.

'Oh right, fab, great. Okay, let me tell you a bit about us. We're an eight-piece band, right, but what makes us different from the rest, right, is we are a kind of comedy band. We do covers but we really jazz them up, right? It's great fun. We've been together for ages now and I've got lots of things in the pipeline for us. We've got a gig confirmed in Battersea next month. Why don't you come down and meet with everyone and see how you get on?'

'That sounds great, when would you like me to come along?'

'Well, why don't you come now? Yeah, that'd be cool, actually. We're all here now and we'll be here until 10:30 tonight. What do you think?'

Jesse's mind went blank with panic.

'Hello, you still there?'

'Sorry, yes of course, I'd love to. Where are you?'

'We're at Running Frog in Windsor. Do you know it?'

'Yes, funnily enough I do.'

'Okay, see you soon, then. Great. Lovely. Smashing. Oh, what's your name?'

'Jesse.'

'Hi Jesse. My name's Justin but you can call me Freddy Valentine if you like. See you soon. Bye.'

'Bye'.

'Freddie friggin' Valentine? What is he on about?' Jesse was rerunning the telephone conversation while changing out of her jeans and T-shirt into her bootlegs and the long black tassel jumper which hid her figure a bit better. Justin/Freddie had sounded a little bit too excitable on the phone but what else was she going to do tonight? No doubt open another bottle of wine and think. She'd done enough of both over the week. After her third trip to the toilet she gave in and took a Diocalm pill, jumped into the car and drove like the wind, heading towards the unknown.

Jesse had recorded her demo CD in the Running Frog and knew the layout and staff well, which was great as she needed to see a friendly face before she went in to meet eight complete strangers. The owner of the studio was sat behind the desk brushing his long hair out of his eyes while smoking a roll-up and talking on the phone. 'Hi Phil, how's it going?'

'Well, hello, Jesse, not bad, not bad. What are you doing here? I've not got you booked in for tonight.' Phil was scouring his diary looking for Jesse's name.

'I'm not rehearsing tonight, actually. I've come to see someone called Justin. He's advertising for a backing singer. Know anything about it?'

'Oh yes, oh yes.' He gave Jesse one of his wicked 'I know something you don't know' smiles before adding, 'You'll find him in number four.' Taking one final puff of her menthol, Jesse asked, 'Any advice?'

'Well. They're a bit controversial but they seem all right.' Phil pulled a face before adding, 'He's got some weird views, though, but they all seem to keep him under control. No harm in having a look, though, is there?'

'All right, thanks a lot.' She meant to say 'thanks for nothing' but didn't want to burn her bridges. She threw her cigarette out the front door to be extinguished by the rain and strode to door number four as if she was brimming with confidence and did this all the time. The reality was this was the first audition she'd ever been to, but Jesse threw on her singing persona, knocked twice and pushed through the heavy soundproofed door.

There was a long pause before a rather tall, exceptionally weird-looking guy shouted, 'Jesse, hi, come on in and meet everyone!' He indicated for her to stand in the centre of the tiny room but she shut the door behind her and stood firmly where she was.

'Okay, this is Amadeus, the drummer.' He gave Jesse a nod and a big smile - obviously the Italian stallion of the band. 'Then we've got Liz on bass.' An incredibly thin slip of a girl with long blonde hair nervously smiled in her direction. 'Then we've got Steve on keyboards.' Never in her life had she seen someone in real life with such dreadful skin, bright red blotches and boils - he had a nice smile, though.

'Duncan on trombone.' Obviously a member of the Sally Army; wonky glasses and a squint, emptying the spit out of his instrument while nodding at the floor rather than at Jesse, who was trying to keep a neutral face. 'Graham on trumpet.' He couldn't have long been a teenager, wearing a surfing jumper and glasses that had tape on the frame, chin fluff and a bit of a leer. 'David on sax.' A rather intense-looking man with black hair and eyes to match with a strange kind of goatee beard going on, bubbling with excess energy. He smiled at her while bobbing up and down on his heels.

'Then we've got Karen on lead guitar.' A broad smile from the anorexic brunette, who had certainly been crying before Jesse arrived. 'And obviously I'm Justin, the lead singer. Pleased to meet you, Jesse!' It appeared Justin thought he was being humorous and there was wavering laughter cascading around the room. Everybody wanted to stare at this new possibility who had just entered their lair, but they seemed too embarrassed to appear curious - except Amadeus, who practically undressed her with his eyes.

'Okay, why don't we play you a bit of the set and you can decide if it's something you want to be a part of? Feel free to join in on any harmonies.' The drummer started clicking his sticks to a count of eight and Jesse nearly fell over to the deafening sound of *Live and Let Die*. She found an unused amp to perch herself on - she should have worn her flat boots - and felt the vibrations travel from the carpet into her feet up to her kneecaps. She'd never heard music played so loud in her life.

Apart from the very fast and loud rendition of *Live and Let Die*, she also had no idea what to make of the lead singer. The fact he was doing high kicks during the entire performance when he was in his late forties was a bit unusual, but his looks actually disturbed her. His hair was jet black and long and was scooped from the nape of his neck to the front of his head so it sat in front of his eyes, held there by half a bottle of hair spray. He had huge bushy eyebrows and black hair on his chin which didn't quite meet his extensive side burns. He was wearing a black cardigan that was covered in holes over what looked like a works uniform and a 'Save the PG Tips Chimps' badge sat on his chest. He freaked her out.

As the last note was played, the sax player bounced over to her with a huge smile and announced, 'I've already set your mic up. Why don't you join in?' She hated him already. Wasn't it patently obvious that the last thing Jesse wanted to do was actually sing?

'Do you know *Walk On By*?' he asked in between Jesse's, 'One, two testing, one, two testing.'

'No.'

'Well, have a listen and join in if you can find the harmonies!' Justin shouted. Of course Jesse knew the song, the lyrics were hardly an obstacle as there were only three of them, but she said no in case they

122

played it in the wrong key. There was no way Jesse was going to humiliate herself when singing. Knowing this, she should have left immediately - she did not.

After she'd sung *Walk On By* in very soft dulcet tones about fifteen times, the band decided she was indeed the one they had been looking for. The excitement from all eight band members was evident and she felt compelled to say, 'I'd love to join you, sounds great.' Jesse's gut instinct told her to find out more before committing herself - she should have followed it. After several more renditions of *Walk On By*, *Copacabana* and *Fly Me To The Moon*, the band invited her to the pub, where the group's name was revealed. Jesse sat in silence among the eight, paying no attention to what was being said, between mouthfuls of pork scratchings and cheese and onion crisps. She was trying to decide if she wanted to be in a band called *The Paisley Wheelchair Experience*. Jesse had very strong views about disability, as she did about ageism, sexism, racism and fatism.

'Excuse me, Justin, sorry to interrupt. Can you explain why you're called *The Paisley Wheelchair Experience*? It isn't a piss-take, is it?'

Justin looked horrified and started flapping his hands about in a kind of 'get away from me' action. 'Good God, no! I love people in wheelchairs. I'd never take the piss out of someone with a disability.'

'Good, I just wanted to check because I can't have anything to do with a piss-take.'

'No, me neither. God no! The name of the band came to me in a dream over ten years ago now. Elvis Presley walked up to me and said, "Create your dream. Call your band *The Paisley Wheelchair Experience*, uh hu hu" and so I did.' Having explained the name away, conversations were picked up again ranging from the music of Frank Sinatra, Elvis impersonations, what was on at the cinema lately and the fact there was a particular kind of circus monkey up for sale on the Internet for £2000 and Justin wanted it. For the most part, Jesse tuned out until the two female guitarists started talking about pink glitter eye shadow and Jesse felt she was with family.

On the dark drive home in the rain, Jesse felt undeniable excitement in her stomach - something she hadn't felt for ages. She would be out at least once a week rehearsing with a big crowd of people. She would have a drink with them every week and get to know them as friends. There would be actual gigs to go to, which would take up some Friday and Saturday nights, and she was now a bona fide singer in an eight-piece cabaret band. She had forgotten to ask what they actually meant by cabaret but figured she'd ask on her next rehearsal. She was a bit disappointed that she was flying to Greece the following Thursday as she wouldn't see them again for two weeks, but felt sure it wouldn't really matter that much. She had been accepted into their group.

She had no idea how much she didn't fit.

CHAPTER 14

Dotty was used to making this journey from her home in Stratford to Liverpool Street on the train, she did it every morning before changing onto the Northern Line to get to Islington. It made a nice change to be getting off after only a twenty-minute journey and, as she felt like a treat, she quickly stepped into Boots on the concourse to grab a Mars Bar before making her way to the front of the station where she was hoping Jesse would be waiting.

Dotty noticed some large steps to the right of the entrance so sauntered over and sat down heavily on the third step, which was a comfortable height for her legs to still reach the pavement. She was enjoying nibbling the chocolate away from the toffee of the Mars Bar, while scanning the road for black cabs, Jesse's choice of vehicle when coming into town.

Dotty had already decided to wait and see what Jesse's mood was like before she told her that she had had phone sex with Ron the night before. Over the past weeks, the text messages had gone from friendly to sexy to almost pornographic. Each telephone call brought them closer together and Dotty felt she had known him her entire life, even though she'd only met him the once. She was very strict about intercourse as she was determined not to give herself to a man until they were married in the eyes of God, but as far as foreplay was concerned, anything and everything was allowed. With his soft Scottish drawl he had asked her to take off all her clothes and lie in bed and then proceeded to tell her in explicit detail what he was going to do to her and what he was doing to himself while thinking about it. She'd never done the phone sex thing before but he had turned her on so much she had no problem explaining graphically what she intended to do to him and what she was doing with her vibrating Rabbit while lying in her bed. She was a natural. She had a fantastic orgasm and slept like a baby after telling him she was falling in love with him.

If she did tell Jesse, she would omit the last bit as she knew Jesse wouldn't understand and would think she was desperate if she told her how her feelings were escalating for Ron. Another five minutes passed before Jesse arrived, calling to Dotty to get in the cab as she couldn't be arsed to walk the three streets to the pub.

The black cab came to a stop on a deserted road opposite a dark alley. 'There we are, ladies, just down the alley on the left.'

'Are you sure it's down there? I can't see anything.'

'Number Two is on the left, ladies.'

'Okay, if you're sure.' Jesse was nervous.

The taxi pulled away, leaving the two girls standing on the pavement in the dark.

'Okay Dotty, I don't like the look of this. If we can't find it or it looks like a dive, let's get out of there and go to Dover Street Wine Bar or something.'

'All right. I'm sure it'll be fine. Come on.' Dotty linked arms with Jesse and started down the alley. After only five tentative strides they could see a doorway that was lit and a freestanding sign on the pavement. As they got closer the sign read 'Big Girls This Way - *Big Belly* magazine & Paradise welcome you.'

'Ah bless,' Dotty said with affection, 'Isn't that sweet?'

'Mmm.' Jesse was unimpressed.

The bouncers on the door didn't look welcoming at all. They looked downright terrifying. The two burly men looked the girls up and down before silently opening the door for them. Music blasted out and the sound of many people chatting flooded into the alley.

'Oh good, it sounds like there are lots of people here,' Dotty enthused as she took her first step on the spiral staircase to hell.

'What kind of people, though, Dotty? That's what concerns me.' Dotty looked over her shoulder and gave Jesse a dazzling smile then proceeded to heft herself up the staircase, where a Bunny Girl on roller skates was waiting for them.

'Hello ladies, welcome to Paradise. Please order your drinks from the bar where you can pick up a complimentary copy of *Big Belly* magazine. The dance floor is down the staircase, along with the toilets. Enjoy your evening.' With that, she parted her glossy red lips, gave a half-genuine smile and skated away.

The bar was immediately to their left and Jesse could see it was one of those minimalist efforts that sold only four kinds of spirit and as many lagers, and charged a fortune for it. It didn't go unnoticed that the bartender hadn't looked either of them in the face when taking and delivering their order of vodka and cranberry juice. Jesse assumed it was the embarrassment of charging them £14 for the privilege.

Jesse and Dotty stood in silence while they were checking the place out. Dotty's assessment was written all over her face - she loved it. For once in her life, Dotty wasn't the largest woman in the crowd - in fact she looked positively average. Nearly all the women were around the twenty stone mark and quite a few much bigger than that and, to Dotty's delight, none had as pretty a face as she did. Jesse, on the other hand, stood out like a sore thumb and they both knew it. Even though Jesse was a good size twenty she looked positively scrawny compared to the majority of women and had noticed more than one dirty look cast in her direction. There were quite a few men scattered around the place but they all looked stereotypically gay; bandannas, chains, leather trousers and vest tops, which only added to Jesse's unease.

'I'm not getting good vibes here. Shall we go downstairs and find a seat?' Dotty looked at Jesse with concern before nodding in agreement. Jesse's heart sank when they reached the room with the dance floor. The entire room was painted black with a black wooden floor, which had bright red coach seats nailed to it along with plastic Formica tables in the middle of them. Jesse felt like the ball in a pinball machine as she was bounced from one woman's huge stomach into another woman's arse and then back again before reaching the safety of an empty seat.

The room stank of sweat and the atmosphere was heavy. What could only be described as frantic underground music played and several huge women were gyrating on the tiny dance floor. Jesse found it hard not to stare in wonder as all of the women were dressed in outrageous clothing. One had a white bodice pushing her huge breasts up to her throat and only a G-string covering her no doubt expensive vajazzle. The arse she had made contact with was wearing a lime green Lycra miniskirt, tottering on white stiletto heels. Another dancer wore a lace gypsy-style top with a long black skirt which would have looked pretty were it not for the split that went up the front of the skirt to reveal the woman's black feather knickers.

Jesse tried not to move her lips for fear of someone lip reading when she turned to Dotty and said with a smile, 'We need to get the fuck out of here now,

Dotty, right now.'

'Oh come on, Jesse, we've only just arrived. Have another drink and loosen up. Look, let's have a leaf through the magazine.' After patting Jesse on the hand in what was meant to be a reassuring gesture, Dotty picked up the *Big Belly* magazine and started to flick through. Jesse watched, intrigued, as Dotty's facial expression gradually moved from one of interest to blatant disgust.

'Oh my giddy aunt, have you seen this?'

Dotty was obviously outraged at the centre-spread of an incredibly large woman dressed only in a bra and panties being fed cream cakes by a very thin man dressed in black leathers. She continued to show Jesse page after page of women being hand-fed wearing next to nothing and it wasn't until they reached the personal ads that it dawned on Dotty what they had unwittingly walked into.

'This is a fetish club!' Dotty said far too loudly. 'Shitty death, we'd better get out of here!' Not another word was spoken as Jesse grabbed Dotty's hand and quickly guided her through the house of horrors and out into the fresh air of a stormy London.

'Oh my goodness! Oh my goodness! That was horrible. Did you see the state of those poor women in there? And the music? I just can't believe it!'

'Keep walking, Dotty, we need to get out of here.' Dotty found it hard to keep up with Jesse's pace but continued to rant between breaths at the humiliation of it all. Just as panic was beginning to set in, a taxi headed towards them, its orange glow as welcome as water in the desert.

***

After their ordeal, dancing had become out of the question and a strong drink was needed, hence their current position in the quiet basement bar of the Glasshouse Stores on Brewer Street.

'I'm not being funny but that is the last time I go to anything but a normal club or pub with you. I can't cope with it all. No disrespect but those women were on a completely different planet to you and I, and I don't think you should lower yourself to that kind of level, Dotty. That place was horrific.' Her heart was still racing just a little bit too fast as Jesse lit her second cigarette from the glow of the last.

Dotty was close to tears, 'I know, I know. Gosh, it really was awful, wasn't it? You know I couldn't see it until I opened that magazine. I suppose I was just happy to be in a room where I felt normal rather than ridiculed.'

'I don't think there's anything wrong with those kind of places if that's what you're into, but we so obviously aren't. I mean, I know I stuck out like a sore thumb for not being big enough, but so did you for having clothes.'

With a nod of her head, Dotty drew her friend's attention to her feet, which were wearing sequined flip-flops, and gave a cheeky waggle of her toes.

'Okay, apart from your feet!' The girls smiled at one another and visibly relaxed.

'Seriously, though, you look really lovely tonight. Is that a new suit?'

'No.' Actually it was a new suit but Dotty knew she'd get a lecture if she told Jesse she'd just forked out £70 on an outfit when she hadn't got the spending money for the holiday yet with less than five days to go.

'Anything new on the Les...sorry, Ron front?'

'Only if you call phone sex new.'

Jesse's mouth hung open as she gaped at the woman sat smugly next to her.

'Oh, it was so good! He described everything to me. He told me how he was rubbing his hand up and down his dick while...'

'Stop! I can't take it.'

'Oh, don't be so prudish. He said he wanted to insert his fingers into my soaking wet...'

'La, la, la, la.' Jesse had her hands firmly pressed over both ears, with her eyes closed.

'What's the matter with you?' Dotty's laugh bounced off the basement walls. 'You're so flaming funny! You've talked about nothing but wanting sex with a bloke for over a year now and you can't even bring yourself to talk about it.'

'I don't mind talking about wanting sex. I just don't want to talk about the actual act itself, thank you very much!'

'What's wrong with the words dick and pussy,

for heaven's sake?'

'Nothing,' Jesse muttered squirming in her seat. 'I just don't feel comfortable using that language with *you*!'

Dotty was laughing again. 'Ah, how sweet, come here for a cuddle.' Before Jesse could respond, she found herself gasping for air in the pillow of Dotty's heaving breasts.

***

Two hours later and Dotty was stood alone in Soho waiting for a taxi to come her way. As usual she'd put Jesse in a taxi first, as Jesse was terrified of being alone in London. The experience of the last few hours had left its mark on Dotty and she was looking at herself with fresh eyes. She absolutely hated being fat and she really wanted a partner to share her life with, but she had no idea how she was going to go about that without losing weight - which was just not going to happen.

She'd tried all the diets; the Microdiet, the Cambridge Diet, the Grapefruit Diet, food combination and Slim-Fast. She'd stuck to them all for at least two weeks, except for the appetite suppressant course - she only managed two days as the trauma of swallowing tablets was too much to bear. She couldn't count calories as that meant she couldn't eat what she wanted, and she couldn't eat less of what she wanted because she felt deprived. The longest she had dieted for was an entire month, and she did lose two stones, but that was for a specific goal and she hadn't managed it since.

No, she was going to have to think of a new plan, especially now it was obvious Jesse was never going to entertain visiting a fat club again. All her hopes were pinned on Ron somehow becoming more palatable to look at, and the holiday. As usual, her only real goal for the holiday was to have a damn good snog. An objective she had met on every holiday she'd been on with the girls. She had only one real worry about the holiday - the plane journey. She had asked her prayer group to pray for her right up until the day she flew to ensure that somehow she would get her huge bottom snugly into the seventeen inches of plane seat she was allocated. She couldn't be bothered to worry about that now so instead she sent her sixth text message of the day to Ron. She found his silence strange. He hadn't returned her messages since the previous night, which was downright rude considering she told him she loved him.

The rest of the journey home was usual for a Saturday night on the tubes: a few drunken teenagers larking about, a couple having a heavy petting session five seats to her left and a smooth-skinned black man sat opposite showing her his nine-inch erect penis.

CHAPTER 15

It was 5:30 am and Mary was on her second strong coffee of the morning. Jesse had answered the door to Mary in her usual flap - 'Hiya. Come on in, make yourself a coffee, I'm nearly ready' - and then jogged up the stairs, obviously not ready at all. Mary's luggage, a large Samsonite case and matching hand carrier, were sitting in the middle of Jesse's small lounge along with a moody-looking Chloe. Normally Chloe couldn't contain her excitement when Mary called and inevitably spread little droplets of pee on the cream carpet, but not this morning. Chloe always knew when Jesse was about to leave her and never failed to play the guilt trip.

Twenty minutes later and Jesse hauled her rather tatty green suitcase into the lounge to join Mary's, leaving Chloe no choice but to jump to the freedom of the sofa. 'Finally. All done.'

'Have you taken your pills?'

'Just about to. Two travel sickness, one Diocalm Ultra and a lorazepam. Do you want one?'

'No thanks, I'll stick to my Kalms.'

'What time is it? Where's Dotty? Has she called you?'

'She rang over an hour ago to say she was getting in the taxi. She'll be here any minute. Sit down and drink your coffee.'

'God, I'm far too nervous. I keep feeling like I've forgotten something.'

'Did you actually go to bed last night?'

'No, of course not! I didn't even hand over the business to Gill until midnight and as usual I hadn't packed a thing and nearly everything needed ironing. I'm bloody knackered.'

'Sit down and try to relax.'

'Oh, I can't yet, you know what I'm like. I'll be all right once the pills kick in. How are you feeling?'

'Not too bad, actually. I think those vitamin B pills are really helping. I actually ate the meal on the last plane journey to Amsterdam.'

'Well, that's much better than last year. For crying out loud, where is she?'

'She's not even late yet, Jesse, calm down. Have you got your passport and money?'

'Yeah. I'm going to get currency at the airport. I just haven't had time to organise it. It doesn't matter, though, we'll have plenty of time once we actually get there. Who's the guy you booked with the minibus?'

'I don't actually know him. Cath used him and said he was very cheap.'

Jesse frowned at the mention of Cath's name.

'He sounded really nice on the phone and he only charged us thirty pounds.'

'Thirty quid to get to Gatwick? That can't be right, it cost us seventy five last time.'

'He said thirty - I double-checked.'

Stamping out her cigarette, Jesse noticed Dotty pulling up outside. 'Right, let's get our cases out onto the drive. We'll never get Dotty's case into the lounge.' Chloe gazed out of the window, watching Jesse drag her suitcase to the end of the drive.

'Morning, darling. I'm so excited. How're you feeling?' Dotty was dressed in a bright yellow dress with a matching scarf tied in her hair, the early hour of the morning not showing in her face at all.

'I'll be fine once the minibus arrives and we're on our way. Excuse me a minute, come in and grab a tea if you want one.' Jesse ran up the staircase shouting, 'These fuckin' pills haven't kicked in yet,' and was out of sight for a further five minutes.

Mary and Dotty were pouring water in the ashtrays as they noticed the minibus pull up outside and a skeleton slowly clamber out of the driver's side and open the side doors, 'Oh crikey, Mary, Jesse's going to throw a wobbly when she sees him.' Mary followed Dotty in crossing herself. The two girls were staring out of the lounge window with dismayed looks on their faces as Jesse arrived from the loo, handbag balanced on her hip and gym bag on her shoulder. Glancing out of the window she nodded her head and went to say goodbye to Chloe. Regardless of all the reassuring noises Jesse made, there was no way she was going to get a kiss from the miserable dog.

'Don't worry, Chloe, Granny'll be here in two hours and then you won't notice I'm gone. Right, all set? ' Looking around her, she intoned, 'All fags out, dog fed, empty bins, keys, money, passport, answerphone on, mobile charged. Tickets?'

'I've got them,' said Mary, tapping her leather handbag.

'Okay, let's go.' Jesse gave the two girls a smile before ushering them out of the house and locking the doors behind them. Jesse made it to the minibus first and helped the bag of bones lift her suitcase into the bus before jumping in and gesturing for the girls to hurry up.

They both let out an audible breath before Mary reached for her luggage and muttered 'Pills must have kicked in.'

'Praise the Lord,' answered Dotty.

***

They rode in silence for the fifty minutes it took to get the clapped-out minibus to Gatwick Airport. The two girls who didn't have the benefit of lorazepam were on tenterhooks the entire time, terrified that the haggard-looking driver would take his last breath and die at the wheel. Jesse, on the other hand, was totally relaxed and thoroughly enjoyed the splendour of the sunrise unfolding before her. As they finally reached the check-in desk after queuing for half an hour with two young children intermittently laughing and screaming behind them, Mary's patience had run thin. This was the only time Mary ever had to queue before getting onto a plane and it irked her. She always flew Club Class for work and hated slumming it in Economy. Jesse and Dotty stood back and let Mary do the talking to the check-in clerk - this was a familiar routine by now.

Showing the clerk her travel agent ID, she made the usual demands: seats near the exits as they had the most legroom, two in front and one behind just in case someone didn't catch the plane, leaving a seat free next to Dotty so she could spread out, and a standby for First Class should there be availability for them to be upgraded. The clerk seemed fairly positive about both an upgrade and a spare plane seat - neither of which materialised.

A few hours later and Dotty and Jesse were standing, heads slightly bent over in front of the exit chairs, while Mary was animatedly talking to an air hostess. The seats they had been allocated did have plenty of legroom. Unfortunately these seats had solid armrests that held the food trays, which meant the arms couldn't be lifted to allow Dotty's girth to spread into the aisle and into the body next to her and were so thin Jesse couldn't fit in either. Before Mary had returned, most of the people in their direct vicinity had been watching the girls intently, and they were both flushed with embarrassment. Rather than waiting for Mary to solve the problem, Dotty took her courage in her hands and asked a rather thin elderly gentleman to her right if he would mind swapping seats. He looked at the two girls with a very smarmy expression before slowly saying, 'Yes, I would' and returned to reading *The Guardian*. Thankfully, Mary arrived before Jesse could react.

'It's no good, I'm afraid, the plane is full. The air hostess is going to walk down the aisle and see if anyone will be willing to move for us.' Mary chose to ignore the dejected facial expression planted on Dotty's face before adding, 'We won't be able to sit together.'

'Shit,' muttered Jesse. Dotty started to cry and neither of the girls knew what to do about it.

'Jesse, I can't sit next to someone else. I'll crush them. I can't do it. I'm going to ask to get off the plane.'

'Don't be silly,' Mary soothed, 'We'll sort something out.'

'No, that's it. I'm getting off the plane.'

Then an unexpected wonderful thing happened. A couple in their early twenties who had been watching what was happening from five rows away simply stood up and sat in the exit seats. No explanation. Just like that.

'I'll sit with Dotty,' Jesse stated. This was obviously not up for discussion. As each of the girls moved past the couple, they nodded and smiled their appreciation. Dotty followed last and gently squeezed the young man's shoulder and whispered, 'God bless you.'

Lorazepam might calm the mind but it does absolutely nothing for pain. For the entire four-hour trip Jesse sat, as she had the year previous, with her elbow on Dotty's shoulder, squashed against the window with her armrest digging into her stomach where Dotty was squashing her from the other side. Dotty even had to cut up her chicken dinner as Jesse couldn't use her left arm so she had to stab her food with her fork in her right hand. Dotty was riddled with guilt and shame and frequently stood looking out of the windows near the toilets, trying to give Jesse some breathing space before turbulence would bring the seating lights on and force her to return. As the plane touched down, laughter erupted from the passengers in reaction to Mary's high-pitched scream, which broke some of the tension and flooded Dotty with relief.

***

The apartment was like any other they had visited in Greece - basic. There were two bedrooms, one of which was open plan in the living room and kitchen area, and the other private with a heavy door - this would be Mary and Jesse's room as no-one would share with Dotty as her snoring was horrendous.

Mary was the first to get her area organised. She was so used to travelling she had it down to a fine art. None of her clothes were creased, everything had its own little bag or section and she was freshened up within twenty minutes of arrival, leaving Jesse and Dotty moaning about the state of their crumpled clothes, which had been packed with their usual 'it'll be all right on the night' attitude.

While Mary was at the supermarket next door to the apartments Dotty and Jesse changed out of their travelling clothes and freshened up. They were discussing which shades of lipstick would be best for their relative outfits when Mary came in carrying two full carrier bags of shopping.

'Ooh, what did you get?' Dotty asked while taking both bags off Mary and shoving her face in to investigate.

'Cleaning products.'

'What, no goodies?' moaned Dotty.

'We've only just arrived. I didn't think you'd be wanting anything,' Mary said.

Jesse and Dotty shared a look of 'why wouldn't we want any...' and then when Dotty removed the contents of the plastic bag, Jesse asked 'Why would you want Cif?'

On the bed lay a bag of J Cloths, two green scrubbers, a bottle of washing up liquid, Cif, bin liners, a small jar of Nescafé, milk, sugar and two tea towels.

'I know you two are happy to live in squalor for the next seven days but I'm not. Don't worry Jesse, you won't have to lift a finger. All I ask is that if you're going to keep your clothes on the floor then just do it on your side of the bed so I can't see them when I come in.'

'Fair enough.' Jesse had made it known years previously that when she was on holiday she didn't lift a finger, didn't wash a cup, didn't empty ashtrays - nothing. Mary had grown accustomed to Jesse's mess over the years and Dotty's inability to store her clothes in a wardrobe. She insisted all her outfits were kept on hangers on the doors and picture hooks, leaving any room looking in complete disarray. Mary had coped with this but not a cup or saucer could be left on the draining board for more than five minutes without Mary drying it and putting it out of sight. They had grown used to living like this, but regardless of how many times they had spent weeks together, Jesse still felt incredibly awkward with Mary and Dotty walking naked around the apartments. Okay, Jesse was the first to get her boobs out on the beach but she had always had a thing about hairy fannies... If they were anywhere near her she got nervous. Despite being someone who normally spoke her mind, she hadn't been able to alert her friends to her embarrassment for fear of them thinking she was prudish. She was happy that they could feel free in her company but it was a daily grind sitting on the balcony waiting for the girls to at least get around to putting their knickers on before she could get herself ready. They each had to adapt and had found ways of coping without causing friction.

One of the first things Dotty did on arriving at any resort was to get a double quota of toilet rolls, as both Mary and Jesse had real problems with not being able to wipe themselves after realising Dotty had gone through yet another entire roll of tissue trying to clean herself. On more than one occasion she had caused the toilet to block, causing much retching from Mary, who was inevitably left to try and sort it out, as Dotty would never claim responsibility for it, even though Jesse and Mary knew damn well she was the culprit. No matter how often the girls tried to drum it into Dotty that you couldn't put tissue in the toilets in Greece, she absolutely refused to use the bins provided as she felt it was unhygienic, but seemed only too happy to allow Mary to get up to her elbows in shit when she continually ignored their pleas.

The last time it had happened was in a taverna in Hersonissos so the girls had finished their drinks in one mouthful and left immediately before the stench was detected. They were practically running until they got out of sight into a cocktail bar, each harbouring visions of Greek waiters stumbling screaming out of the taverna, eyes streaming and gagging, pointing at the three figures running for freedom and shouting something along the lines of 'Fat English Bastards!'

***

Jesse was on her second vodka and tonic by the time her two friends arrived to join her at the apartment pool bar. Dotty had changed into a flowing green crinkle dress with red Jesus sandals and bag to match. Mary had opted for a navy twin set with classic-cut trousers, finished off with navy pumps. The two girls were a good half an hour behind Jesse, neither one of them being able to decide on which outfit was appropriate for the first night's drinking. Jesse, on the other hand, had only black-and-white clothes packed for her holiday to keep it simple, black for night, white for day, so she had no difficulty choosing a pair of black trousers and a shirt, finished off as usual with her black suede boots. Jesse never wore sandals or shoes, regardless of the weather, and hardly ever went without a jacket, regardless of the heat.

'Hello ladies, my name is Niko, welcome, welcome! What can I get you two lovely ladies to drink?'

'Hello Niko, I'm Dotty. I'll have a dry Martini and lemonade please, tall glass, lots of lemonade and ice and lemon. What about you, Mary? What are you having?'

'I'll have a Diet Coke, please.'

'No you won't!' screeched Jesse, nearly choking on her cigarette smoke. 'You're on holiday, Mary, you've got to loosen up, girl. Have a vodka and chill a bit.'

'I don't want vodka. Diet Coke'll be fine. I'm more than capable of having fun without being drunk, Jesse.'

'Yes, I know that, but not on our first night, okay? Please, I really need to let off some steam and I can't do it properly unless we all get a little tipsy. Okay?

Deal? Just for tonight? You can have Diet Coke for the next six days. Come on, Mary, have a proper drink.'

Mary took a moment to think about it, the pleading look on Jesse's face being the clincher. 'All right, just the one, though. I'll have a vodka and slimline tonic please, Niko.'

The girls sat in a row of contented silence around the bar watching the gorgeous Greek barman Niko mix the drinks. Jesse clocked the wedding ring within seconds of taking her seat at the bar so had no interest in him whatsoever. The two girls next to her were obviously oblivious to it as they both eyed him up and down as if he was a bar of Dairy Milk. After giving each of the girls their drinks, Niko then produced four small shot glasses with clear liquid in, handed one each to the girls, tilted his head and said 'Yamas' and drank the drink down in one. Jesse was the first to follow suit, leaving Mary and Dotty looking suspiciously at the liquid.

'Just get it down you,' Jesse moaned, failing to mention they were about to drink neat raki.

'Come on then, Mary, Yamas,' said Dotty and downed the shot. Her face turned pink. Mary followed with a silent grimace. Happy to have been of assistance, Niko smiled and busied himself changing the music playing on the CD.

'What are we going to do for food tonight?' Dotty asked after ordering a lemonade to water down her Martini so it was drinkable.

'I think we should turn right and have a wander and see what we come to,' suggested Mary.

'Sounds good to me,' Jesse agreed, 'traditional Greek tonight. I don't care what we have so long as it's loaded with tzatziki. It's far too early to go yet, though, so let's just settle down and have another drink here.'

Dotty spotted a bar immediately across from where they were sat. She could see it had huge cane chairs with comfortable-looking padding, the candles were lit and she had noticed a few shadows from around the bar, very obviously members of the opposite sex. 'Why don't we go across the road to that cocktail bar? I fancy a cocktail now.'

Jesse leaned back on her stool to investigate the bar, deciding it looked dark and atmospheric she downed her vodka and made to leave.

'See you later, Niko. What time are you open till?'

"Til you decide to go to bed!' he announced with a broad smile and a shrug of the shoulders.

'You'll regret saying that,' Mary mumbled as she gathered up her purse to follow the girls.

Dotty managed to get herself comfortable in one of the cane chairs without too much of a struggle. Mary looked decidedly petite surrounded by the huge chair and Jesse looked quite uncomfortable having to lean back with her legs crossed. These chairs were perfect for skinnies as the backs were set at an angle to allow you to relax back, but when you were horizontally challenged all that did was light up your spare tyre and encourage your double chins to come out to play. Had Jesse noticed any good-looking talent, she would have point-blank refused the chairs and chosen a stool at the bar instead. However, the bar was empty except for the barman and drinks waiter so she had to follow Dotty's suit.

'Hello ladies. You stay at Maria Apartments?'

'That's right. How did you know?' smiled Dotty at the man now standing beside their table.

'How could I not notice three beautiful women from such a distance? I would be blind.' He took a bowl of salted peanuts off his tray and put them next to Dotty on the table. Giving her a smooth smile he said, 'What can I get you to drink, lovely lady?' Jesse coughed loudly and rolled her eyes at Mary.

'Call me Dotty, please! What's your name?'

'My name Stavros.'

'Stavros, what a lovely name!'

Jesse had two fingers in her mouth but was polite enough not to accompany the action with a gagging sound.

'What would you recommend, Stavros?' It seemed Dotty was oblivious to her three chins being lit in neon from the bar sign as she gave the waiter an eyelash flutter.

'I recommend a Slow Screw Up Against the Wall.'

'How original,' Jesse muttered, but only to

herself, not even Mary heard her.

'Although I'm sure that's very nice....' flutter, flutter... 'I'll have the Antonio Special please.'

'Very good choice.' Before he had a chance to turn fully to look Jesse in the eye, she gave him her order.

'Champagne cocktail, please.'

'Okay, and for you, lady?'

'Black Russian, please.' Mary didn't need to look at Jesse to know she had pleased her. She really didn't want to get drunk but knew it was par for the course on the first night on holiday with Jesse to have a few drinks.

'I'll be right back, ladies.' Dotty actually turned in her seat to watch him leave. 'Mmm,' Dotty sighed.

'You've got to be joking, Dotty. He's foul!'

'No he's not!'

'Er, yes, he is! All that slow screw up a wall bollocks, he obviously trots that one out every night, for Christ sake. He was so smarmy.' Jesse made a face and visibly shuddered.

'He's Greek, for goodness' sake. That's how they are, Jesse! He isn't smarmy, he just can't communicate as we do.'

'I can't believe you're making excuses for him and you've only ordered one drink off him. You'll be wanting to marry him by day two!'

'Well, I couldn't do that as he's probably not a Christian, but I wouldn't mind a damn good snog.' All three girls started to giggle.

'Why don't we go and sit at the bar so we can talk to him?' suggested Dotty.

'Anything to get out of this friggin' chair,' said Jesse, trying to get enough momentum to swing herself out of the cane monstrosity. She discreetly stood at Dotty's side and offered her hand to help Dotty heave herself up.

Once up, Dotty took the lead, hefting herself up on a high bar stool and declaring, 'I thought we'd move so we could come and talk to you.' Mary whispered to Jesse, 'Nothing like keeping him guessing.' Jesse smiled and sipped her drink.

Jesse and Mary tuned out of the conversation with Dotty and Stavros when the sexual innuendo began being bantered between the two of them.

'I can't believe how quiet it is. It's nearly eight o'clock and there's hardly anyone around.'

'I know. I don't actually know how far away we are from the town but I'm guessing we're on the outskirts here. We'll see if we can find some buzzing bars after dinner close to home. If not, then we'll go into the town and see what's happening there.'

'Okay. I'm a bit knackered from the flight, actually. I don't feel much up to dancing or clubbing it.'

'Me neither, to be honest. I'm quite happy sitting at a bar drinking all night. I'm not that bothered if we stay at the apartment bar. Niko seemed nice enough. I'm sure we could get him to play some good tunes and have a boogie on the patio.'

Mary smiled knowingly. They'd been here before. Every single first night on holiday they all felt pooped from the flight, but Jesse would turn into disco diva after ten shots and boogie the night away until the early hours of the morning, not letting anyone go to bed. Annoyingly, she was always the worst for wear, drank at least three times more than the others, stayed up later and yet awoke first thing full of life and incredibly perky.

'If we can drag Dotty away from Romeo over there then I'm up for it.'

Jesse finished her drink in one go and said, 'Anyone for food?'

Dotty nodded, gulping down the last of her colourful cocktail, while Mary gathered the cigarettes and they were off.

It was a warm evening and there was a slight breeze tousling the girls' hair as they strolled. Unusually for Greece, there was a pavement on one side of the road so they kept to it while examining the tavernas along the dusty road. They had passed several with no-one in, completely unacceptable to Mary as she had to have atmosphere while she ate. They had passed two that looked very inviting but were a no-go, as the flimsy chairs would not support Dotty. They passed a pizzeria and a Chinese, which was out as it had to be traditional Greek on the first night for Jesse. It was a while before they came to a lovely-looking candlelit taverna, canopies pulled down the sides with the front open to give a feeling of eating alfresco. There were five tables occupied. The chairs were solid wood with no arms and the food was Greek - perfect. Not one compromise had been made and everyone settled onto their table happy.

They never normally drank the wine. Both Dotty and Jesse had a particular sense of taste and would normally only drink Sancerre, chilled to perfection. But as it was their first night they had to get drunk and as the years wore on, it was getting harder and harder for Jesse to get drunk without mixing her drinks. Wine never failed in doing the trick. The wine came as expected, in a brown pottery jug with three small glasses. Both Dotty and Jesse wrinkled their noses as they took their first sip. It was more medium than dry, had a bitter aftertaste and was not quite cold.

'Ugh, oh well, it'll be fine after the first glass. Cheers everyone, here's to a good holiday,' toasted Jesse.

'No, here's to a bloody great holiday!' seconded Dotty. They each ordered a starter suitable for sharing. Jesse had two but said tzatziki didn't count, as she had to have it with everything and wouldn't share it. They had all decided on Kleftiko, all secretly hoping it would come with roast potatoes rather than the traditional rice. Two extra baskets of pitta breads were ordered and then there was the usual forty five minute wait until the main course, which gave Dotty plenty of time to annoy Jesse by taking endless photographs of the trio. Five cigarettes later, the main course arrived and Mary was half-drunk.

Mary never normally touched wine as one glass was enough to get her tipsy. You could never normally tell when Mary was tipsy. If she didn't insist on telling you every five minutes that she was pissed then you'd never know. She never slurred, fell over or made a fool of herself. Only her closest friends would know because she became flirtatious, something she never did when fully sober. Mary hadn't informed them she was getting drunk, but Jesse realised once the waiter came over with some complimentary shots of Metaxa.

'Aren't you going to join us in a drink?' Mary lifted her glass and batted her eyelashes.

'Oh yes, yes of course!' The waiter scurried off to get himself a glass.

'Grab us that chair next to you, Jesse, so he can sit down. He's been on his feet all night, poor thing.'

Dotty looked at Jesse and smirked. 'Here we go,' said Jesse.

'Here you are, we've got a chair for you,' Mary said, lounging over the back of the empty chair. As the waiter sat down, Mary rubbed him gently on the arm and said, 'Ah you poor thing, sit down for five minutes and have a break. You must be knackered.'

'Yamas!' The waiter downed his drink, looking a little nervous.

Mary transferred her hand from the back of his

chair to his knee and said, 'So how long have you worked here?'

She was met with a blank expression followed by a smile.

'It seems a quiet area. Is it normally this quiet this time of year?'

Another smile.

'Oh for heavens' sake, Mary, he doesn't speak a bloody word of English!' Jesse said, amused.

'English? No.' He shook his head with a look of mock misery.

Mary pointed to her chest, 'Me Mary. You?'

A big smile, 'Carlos!'

'Carlos, this is Jesse and this is Dotty.' He nodded to each.

'Carlos, do you understand a word I am saying to you right now?' smiled Jesse.

Carlos looked confused for a moment and then smiled, nodding his head.

'Good. So if I said to Mary, 'Don't even consider going with this guy because he's obviously all of seventeen, can't understand a word you're saying and probably is absolute crap in the sack' would you nod your head like a moron and agree?' Jesse smiled and nodded her head. 'Yes?'

'Yes, yes,' nodded Carlos.

Dotty let out a muffled snort and then tossed her head back and roared for England. By the time she had stopped her laughter and got it down to a

consistent giggle, she had tears of mascara rolling down
her face. Had Carlos not joined in with her laughter it
might have got under control sooner, but watching the
poor bastard laughing set her off even more. Jesse sat,
smiling to herself with the realisation that Dotty and
Mary had already partnered themselves off for the night
and she was going to end up pissed at the bar talking to
Niko while her two friends were getting some.

It was late by the time they left the restaurant.
Carlos had given them three extra rounds of Metaxa,
which had turned Dotty's face pink and kept Mary's
hand firmly on his thigh. Mary explained with hand
signals where to meet them after he finished work and
at what time. In the end she drew a map with Jesse's
eyeliner onto a white napkin showing the Maria
Apartments, the bar opposite and a picture of a clock
with its hands on midnight - a nice touch, Jesse had
thought.

'See you later, Carlos,' Mary cooed, after kissing
him on the cheek and giving him a dirty wink.

With Jesse in the middle, the girls all linked
arms and strolled back up the street to the bar. Jesse
wasn't sure if it was her who was stumbling sideways or
Dotty. Either way, it took a lot of zigzagging to get
back to the bar. Jesse and Dotty had humoured
themselves along the walk recounting the evening's
events with Mary and Carlos, mimicking Mary and the
poor hapless bugger she'd ensnared. They were still
laughing as they hauled each other up the four steps

into the cocktail bar that contained Stavros. The bar was almost as deserted as it was three hours previously. There was a young couple sitting at the front drinking cocktails and four men sitting behind them in a ring, working their way through beer and tequila, and another local had joined Stavros behind the bar.

The additional barman was Antonio. He was very tall, had a dirty look about him as though he hadn't washed, very yellow teeth and blood-red veins surrounding his brown eyes. He obviously drank a lot and Jesse guessed that this evening was no exception. After organising the girls' drinks, Antonio became their host for the evening by performing endless magic tricks with cards. Stavros had joined Dotty and as they were getting friendly, whispering and giggling to each other, Antonio focused on Mary and Jesse. Jesse kept kicking Mary's ankles as her chant of, 'Oh how did you do that? Show us another one,' was getting on her tits no end. Mary, a little tipsy, paid no attention.

Midnight came and went and Jesse found herself constantly turning in her seat to look at the entrance just in case Carlos was coming up them - she needed some light relief. By the time Carlos eventually arrived at half past one, Dotty and Stavros were smooching on the dance floor, Jesse was searching her vodka and tonic for the meaning of life and Mary and Antonio were holding hands across the bar talking smut.

'Hello Mary,' Carlos said sheepishly.

'Oh Carlos! I've been waiting for you! Let's dance,' she jumped off her stool and dragged a happy Carlos to the dance floor, leaving Antonio looking after her bewildered.

'Can I get you another vodka, Jesse?' Antonio asked, obviously wanting to distract himself.

'No thanks, I'm off, actually. I'll maybe see you again tomorrow.'

Jesse stepped down from her stool very gently and was surprised to find her legs did actually support her and didn't buckle under the amount of alcohol she had consumed. She looked at the two couples smooching on the dance floor and decided they wouldn't notice if she left, so just walked quietly to the exit and left them to it. Focusing on her walk, she managed to cross the road to the apartment bar without stumbling which, given the potholes in the road, along with her being pissed, was something to be proud of in itself. There were four men sitting around the bar drinking shots, the same ones who'd propped up the bar across the road earlier, and a middle-aged couple sat in the corner with coffees. She had intended to walk straight past the bar and head to bed until she heard Robbie Williams blaring out of the bar's large speakers, which made her pause.

Niko came running around from behind the bar, shouting, 'Jesse, Jesse!' and threw his arms around her. 'Everyone, you must meet my friend, Jesse! Isn't she lovely?!' Jesse couldn't help but laugh at his behaviour. She hadn't spoken more than five words to him and already she was his friend. 'Come, sit down and join us for a drink.' With that he pulled up a stool and put it right in the middle of the four men at the bar. Jesse was mortified. She knew she was pissed and the last thing she wanted to do was try and be sociable to a bunch of men who had probably been having a perfectly nice time until she crashed the party.

'Thanks Niko but I really can't stay.'

'Nonsense. Sit down and have a drink with us.' Jesse turned to the man on her right who had taken her arm, stopping her from getting off her stool. She examined his face and decided he looked rather nice. His voice had been soft and his features matched. He had a kindness about his brown eyes to which she warmed and he gave her a gentle smile.

'Let's have some tequila!' Niko shouted, throwing his arms in the air. He turned the music up louder and everyone started to sing aloud to Angels, Jesse included. Each of the boys she was sitting between bought rounds of tequila slammers. Between each round, Niko gave a complimentary shot and no-one let Jesse touch her purse. After Jesse said she couldn't do it anymore as the salt was making her sick, Niko made hers with sugar and orange rather than salt and lemon, and the party continued.

Robbie Williams turned to Bryan Adams, which led on to Queen. By the time Mary and Dotty had decided to call it a night at three am and stumbled over to the pool bar, they found Jesse dancing around the pool with four men, an elderly couple and Niko singing Fat Bottomed Girls at the top of their voices.

On spotting the two girls, Niko shouted, 'Ladies, come dance!' Within moments the entire circle of eight pissheads surrounded them, jumping up and down and thrashing their heads around laughing and singing, and the eight became ten.

Jesse had become one of the men, screaming and shouting at the two girls to 'down in one' when they were handed tequila after tequila. It was after five am when the music slowed to Celine Dion and Jesse took it in turns dancing with the group of men, slowly staggering in a circle, head on shoulder, eyes closed. Mary danced slowly with Niko and Dotty bored the couple, Frank and Annie, by talking about Christianity and her new found love - Stavros.

Just before six Jesse announced, 'That's it. Enough! See you in the morning.' She ignored all the pleas of 'the night's still young', kissed every single one of them on the cheek and managed to get around the pool to her apartment without falling over.

When Dotty staggered home some time later, she stepped carefully over Jesse, who was lying on the floor naked with her head in the open fridge, and fell on the bed into an instant sleep.

Both of the girls were unconscious when Mary came to bed more than an hour later. As they were both snoring loudly, Mary was quite happy to leave

Jesse where she was and have the bedroom to herself. She pulled the curtains shut to keep out the morning light and got out of her blouse and trousers, changed into her teddy bear pyjamas and fell into a deep sleep. As well as forgetting to brush her teeth, she also forgot to remove her bra and panties out of her handbag, where Niko had placed them only ten minutes earlier.

CHAPTER 16

It was past noon when Mary managed to drag herself out of bed. After popping two paracetamol she grabbed two chocolate croissants from the fridge and took her freshly-brewed Nescafé and cigarettes out onto the balcony. She was still wearing her teddy bear pyjamas and added Ray-Ban sunglasses, finished off with pink flip-flops.

As Jesse had not been in the fridge when Mary reached for it, she knew she would find her sunbathing. She was easy to spot, sitting upright on a sun lounger, pure white skin glistening with lotion, reading a John Grisham book. She was bulging out of a skimpy black triangle bikini and had on a black baseball cap with the word Justice inscribed in pink. Mary was pleased to note that the beds on either side of her friend were strewn with items: dress, book, bum bag, towels, cigarettes, very obviously on hold for herself and Dotty, which was good as the pool area was packed to capacity.

She looked from her friend to the pool bar, wondering if Niko was working yet, but in his place stood a petite tanned blonde in a yellow bikini top, squeezing fresh orange juice.

Mary watched Jesse approach through her darkened lenses and inwardly groaned. Standing on tiptoes to rest her arms on the ledge of the balcony, Jesse greeted her friend.

'Hi Honey, how ya doing?' Jesse was chipper as usual on a hangover.

'Mmm. I'll be better once I've had a few more coffees.'

'You're looking a bit grey. Better get yourself lotioned up and get in this sun. Isn't it fantastic!'

'Mmm. I don't know how you do it. Don't you feel like shit?'

'I feel fine, actually. Had the trots as usual this morning after breakfast but I'm fine now. In fact I think I'm ready for a beer. Want one?'

'Not on your life, I'm not drinking again. Ever.'

Jesse laughed. 'You'll be fine once you've had some sun. Where's Dotty?'

'Still in her pit snoring her head off.'

'Hasn't she gotten up yet?'

'She's been wandering around. The chocolate is by her bed so she's had breakfast. What did you have?'

'I got Niko's wife to make me a cheese and ham toastie. It was lovely, actually. Are you going to come next door for some lunch?'

'Lunch? Jesse, I've only just got up.'

'Did someone say lunch?' came a voice from inside the apartment. The two girls were silent as they heard Dotty's heavy feet on the marble floor, walking to the patio window. The curtain opened just enough for her to stick her head out. 'Did you say lunch, Jesse?'

'Yes, I thought I'd go next door to the taverna and have a Greek salad and kebab. Fancy it?'

'Oh, do you think they'll do me a fry-up at this time of day?'

'I don't see why not, but I'm starving. How long will you be?'

'Two seconds, luvvie, give me two seconds.' Dotty's head was out of view before Jesse could respond. Jesse turned her attention back to Mary, who was eyeing up the blonde in the bikini at the bar.

'Who's the blonde?'

'That's Niko's wife. I told you, she made me the toastie this morning. She's a bit pissed off at having to do the bar, I think. She said Niko didn't get in until gone seven this morning. I didn't realise we'd been up that late. What time did you and Dotty get in?'

'Dotty left as soon as you did and I followed her in, after saying goodnight to everyone. The bedside clock said quarter past seven.' Mary was glad of her covered eyes as she lied to her friend.

'Quarter past seven! Blimey, where did the time go?'

'Where are the guys from last night? Seen them yet?'

'No, not that I'd recognise them if I did see them.'

Mary raised her eyebrows.

'You know me, I don't remember sod all past midnight. I've been trying to remember their names and buggered if I can. I don't even remember saying goodnight to anyone.'

'Oh don't worry, you did.'

'What does that mean?' Jesse instantly looked anxious.

'Don't worry. I'm only messing with you. You just kissed them all on the cheek.'

'Thank heavens for that, I can't stand it when I don't remember having a tongue in my mouth!' Jesse laughed just as Dotty appeared from the side of the building, hair in a ponytail, looking like death in a yellow sun dress.

'Ready!'

'Blimey, you were quick. Give me a second to get my dress on.'

'Don't worry. I'm sure they won't mind you in your bikini.' Dotty was only half joking.

'Bugger off! I know what I look like, Dotty. Besides, I don't want a pattern from those bloody seats on my arse and thighs for the rest of the afternoon, thank you very much.' With that, Jesse trotted back to her lounger for her cover-up.

'How are you feeling, Mary?' Dotty enquired.

'Like crap, actually. I'll be all right once the paracetamols have kicked in. What about you?'

'The same. Crap.' They both watched Jesse

stride towards them with her white dress blowing in the breeze.

'I don't know how she does it.'

'Nope, me neither. See you later, Mary.'

'See ya later!' Jesse waved as she passed the balcony, linked her arm with Dotty's and off they went.

***

When Mary returned to her seat on the balcony, she had showered and changed into a flowered bikini, which she wore under a towelling white robe. Her headache was starting to subside as she dipped Dairy Milk into her second cup of Nescafé, not being able to take her eyes off the beautiful blonde whom she now knew to be Niko's wife.

Mary was in two minds about how she should be feeling. Her thought process was exhausting her.

I can't believe you've done it again with a married man.

I didn't know he was married.

Of course you did.

He didn't tell me.

You saw the ring.

No I didn't.

Excuse me?

Okay, I saw the ring but don't they wear them on the other hand in Greece?

Nice try.

Well, he was the one who made a move on me. It wasn't my fault.

You mean you didn't for an instant egg him on?

No!

No?

Really?

Weren't you the one who brushed against him first?

No, I don't think so.

I think you'll find you did. Weren't you the one who asked to dance with him?

I don't remember. Yes you do. It was Celine Dion and you even went behind the bar to bring him out.

Well, everyone was dancing.

Dotty wasn't.

Everyone else was.

You mean Jesse was.

She was!

She was dancing with single men.

How do you know that?

Because you know she'll hardly talk to a married man, never mind dance with one. Besides, Jesse had her hands on their shoulders. You had your hands on Niko's arse.

I'm just shorter than he is, that's all. It was uncomfortable to put my hands on his shoulders.

Pull the other one. You fancied him and you wanted him to know you were available.

So what if I did?

He's married.

So?

So, what does that make you?

A tart.

Ah, don't be so hard on yourself! You do realise you have a problem with commitment.

Ha, rubbish. Why else, then, do you dance with the only married man? Because you know he's not yours to keep, easy, no hassle, no commitment, no heartbreak... but there always is heartbreak, isn't there?

No, I'm not in love with Niko. Not yet. Come on, it was only one night, a few hours, even - not long enough to get attached.

That's what I'm saying. You're afraid of commitment. If he had been single it wouldn't have only been one night - it might have been the next seven nights and then what?

Then nothing, because it didn't happen.

But you know what I'm getting at?

Yeah, I guess.

You had the pick of four single men last night. You have to ask yourself why you went for the only married one.

I didn't have a pick of four men. Jesse had them.

Jesse had a choice of four, which left three single men unaccounted for.

But she didn't pick one so how would I know which one to go for without upsetting Jesse?

She didn't pick one because she never does, and you know that.

Yes and what is that all about?

Think about Jesse later - we have to deal with you right now.

Well, I don't need this shit. He was married, it happened, over.

Well, so obviously not over otherwise you wouldn't be comparing yourself to the bikini-clad blonde over there.

Well, that's only natural. If she wasn't Niko's wife I'd still do that.

Really? What about the other twelve or so women sat around the pool? You haven't even glanced at them.

Point taken. I'm bored of this now.

Okay, just remember, though, if Dotty finds out, there'll be trouble.

She won't find out.

No? You've already lied to Jesse about this and you know you can't lie to save your life.

It won't come up again.

You'd better decide what to do if it does.

If it does then I'll tell them.

Brave girl, do you think that's wise?

They'll understand.

They'll be pissed off.

Why should they? It's got nothing to do with them.

They love you and they're frustrated with you constantly ending up with married men.

It's my business.

No, it's their business. They have to pick up the pieces and put you back together again.

Oh come off it, it doesn't affect me.

No, correction, it didn't affect you a long time ago. The last two times it has affected you.

No.

When was the last time you went out before this holiday?

What's that got to do with it? It's been winter.

Think about it. When was it?

I went to the cinema with Jesse.

How long ago was that?

I can't remember, a few weeks, maybe.

Make that well over three months ago.

I go shopping all the time!

Shopping is not going out and you know it. You've hidden yourself away.

No, I just don't like going out any more.

Why is that?

I don't know.

Yes you do.

Because I can't be bothered.

Because you don't want to meet a man in case he happens to be married and he happens to break your heart again.

My heart isn't broken.

No, it's completely closed now - you've locked it away and have hidden the key.

Oh, very poetic.

Come on, don't laugh this off. It's about time you dealt with this.

Right now, on a hangover?

Why not?

I'm not in the mood.

You need to sort this out before it ruins your life.

Nothing is ruining my life. I'm perfectly happy, thank you very much.

No you're not.

Yes I am.

Tell me one thing you're happy with.

My house - my house is lovely and perfect and it belongs to me.

Bricks and mortar.

I worked damn hard for those bricks and mortar, my parents can be proud.

They'd be more proud to see you married.

Maybe they will one day. I'll meet someone and fall in love and get married, it happens all the time.

How will you meet someone?

If it's meant to be he'll come to me.

So you want to be married to a postman.

No!

Well, that's the only way a man is going to come to you. You never leave the house. If it's meant to be, it will be. That's a great way of giving up all responsibility of what happens to you.

Oh shut up, you sound like Jesse now.

She might have a point.

Look, when I'm ready to meet a man, I will. He will come to me and that's it, no more. I've got a headache and I want to relax.

Okay, make yourself another coffee.

Good idea. You might want to get some more chocolate from the fridge while you're at it.

Well, I am on holiday. Yeah, go on. Treat yourself, then. You can feel guilty about something else other than fucking Niko.

Give me a break!

Mary stood for a while, breathing deeply, concentrating on silencing her inner voice. Happy that the discussion was over, she ventured back into the cool of the apartment for her third Nescafé-and-chocolate fix.

***

From her sun lounger Mary watched Jesse and Dotty pass the pool, heading for the apartment. As usual Dotty pretended to ignore how noticeable she was and drew more attention to herself by shouting across the pool, 'Mary, do you want anything from the room?!' Mary nodded and made a smoking motion with her hand.

'Are they in your bag?' Again Mary nodded and put her head back in her Danielle Steel novel.

Jesse plonked herself down on the lounger next to Mary. 'Where's Dotty?'

'She's gone to have a lie down. Probably won't see her for another hour or so, I reckon.'

'What did you have to eat?'

'Greek salad, tzatziki and chips. Dotty had a huge fry-up and an ice cream. That's why she's gone to lie down. She's eaten too much.'

'That's the one thing that pisses me off about her, she sleeps her life away. It really annoys me that we're on holiday and she spends it sleeping.'

'Don't let it bother you, Jesse. So long as she's happy .'

'Yes, I suppose so. What about you?'

'What about me?' asked Mary.

'Are you happy?'

'Of course.'

'So would I be if I got shagged last night as well.' Jesse tossed Mary's cigarettes into her lap.

'What are you talking about?'

'I'm talking about your bra and knickers in your handbag.' Jesse took a drag of her cigarette and watched her friend's face carefully. Mary lit a cigarette of her own to give herself a few seconds' pause to decide what to say. One look at Jesse, who had purposefully removed her shades, told Mary she didn't have a hope in hell of getting away with this.

'I didn't get laid. I just had a grope.'

'Who with?' Jesse was very matter-of-fact.

'No-one you know.'

'Niko.'

'What on earth makes you say that?'

'It was Niko, wasn't it?'

'Tell me why you'd think that and then I'll tell you.'

'Because he's the only one who was married from last night.'

Mary was disappointed she was being so predictable. 'I didn't know he was married until this morning.' It was a lie and they both knew it, but they both knew to let it go if this day wasn't going to be spoiled.

'So what are you going to do about it now?'

'Nothing, of course. It's done. That's that.'

'It's going to be a bit embarrassing when he turns up later.'

'Why? I was pissed. We didn't actually have sex. It's really not a problem.'

'So where were you when you had your grope? You said you followed us to bed.'

'I did, eventually. As soon as you left, everybody went home so I helped Niko clear the glasses up and close the bar. He poured us both a nightcap and before you know it, we were kissing.'

'You were kissing at the bar? What if someone had seen you?'

'Well, actually, no, it wasn't at the bar. We'd moved into the reception of the hotel.'

'You lost your bra and knickers in the reception area?' Jesse was incredulous.

'No! After we were in the reception, I popped down into his room for a few minutes.'

'What room?'

'They have a room downstairs for if they stay on duty until late so they don't have to drive home too tired or pissed.'

'Who's they?'

'Niko and his brother.'

'Is his brother single?' Jesse asked hopefully.

'No, apparently he's engaged.'

'Shame. If he looks anything like his brother I

173

wouldn't mind having a go.'

The two girls smirked at each other and then smoked in silence for a while.

'Was he any good?'

'Actually, he was a good kisser and he was very romantic. He wanted me to put it in my mouth, though. That's when I decided we'd gone too far and it was time for me to leave.'

'Mary, you do make me laugh. I've never known anyone with such an aversion to oral sex.'

Mary put on her Eliza Doolittle voice, 'You know what I'm like, I'm a good girl, I am.' The irony of this comment was not lost on either of them.

'Are you going to tell Dotty?'

'I don't know. What do you think I should do?'

'Well, I'm not comfortable lying to her. I'm happy not to proactively tell her but if she asks me I'll have to tell her the truth, but I'd prefer it if you did.'

'You know what she's like with all this sex before marriage and adultery shit. She'll have a right go at me.'

'There is one way around that.' Jesse puffed her cigarette miserably.

'What do you mean? What's the matter?'

'This Stavros guy that she's been gushing over all fucking morning, the one she was getting off with last night? Apparently she's arranged to meet him tonight and she said they've already gone past first base.'

'What's that got to do with me?'

'He's married.'

Mary's hand flew to her mouth in shock. 'No!'

'Yup. She'll be gutted when she finds out.'

'How do you know? He wasn't wearing a ring.'

'Niko told me last night when I arrived at the bar. He wasn't wearing a ring because he takes it off every evening before he starts work.'

'You obviously haven't told Dotty.'

'No. I'm hoping to get a word with Stavros somehow and tell him to come clean.'

'Just how do you propose doing that without her finding out?'

Without realising it the girls had lowered their voices to a whisper. Their apartment was on the other side of the pool but Dotty's hearing was pristine and they weren't taking any chances.

'Well, Dotty's bound to be in bed for hours yet and apparently they start setting up across the road at about five o'clock. If she's around, maybe you could take her to the shops or something.'

'What're you going to say to him?'

'I'm going to tell him to leave her alone, of course.'

'But Jesse, she's really happy. You can't make that decision for her. She'll be miserable.'

'Well, what the hell else am I supposed to do? You know what she's like. She's probably already fallen head over heels for the prick. If she goes any further

175

with him and then realises he's married, she'll be repenting for the next two years.'

'I think you should tell her yourself and not talk to Stavros.'

'What, so I get it in the neck? You know what she's like, she'll shoot the messenger. Besides, how do I get away with the fact I've just spent the last two hours listening to her guff on and on about him and not told her, then?'

'Why don't you wait until Niko comes back on duty, and say he told you then?'

'But that would be a lie.'

'Only a white lie.'

'I'll think about it.'

The conversation stopped while Mary applied lotion to Jesse so she could lie on her belly and tan her back.

'Did you enjoy last night?' Mary asked.

Jesse had put her shades on again so Mary couldn't see her expression clearly, but she thought she saw a flicker of anger.

'It was all right. I was bored at the bar, I have to say.'

'You should've danced with Antonio.'

'Give me some credit, Mary, he's married. Besides which, he was foul!'

'He was lovely.'

'Lovely? So lovely you cast him aside without a moment's hesitation when Carlos turned up.'

'Okay, so he wasn't as lovely as Carlos, but there was nothing wrong with him.'

'You wait until you get over there again tonight without drink in your system and see if you can say that without crossing your fingers behind your back! Come to think of it, what happened to Carlos last night?'

'Nothing really.'

'Meaning?'

'Meaning we had a few snogs and a dance and that was that.'

'When are you seeing him again?' Jesse dreaded the answer.

'Tonight after work.'

'I'm not being funny, Mary, he was reasonably cute but he can't speak a word of English. What the hell are you going to do with him?'

'I don't know. Go for a walk or something.' Jesse's facial expression made Mary laugh. 'Don't be so cynical, Jesse, I can go for a walk without getting up to naughties, you know.'

'I wouldn't put my mortgage on it, darling, not in a million.'

'What about you?'

'What do you mean?'

'You were dancing with all those blokes. Didn't you get off with any of them?'

'God, no! How tacky!'

'What's tacky about it?'

'I don't know. I'm not into all these public
177

displays of affection. Besides, I was pissed.'

'All the more reason for you to get off with one of them, I would've thought.'

'You'd think so, wouldn't you?' Jesse got up from her bed, placed her towel over her stomach to hide her rolls of flab and sat on the edge of the lounger to face her friend. 'I know I was pissed last night and don't remember a lot of the evening, but when I was sat in the bar I got to thinking about my situation with men. For the last two years, nearly, I've been desperate for a man, any man, and yet I haven't found one. All this time I've been thinking I'm desperate for a shag, but when I think about it, I'm not.'

'Yeah, right, pull the other one, Jesse.'

'No, seriously, hang on a minute. I've had plenty of opportunities to get laid. I've actually spoken to quite a few single men. I go out as often as I can. I can list a hundred things I want in a man but I can also list a hundred things I don't want. I think I've finally come to the conclusion that what I want *is* actually out there, but it is also coupled with a lot of what I don't want.'

'Not quite with you yet, honey.'

'Okay. Bear with me. I say I want to get laid but, seriously, and I know you are going to think this is gross, but I have better orgasms with my vibrator than I ever have done with a man.'

'You just haven't found the right man.'

'I know, because I don't think I really want one.'

178

'Oh come on, Jesse, you never stop talking about wanting a bloke.'

'I know this, but I think I've had a breakthrough.'

'Breakdown, more like!'

'No, breakthrough. I think the only reason I think I want a man is to break up the boredom of my own life.'

'Doesn't everyone?'

'I don't know, do they? If so, that doesn't make it right, surely? No wonder all my relationships have turned to shit. I expect a man to come in and turn my life around. I've finally come to the realisation that only I can do that.'

'Jesse, what are you talking about? You have a great life.'

'It may appear to be great but I'm bored out of my skull killing time.'

'But you have everything!'

'Look, I don't want to sound ungrateful, because I know I'm in a great position: my own home, brand new car, my own business, a glamorous hobby with the singing, lots of money to throw around. But I have no stimulation at all, nothing to be passionate about. All this time I've thought I'm missing a man. I don't think I am. I think I'm missing passion.'

'What about intimacy? Don't you miss that?'

'Oh, you mean the cuddles at bedtime and the farting openly under the sheets?'

Mary laughed. 'You know what I mean. I love falling asleep tucked under a man's arm. It makes me feel really safe.'

'I feel safe with my dog next to me, Mary. I can't stand sharing my bed with someone and I've never liked the feeling of a man trying to protect me. That's never sat well with me.'

'That's because you can look after yourself.'

'Exactly! I don't actually need a man for anything. That's why I can't find one. I don't need one. I only think I want one. What the hell can a bloke actually offer me?'

'Security.'

'I have that. I can provide for myself.'

'Company.'

'I have you and Dotty and Chloe.'

'Sex.'

'Rabbit.'

'Conversation.'

'When was the last time you had a half-decent conversation with a man you were involved with? I only find men interesting because they have good looks, because I'm attracted to them, not because of what they have to say. I really think I'm onto something here. If I'm happy with my life then maybe a man can come in and enhance it. But up until now I've wanted a man to come in and change it and I don't think that's possible. What do you think?'

'I don't know, I suppose you've got to follow

your own instinct.'

'I think so, too, and my instinct today is saying lay off the men, sort your life out, find your own happiness and then anything else is a bonus.'

'Just how are you going to turn your life around, though, Jesse?'

'No idea. That's the hard thing. There are lots of things I should feel passionate about, but frankly, I really don't. I really don't know what makes me happy...'

'Chocolate.' Mary smirked.

'Yes, there's always that... I know what makes me comfortable - watching videos, drinking wine, going to the cinema, but I'm not sure I know what makes me actually *happy.*'

Mary lit another cigarette and pondered for a while.

'Now you've said all that, you've made me thoroughly depressed.'

Jesse laughed loudly and patted her friend on the knee. 'Don't be so morose! Come on, time for a tacky cocktail. Let's show ourselves up by having a Piña Colada with one of those umbrellas stuck in the top.'

'I'll have an orange juice, thanks.'

'Hair of the dog.'

'I wasn't drinking cocktails last night!'

'It's alcohol. What's the difference? Come on, cheer up. One thing I do know is spending time with you makes me happy.' As she got up, she planted a big kiss on Mary's forehead and trotted to the bar as if she didn't have a care in the world and, for about ten minutes, she didn't.

***

Dotty was sipping an orange juice beside Mary, who was reading Dotty's *HELLO!* magazine. She looked a bit like Jackie Onassis with the black oversized sunglasses. The only detractions from this image were the orange shorts she had placed on her head to protect her hair from the sun and the blue-and-yellow sarong she had tied across her body. Dotty's skin was almost blue where it had been deprived of sun most of its adult life. She was currently wearing factor twenty five on her shins, arms and face. She didn't bother putting lotion on any other part of her body as she had no intention of baring it. She hadn't yet decided whether to get in the swimming pool. The plastic steps didn't look very strong and she was concerned she wouldn't get back out once in. The memory of last year's disaster in the pool still burned strong and it pained her to recall it now.

She had got into the pool without too many problems. She had been gently swimming the small length of the pool, when the pool area seemed to suddenly fill with people. She noted all the skinny babes and tanned young men and was too embarrassed to get out. She was in there a full two hours before Jesse realised what was going on and came to her rescue. Jesse's plan was to get in the shallow end, have Mary standing by with her towel and Jesse standing directly behind Dotty so the full view of her backside wouldn't be for more than a few seconds. It had worked and she'd managed to keep some of her dignity, but her face had burnt severely in the water so she had a constant reminder for several days afterwards. There had been no nasty comments from people around the pool but she wasn't sure if the hushed silence was worse. She had felt hundreds of eyes upon her, although she didn't actually make eye contact with a single pair. Sometimes she absolutely hated herself, but she was practised at pushing these feelings aside, which is what she chose to do now.

'Fancy going to the beach, Mary?'

'Not today, Dotty, it's too late. The sun will be in soon.'

'What about tomorrow, then?'

'If Jesse doesn't get too drunk tonight, I'm sure that'll be okay.'

'Why does it matter if Jesse drinks?'

'You know what she's like, she'll need to be near a toilet.'

'Where is she now?'

'On the toilet.'

'Ah, I see! Well, why don't we go down and investigate and see if there are any bars or anything on the beach where they've got toilets?'

'You know what she's like, Dotty. She won't go

from the apartment if she knows she's going to get the shits. I don't blame her, it must be horrid.'

'Yes, I suppose so. Mind you, knowing Jesse she won't be drinking tonight, after last night.'

'She's already started.'

'Oh! I was hoping for an early night, after last night.'

'I'd have thought you'd had enough sleep today to catch up?'

'Oh I wasn't sleeping. I've just been resting.'

'Mmm.'

'What time are you going across the road tonight?'

'I'm not sure, actually. Jesse's putting me off Carlos a bit.'

'Why?'

'Well, he doesn't speak a word of English.'

'Didn't bother you last night.'

'No, but I have a feeling it might tonight. What about you? Are you meeting Stavros?'

'Yes, I said we'd go over before we go out to eat.'

'Have you spoken to Jesse about that?'

'No, why?'

'She said she found the bar boring last night so I'm not sure she'll want to go in there before dinner *and* after. I think we've got a better chance of getting her in there after dinner, to be honest with you, once she's had a few drinks.'

'Oh, but I've told him I'd see him,' Dotty whined.

'I'm sure he'll understand. Besides, you'll see him. Just not until later.'

'But I want to see him before dinner!' Dotty wailed.

'Why don't you see him before dinner, and Jesse and I will stay here and chat to Niko? That way everyone's happy.'

'But I'll have to walk in there on my own. I can't!'

'For heaven's sake, Dotty, you can see the bloody bar from here. It's not as if you won't know he's there to meet you.'

'True. Okay, so what time did you get in last night?'

'Straight after you.'

'You didn't get up to anything with Niko?'

'Why on earth would you say that?'

'I don't know, I just thought you were getting a bit friendly with each other.' Mary chose to say nothing. 'You do know he's married, don't you, Mary?'

'Yes, Dotty, I know.'

'Good! Fancy a toasted sandwich?'

'No thanks, it won't be long until dinner.'

'Okay, I'll get one for Jesse, though, just in case she comes back soon.'

'I don't think she will, Dotty.'

'Just in case.' In other words, thought Mary, *I'm*

getting two toasted sandwiches, so please let me live in denial that they are not both for me.

***

Jesse had waited until late afternoon before checking in with Gill, who was looking after her business. She drained the last of her Piña Colada, lit a menthol cigarette, got her pen and paper ready and rang home.

'Good afternoon, Monroe Transcriptions, how can I help you?'

'Hi Gill, it's Jesse. How's it going?'

'Hiya! Hang on a minute while I get a fag so I can chat.' Jesse heard the phone clatter onto the desk and could easily visualise Gill rummaging around the office trying to find where she'd thrown her cigarettes. Gill was a fantastic businesswoman, but she was a messy one. Jesse heard the lighter flick and Gill take a large drag and exhale before coming back on the line.

'Sorry about that. What's the weather like?'

'It's in the nineties. Sheer bliss.'

'Did you go out last night?'

'Oh yes.'

'Hung over?'

'Oh yes.'

'Glad to hear it. So what're you doing calling me when you're supposed to be enjoying yourself?' Gill's tone was mockingly stern.

'You know what I'm like. Just wanted to make sure everything was all right. Any problems?'

'Nope. Not at all. Everything's arrived that was meant to and all the girls are working. The phone's been a bit quiet but apart from that it's all fine.'

'Any post?'

'Only the tapes that you were expecting and it looks like you've got a few cheques here and the odd bill. I did accidentally open a personal package for you, though.'

'Oh, what's that, then?' Jesse was fierce about her privacy and anything that didn't look like it had cassettes in it was not to be opened, on pain of death.

'I only opened it because it was in a padded envelope and it felt like it had a cassette in it, but it was actually a music CD. It had a note in it from Henry Crud.'

'Who?'

'Henry Crud. It sounds like he's a member of some band. I've got the note here somewhere, hang on'. Annoyingly Gill was gone, rustling papers again.

'Here it is. Right, I'll read it to you. "Dear Jesse, lovely to have met you the other night. Am thrilled that you will be the touch of glamour we were needing at *The Paisley Wheelchair Experience*. I thought it would be helpful to give you the attached CD, which has our entire set on it. I've also attached the lyrics so you can get to grips with some numbers before we see you again in two weeks. I find myself looking forward to the next rehearsal with renewed enthusiasm - Henry Crud." He's also given you his email address. So who's

Henry Crud, then?' Gill sounded amused.

'I'm assuming it's Justin, the lead singer from that band I've just joined. Bloody weird guy, though. He said his name was Justin. Then he said I could call him Freddie and now he's Henry bloody Crud! Talk about multiple personalities!'

'He sounds a bit weird.'

'Mmm, I'm assuming he's harmless, though. I'll have to have a rethink when I go there next.'

'So do you want me to email him and let him know you've got the CD but you're still on holiday?'

'He knows I'm on holiday but it won't hurt to send him a message.'

'Who should I address it to? Dear Justin, Freddie or Henry?'

'Let's go for Justin. Just write, 'I enjoyed the rehearsal, looking forward to next time, ya de ya, blah, blah, thanks for the CD, bye.'

'No problem, I'll do it later today. So what's the plan for this evening, then? Any men on the scene?'

'Not for me. Dotty and Mary seem to be getting their fair share, though!'

'You mean you haven't met anybody yet?' Gill sounded confused.

'Nope.'

'I don't believe it. You've been there two days!'

'You know what, Gill? I'm not in the mood for them. I'm just going to chill out, get drunk and catch up on my reading. Full stop.'

'Sounds like my idea of heaven. Actually, that's a lie. My idea of heaven is David Beckham in a hot tub!'

'Tart!'

'I know, I can't help myself. What about Dotty and Mary, then? Who did they manage to pull?'

'Two locals. Actually Mary's pulled three.'

'Three? Blimey, that girl's a dark horse.'

'You're telling me. She's meeting a guy tonight who can't speak a word of English.'

'Do they need to?'

'Apparently not. Anyway, I'll tell you all about it when I get home. I'd better go, as this will be costing me a fortune. Are you sure everything's all right?'

'Yup, no problems.'

'You're all right?'

'Yeah, although Chloe keeps giving me funny looks.'

'You're just paranoid. Mum's walking her, I'm assuming?'

'Yeah, twice a day. She's doing fine, nothing to worry about. Go and have a drink and enjoy yourself and stop worrying about things here.'

'Okay, I'll call in a few days. You've got the number if you need me.'

'There's no need to call, Jesse. Just enjoy yourself.'

'I will. I'll speak to you in a few days.'

'Okay, speak to you soon. Take care.'

'And you.'

Jesse sat on the balcony overlooking the pool. She took a glug of the beer and a drag of her fag and settled into the hot plastic chair, crossing her legs on the balcony ledge. Henry Crud. What a name. The fact that the man had her home address was a bit worrying and she realised he completely creeped her out. She was no longer sure about the band at all.

***

From where she was sitting, she could see Mary and Dotty deep in conversation. They looked like they were whispering, heads close together, eyes flicking over to the bar where Niko and his wife stood washing glasses.

Mary looked over to where Jesse was sat, and waved. Dotty and Mary exchanged a few words before standing up and gathering all their belongings from the sun beds. Arms laden with towels and bags, both of the girls said 'See you later' to Niko and headed for the apartment to join Jesse.

Jesse heard the apartment door close from behind her and looked over her shoulder in time to see the girls throw their towels down, grab a handful of chocolate from the fridge and scuttle over to the balcony. The two friends took their time arranging their towels over the plastic chairs on either side of the small table. Dotty started on the chocolate, while Mary applied another layer of sun lotion. Jesse was the first to break the silence. 'Niko's back, then.'

'Oh yes,' whispered Dotty with a smirk on her

face, 'You should've seen the look his wife gave him when he arrived! You could cut the atmosphere with a knife!'

Jesse looked at Mary over her sunglasses and Mary shrugged her shoulders as if to say 'Nothing to do with me.'

'What time are we going out tonight, Jesse?' Dotty asked.

'Whenever. I'm not bothered. You say a time and I'll be ready. What time are you thinking, Mary?'

'Not too early. I'm thinking eight o'clock. What do you think?'

'Eight sounds fine to me.'

'Me too,' chirped Dotty. 'That gives us just over three hours so I'm going to go and have a sleep. Wake me up at seven, will you?'

'I'll set the alarm and put it next to your bed.'

'Okey dokie. I'm off, then. Night night.' Dotty blew two air kisses to her friends, left the balcony, crossed the apartment and nearly broke the bed when she scrambled onto it.

Almost three full minutes had passed before Dotty could be heard snoring loudly.

Jesse got up from her chair and pulled the sliding door to the apartment closed in order to block at least some of the noise coming from Dotty's mouth. Moving her chair close to Mary, Jesse whispered, 'Did you say anything to Niko?'

'No. Well, I said hello but that was it.'

'Do you think his wife has any idea?' Both girls were looking at the bikini-clad goddess through their sunglasses. 'I don't think so but she's in a foul mood.'

'Well, maybe that's just because he was late in and she's had to work.'

'Mmm, maybe.' Mary sounded doubtful.

'So what're you going to do about it?'

'Forget it.'

'Really?' Jesse wasn't convinced.

'Yeah, I don't want to get anyone into trouble. Besides, I'm meeting Carlos tonight.'

'Mmm, gorgeous Niko or no-English Carlos? Hard decision girl.'

'I know what you mean. Still, that's that.'

Jesse nudged her friend's arm affectionately. 'Why don't you blow off all of them and start again tonight? We'll go somewhere new and pick up some fresh blood that can speak our own language. What do you say?'

'There's no way Dotty's going to be persuaded to go anywhere else. She's got it in her head to meet Stavros, no matter what.'

'Oh shit, I completely forgot about him. Do you think I should go over there and talk to him?'

'I wouldn't, if I were you. I'd say Niko told us he was married.'

'But Dotty knows you haven't spoken to Niko. She'll never fall for it.'

'Why don't you go over to the bar, then, and get

a few more beers and then you can say you were talking to him? That way you're not lying.'

'Not much!' Although no decision had been reached, both girls started to glug on their beers rather than play with them.

'Okay, Mary. I think you should go over to the bar and get the drinks, that way you can break the ice with Niko and find out about Stavros at the same time.'

'You're only saying that so you don't have to tell Dotty he's married!'

'I promise I'll be the one to tell Dotty but I think we'd all have a better night if you break the ice between you and Niko. All you have to do is go and order some drinks and casually ask about Stavros.'

'But he's already told you he's married, so why ask?'

'Because I can't tell Dotty that. It has to be new information. We can't let Dotty know we've known all bloody day, can we?'

Mary couldn't take her eyes off the bar, 'Mmm, I suppose you're right.'

Jesse gave Mary a gentle nudge. 'Go on!'

'Oh for crying out loud! I'll be back in a minute.' Taking the beer bottles with her for support, Mary left the apartment and travelled the long walk to the bar. She was thankful her Italian skin tanned easily as she could feel her cheeks burning as she approached.

'Hi Niko, two Buds, please.' Turning to the goddess, she smiled and said, 'Hello, I'm Mary.' The goddess smiled back. 'I'm Nicola, are you having a nice holiday?'

'Lovely, thanks.'

Niko handed the beers to Mary and placed his arm around his wife's shoulders, 'Mary is one of the reasons I was so late coming home this morning. Whatever I did, I could not get her to go to bed!' The double meaning was not lost on Mary and she inwardly smiled.

'Well, we're all paying for it now. Jesse's been in bits all morning and Dotty's gone back to bed.'

'You're on holiday, that's what you're supposed to do!' Nicola smiled at Mary but it didn't quite reach her eyes. 'What do you have planned for this evening, more partying?'

'I'm not sure, we'll see how it goes. We're going to have a meal and then go back to Antonio's bar.' Mary chose her moment. 'Dotty has taken quite a fancy to one of the barmen, actually. Stavros.'

'Stavros!' Nicola turned around to her husband and spoke angrily in Greek. Niko put his hands up in the air and used a gentle tone to calm his wife. Mary had no idea what had just been said but curiosity was killing her. Nicola turned her back on her husband and walked towards Mary,

'Stavros is married man. He has been bad before. You must tell this friend of yours to leave him alone. He not a strong man. His wife is my friend. She must leave him alone.' She looked fiercely over her shoulder at Niko before throwing down a bar towel and striding away from the bar.

From the other end of the bar Niko poured two shot glasses full of turquoise liquid and returned to Mary. 'Yamas.' After downing his shot, Niko shrugged his shoulders and said, 'Stavros is a very stupid man. He plays around with English women under the nose of all his friends and family. He is not very careful.'

Mary could see Antonio's bar from where she was sitting but couldn't see any movement in the shadows, 'I feel sorry for his wife.'

'What she doesn't know won't hurt her.' As Niko retrieved Mary's shot glass, his finger brushed against hers and the expression on his face said they had unfinished business. It took all her strength not to yell out 'Yippee!' before gathering her butterflies together and saying, 'I'd better get this beer to Jesse. See you later.'

'I'm looking forward to it.'

Jesse had been watching everything from the balcony and knew even before Mary turned her face in her direction that she would be smiling. Mary waggled her way to the balcony like a model on a catwalk. Handing the bottles over the balcony to Jesse, she whispered, 'Looks like I'm on a promise tonight!' She didn't catch Jesse's expression as she turned to walk around the back to the apartment, which was just as well as it took Jesse a few seconds to remove the look of distaste from her face.

***

Jesse was wearing white this evening, as she had already decided she wouldn't be getting drunk so wouldn't be spilling her drink down her top. She wore an ivory knee-length chiffon granddad shirt with linen trousers and pumps to match. She didn't have a matching handbag so hid her money and lipstick in her bra and carried her cigarettes. She was drinking a vodka tonic while waiting for Dotty and Mary to arrive. Ordinarily she would be sitting at the bar, but such was her distaste for the situation with Niko and Mary that she was on one of the cane chairs that were dotted around the pool-side.

Dotty was the first to emerge from the apartment in a cloud of Chanel. She got a dry martini from the bar and dragged a wooden chair over to where Jesse sat. She really was oblivious to how much noise she made. Tonight Dotty was wearing a navy blue sundress with matching Jesus sandals, which made a loud slapping noise on the tiles as she stomped over to Jesse.

Dotty retrieved a packet of peanuts from her purse and started to eat them one by one in between sips of her martini. She was quite happy sitting in silence with her friend while Jesse tried very hard not to look at her freshly-painted stubby toes poking through the worn sandals.

'Mary's taking her time.'

Dotty nodded. 'Yes, she's actually putting on make-up for a change. She's obviously making an effort for Carlos.'

Jesse said nothing and glanced towards Niko as she took a sip of her vodka. Jesse had to put her feelings about Niko and Mary aside and deal with the Stavros issue. Jesse knew she could be brutally blunt and didn't want to hurt Dotty unnecessarily, so had conversation after conversation in her head until she decided on the soft approach.

'Dotty, you do realise Stavros is married?' Oops, that hadn't come out the way she'd planned. Dotty's peanut hovered an inch away from her mouth for a moment before she popped it in and started crunching, staring at Jesse with a frown on her face. 'Niko told Mary earlier.' Still there was silence. 'Apparently he's had affairs before.' Jesse decided Dotty's toes were actually easier to look at than the frown on her face. 'What are you going to do?'

Dotty tipped back her head and emptied the entire contents of the packet of peanuts into her mouth. Between chews she said, 'I don't know about you, but I'm getting pissed.'

***

Dinner was a disaster. Mary couldn't settle and Dotty was pissed. Jesse had switched from vodka to Diet Coke but, frankly, wished she hadn't. All evening Dotty had ranted about Stavros and what a bastard he was.

Mary had stayed quiet, embarrassed in the knowledge that she would be entertaining a married man later that very evening. Jesse was bored of it all and wanted to draw a line under it and start again - it was obvious though that that wasn't going to happen.

During the course of the evening Dotty's emotions seemed to move from disappointment to disbelief to rejection and then finally to have settled defiantly on anger. Dotty never had a bad word to say about anyone and lived a very peaceful life. She was also, however, her father's daughter and that was whom Jesse and Mary found themselves running behind on the way to Antonio's bar.

No matter how many times Jesse shouted, 'For fuck's sake, Dotty, slow down, will you?!' she never broke her stride, and it was long and fast.

Dotty disappeared out of view as she turned left and started up the marble stairs to the bar. Mary and Jesse both muttered 'Fuck' before slowing their pace to take the turn, only to find Dotty standing above them at the top of the stairs and not, as fully expected, bashing Stavros over the head with a huge fist.

Mary stayed behind as Jesse made her way up the stairs and stood beside her friend.

'Everything all right, Dotty?' Jesse whispered. Dotty never took her eyes off the bar but said, 'One drink and we're out of here.' Before Jesse could respond, Dotty moved towards the bar and stepped up onto a bar stool. Jesse linked arms with Mary and muttered, 'Here we go.'

Mary clocked the problem instantly. The only reason Stavros still had the ability to walk was that he was sitting in between Niko's wife and his own. His wedding ring was on and the dark slender beauty beside him had her arms around his shoulders. Nicola nodded to them and said, 'Hello ladies' and all three chorused back, 'Evening.'

Antonio served them with an apologetic look on his face, but not once did Stavros make eye contact. Jesse could feel the heat pouring from Dotty but, to her credit, her facial expression was a mask of normality. The only thing that unnerved Jesse was that every time there was anything remotely amusing said between the girls, Dotty threw her head back and screamed with laughter as if she was having the best time of her life. This miserable drama was drawn out for a full twenty minutes before Mary put an end to it by suggesting they go and have a boogie somewhere.

'Oh if we're going dancing, I just want to pop back to the apartments to change my shoes.' With a delicate wave, Dotty strolled out of the bar, crossed the road, expertly ignored Niko at the bar and went directly to the apartment. Mary and Jesse both stopped at the pool bar rather than follow Dotty.

'Should we go after her?' Mary asked.

'No, let's give her ten minutes to compose herself. We'll wait here and have a drink and see what she wants to do.'

'Okay, are you still on Diet Coke?'

'To be honest, I think I need something stronger now. I'm going to go for a whisky and lemonade.'

'I think I'll have one as well.'

Jesse raised her eyebrows at Mary and nodded. 'You know what? Let's have two.'

'Yes.'

They pulled up a bar stool each and sat shoulder to shoulder fiddling with their cigarettes in the ashtrays, watching the clock tick.

Three whiskies later and still there was no sign of Dotty. 'I shouldn't have told her.'

'Thank God you did, though. Imagine what would have happened if she'd been expecting to get off with him tonight and found him sat there with his wife. She'd have been crushed. At least this way she had warning.'

'You do realise this is going to ruin the holiday.'

'No it won't, she'll be fine!'

'No, Mary, she won't.'

CHAPTER 17

Due to the lack of excitement and alcohol the night before, Jesse and Mary had got up very early and taken the pick of the beds around the pool enjoying fresh orange and a croissant each for breakfast. Dotty eventually got out of bed but it took a bribe of a ham-and-cheese toasted sandwich, which Jesse wafted under her nose and then placed on the balcony to tempt her out. Dotty emerged, looking haggard.

'Morning, Dotty, how're you feeling?' asked Jesse.

'Crap.'

Jesse envied Mary, who was hiding behind her novel on the pool-side opposite. She tried to inject some positivity into the situation. 'Don't worry about Stavros. He's obviously a wanker. Anyway, you've got Ron at home waiting for you.'

Jesse wasn't prepared for the tears rolling down Dotty's face. They sat in silence while Dotty composed herself. Jesse was burning holes with her eyes into Mary's book, but she didn't shift it an inch.

'I always pick the bastards.'

'What's happened with Ron?' Jesse asked.

'Nothing! That's just the point. I told him I loved him and I haven't heard a word from him since.'

'You told him you loved him?'

'Yes, I did.'

'You can't be serious, Dotty, he was foul!'

'I know!' Dotty wailed.

'Why the hell would you tell him you loved him if you think he's foul?' Jesse asked.

'I don't know. I suppose I just wanted to move it up a level.'

'What do you mean by that?'

'Oh for heaven's sake, Jesse. Sex. I want sex.'

'But not with Ron, Dotty. He was Les Dawson without the sense of humour.'

'I don't care what he looks like, I want sex! I haven't had sex - ever.' Dotty started crying again.

'You haven't had sex because of your bloody religion, nothing else. Not being funny or anything but if you've held out this long, why ruin it for an ugly bug like Ron?'

'He was the first one who paid me any attention in ages. I was really starting to get used to his face and he was romantic.' Dotty blew her nose into the napkin which had held the toastie.

'So romantic that the minute you tell him you love him, he clears off.'

Dotty just looked at Jesse miserably and blew her nose again.

'Dotty, your problem is not men. It's the way

you react to them. No disrespect, but you're like a stalker once you've got your eyes on someone.'

Dotty's mouth fell open in astonishment, but she remained silent.

Jesse continued. 'You've already admitted you didn't love Ron at all and thought he was disgusting and yet you text him four times a day and call him all evening. Then when he doesn't return your calls, you tell him you love him! You deserve better and you damn well know it and yet you humiliate yourself time and time again on losers. I know you're not really desperate, Dotty, but it really looks like it from an outsider's point of view. Anyone so much as sniffs in your direction and you're planning your wedding.'

'No I'm not.' A few people from the pool-side glanced in their direction at Dotty's raised voice.

'Calm down, Dotty, there's no need to get angry.'

'That's easy for you to say. No-one's calling you bloody desperate!'

'I didn't say you were desperate. I said it might look that way.' Truth be told, Jesse was regretting saying anything at all.

'Well, however it looks, I'm not bloody desperate.' Dotty's chin started to quiver again.

'Exactly! I know you're not but other people may think you are and if that's the case, you'll never get a decent guy. They can smell desperation a mile away.'

'Well, what do you suggest I do?' This wasn't a

question, it was an accusation.

'Reassess how you're feeling. Ask yourself what you actually want from a man.'

'Brad Pitt.'

'Within reason, Dotty.'

'Well, Brad Pitt is what I want,' mumbled Dotty.

'Well why the hell drop your standards so bloody low that you settle for Les fucking Dawson then?!' It was Jesse's turn to raise her voice.

'Point taken,' said Dotty.

They sat in silence for a while, each comparing themselves to the leggy blondes glistening by the side of the pool.

In a resigned voice Dotty said, 'I'm never going to find a man, am I?'

'Dotty, you are only fat, that's it. You don't have a disease. There is nothing wrong with you. You're just fat. Fat is just what you are, it's not who you are. You might do well to remind yourself of that every now and again and stop beating yourself up all the time.'

Dotty thought about this for a while and smiled at her friend. 'Thanks Jesse.'

Jesse lit another cigarette and took a long hard drag. 'No problem.'

'Well, I don't want to hang around this place tonight. Can we go into town and find a club or something?' Dotty asked.

'Sounds like a good plan to me.'

'Okay, I'm going to go and shave my legs and put my cossie on.' Dotty looked down at her dry flaky feet and toenails, which she'd been inadvertently picking whilst talking to Jesse. 'Fancy putting another coat of polish on my toenails, Jesse?'

Jesse started coughing violently on her cigarette but still managed to shake her head, smile and go bright red all at the same time.

Dotty turned on her crispy heels and headed for the bathroom. 'I'll take that as a no, then.'

***

Although Jesse and Mary had been sunbathing happily before Dotty appeared, they were forced to leave their prime spots by the pool-side and venture to the beach. Dotty knew that Jesse wasn't drunk the night before, which meant they could move away from the apartment toilets. The fact that both Jesse and Mary were quite happy where they were was irrelevant. Dotty had had a hard time and was trying to perk herself up and anything she wanted, she was damn well going to get.

Dotty stood at the bar in her yellow sundress, drinking freshly-squeezed orange juice while she waited for the girls to get their beach attire together. It was only a short walk from the apartment to the beach but it took just minutes for Jesse's thighs to blister, hence the denim shorts and T-shirt she'd put on over her leopard print halter-neck bikini. Mary didn't have the same problem as Jesse with her thighs, but she suffered with a mass of cellulite which jiggled ferociously above her knees when she walked, so she had changed into a white floaty dress and pumps. Beach bags filled with water, sun lotion, toilet paper, books and towels, the three set off down the dusty track to the side of the apartment.

The girls said hello to a tied-up goat, which looked miserable in the centre of the barren field they had to cross to reach the beach.

The sea looked rough but inviting in the distance. The warm breeze was pushing against their skin and lifting the hair from their necks and they all took deep cleansing breaths of sea air. They passed between two white concrete buildings and reached the hot sand.

They were used to this scene. Yellow-and-blue plastic sun loungers and thatched umbrellas littered the beach. They stood for a while scanning for an empty bed then Mary pointed and said, 'Follow me' and dashed across the pebble-riddled sand. Mary strode ahead of them, threw her beach bag onto an empty bed and continued for another fifteen or so paces before grabbing the second bed she'd spotted and then dragging it through the sand to where Dotty and Jesse stood. Mary and Dotty immediately claimed the beds as theirs, placed their towels on the hot plastic and started to undress.

Within minutes, all the girls were lotioned up and reading books in the glare of the midday sun. Jesse had lost out with the sun lounger so had taken a little longer in weeding out the big pebbles from the smaller ones under her towel. She had made a large dent in the sand for her bottom to fit into and was using her friend's bags as a pillow to keep her upright while she read. There was no umbrella for protection from the sun so Jesse was wearing her baseball cap, Mary, a large-brimmed straw hat and Dotty, her pink shorts and Gucci sunglasses.

Dotty relaxed more at the beach than anywhere else. By the pool you couldn't get her long sarong off her body. Within a little while of settling into her book on the beach, the sarong was off and Dotty's white-and-blue flowered costume was revealed.

They heard the gentle tinkle of a bell. They hadn't been to Greece in a year but they all recognised the sound and immediately started rummaging around their beach bags looking for money. Mary panicked as the man with the bell started to pass beyond the girls. 'Quick, just give me the money!' With a quick exchange of cash, Mary was off limping across the hot sand, trying to catch up with the doughnut man. The doughnuts were huge, stuffed with chocolate and then covered in even more chocolate. The girls all 'ummed' and 'ahhed' and nodded their way through the doughnuts.

Jesse had been silently enjoying licking the remnants of melted chocolate off her fingers but the quiet was shattered when a wasp decided it would also enjoy the chocolate. She was up and running full sprint towards the sea before the girls had time to realise what the problem was. The large wasp she was running from stayed where it was at the girls' camp and hovered around Jesse's Diet Coke can. In spite of this, Jesse could still hear it buzzing around her hair, trying to get into her mouth as she shouted 'fuck off' several times and ran into the freezing sea, violently shaking her head until she'd dived into the water, nearly losing her bikini bottoms in the process. She swam under water until she had no breath, believing she might have evaded the wasp. As her head slowly came out of the water, she could hear Dotty and Mary's loud laughter. Dotty only added to her humiliation by pointing at Jesse and then throwing her head back laughing, crossing her legs so as not to pee herself.

Giving both girls the finger made Jesse smile and she realised the cool water was actually lovely on her warm skin. She floated on her back in shallow water, feeling the sun pull the moisture from her face and chest. It wasn't long until she could hear her name being called. She spotted Dotty standing by the edge of the water in her costume and Jesus sandals, waving for Jesse's attention. Dotty stood with her hands shielding her eyes from the blazing sun and shouted to her friend, 'What's it like?!'

Jesse was bouncing on the water's surface, holding herself up with the palms of her hands, with her legs floating behind her. 'It's lovely!' Dotty looked at the water suspiciously and Jesse realised there could be a problem.

'Dotty, there's quite a steep drop as you come in and it's covered in hard stones. My feet are killing me, actually. It might be hard to get in.'

Dotty stood for a while longer weighing up the pros and cons and decided to take the risk and go for a swim. She left her sandals a few feet away from the water and tiptoed in, face screwed up in pain as she stood on the hot sharp pebbles that gathered at the water's edge. Once the water was knee-high, the breaking waves knocked her over and she was in. The girls played in the waves for ages. Jesse did a handstand, forcing salt water up her nose and causing her to choke and eyes to sting. Dotty swam breaststroke with Jesse on her back. Onlookers might have thought them reminiscent of a mother and child. After a while, Dotty left Jesse floating gently on her back so that she could pee in private. While moving her arms under water and flapping her legs to disguise the fact she was having a wee in the sea, Dotty realised they had a situation on their hands. Leaving her circle of warmth behind her, Dotty made her way to Jesse and pointed at a middle-aged couple trying to get out of the sea. Jesse giggled quietly as she watched them try and drag each other out. The waves were breaking strongly just at the point where the sand took a sharp rise upwards. The water at this point was only knee-high but the tide was strong and the sharp stones underneath, vicious. The man eventually managed to stand and get hold of his woman and dragged her up the steep sand, and they made it to the beach with some dignity. The smile quickly left Jesse's face.

'Shitty death,' Dotty said sombrely. 'I'm not gonna be able to get out!'

The girls swam back to where they could see Mary across the beach - only to find an empty sun lounger. They were on their own in this.

Jesse took in a large breath and blew it out noisily, turning to Dotty. 'Okay, what do you want to do?'

Dotty was clearly terrified. 'Let's go to where the waves are breaking and just try to stand. Not get out, just stand.'

Jesse nodded and they both made their way on their hands, with legs floating out behind them, to where the sand sloped upwards. This was a mistake. As soon as Dotty got in the wake of the breaking waves, she couldn't get out of them. The waves broke against her head time and time again and her bursts of laughter soon changed to tears of fear and pain.

'For fuck's sake, Dotty, stand up!' Jesse laughed. It wasn't at all funny but there was no way she was going to show everyone on the beach what pain they were in - Dotty's physical, Jesse's mental.

'I can't!' Dotty wailed.

Each wave that crashed over her head caused her to catch her breath and swallow salt water. Her eyes were stinging and the palms of her hands were sore with trying to keep her stomach above the sharp stones. She had too much body fat to put her knees down and straighten up. She was bobbing like a cork.

Jesse tried holding her up by the arms but she just got dragged underneath her friend and choked in the water every time. 'Lie on your back and try and straighten up,' Jesse said.

It looked like it was going to work until Dotty yelled loudly. The stones felt like shards of broken glass under her feet.

'Stay there, I'll get your sandals'. Jesse turned her back and literally clawed her way up the slope, digging her fingers in the sand to help her gain momentum until she was free of the dragging waves. Her thigh muscles were exhausted with the effort. She grabbed the sandals and took a moment to gather her courage as she realised she had to go in again and help her friend, who was struggling to breathe. She never thought to cover her own feet before she painfully made her way back.

Dotty couldn't possibly reach for her own feet so Jesse tried time and time again to grab a foot one at a time and to do up each sandal, before being thrown forwards by a wave. All strength had left them by the time both sandals were on. Dotty's eyes were not visible as her hair was all over her face, but snot was clearly everywhere. Jesse gagged more than once when she saw that somehow in their struggle there was a thread from Dotty's nose attached to her own shoulder.

The water was strong enough to throw both of them over, but not strong enough to break a thin web of snot binding the two girls together.

They had to get out. They were losing strength and several people on the beach who had been openly laughing and pointing at the girls were now starting to look concerned. This situation was going to get out of control if they didn't take action.

Jesse knew she had to be tough to get Dotty to move. She grabbed Dotty by the armpit and growled, 'Get your fucking legs under your arse and get out now!'

A wave broke, taking both girls' legs out from under them but on its return, the wave helped pull their feet underneath them. Jesse stood, grabbing and pulling the soft flesh of Dotty's underarm with her. Dotty pedalled forward for three painful steps until she fell onto her knees, but she was on the slope; a few more feet and she'd be away from the breaking waves. Jesse was on her hands and knees grimacing in pain as she continued to pull at her friend's skin. Dotty gave up trying with her feet and tried to get up the slope on hands and knees, crying quietly all the way. Jesse got to the top and reached a hand down to pull Dotty up. Another hand grabbed her other wrist and she was yanked up away from the sea and back onto the flat beach, where she flopped forwards onto her belly face first in the sand.

The embarrassment hit Jesse first and she sprung up from the sand and stood defiantly, hands on hips, glaring at all the eyes that were upon them. She started to quietly laugh and nudged Dotty with her bloodied foot. Dotty was still face down in the sand, breathing heavily. 'Come on, Dotty, fun's over' and then very quietly added, 'everyone's watching you.' Dotty started laughing loudly and rolled over to sit up on her behind. She grabbed Jesse's outstretched hand and hauled herself up onto her feet. The middle-aged man they had previously laughed at stood in front of Dotty looking concerned. 'Are you all right, love?'

Dotty wiped her face with her hands and said, 'Yes, I'm fine now. Thanks for your help.'

'Yes, thanks a lot,' Jesse smiled.

They both hobbled arm-in-arm to their sun loungers and sat down heavily. Jesse watched the blood from her knees slowly make its way down her shins to her ankles, where it was absorbed by the sand. The palms of her hands were grazed but there were only two spots of blood visible. She had expected far worse. She didn't wish to look at her sore feet, so she buried them deeply into the sand, as it was cooling once you broke through the dusty top layer which had been scorched by the sun.

Jesse took a long swig of warm water from the bottle before passing it to Dotty. Breathing heavily, Dotty took a mouthful and poured the rest over the top of her head, washing the sand and hair away from her face. She too had patterns of blood running from her knees to her ankles and had snapped all but one of her long fingernails. Each sat looking miserable, taking in the other's injuries.

Dotty spotted Mary over Jesse's shoulder walking towards them with three ice creams in her hands. She looked full of the joys of spring as Dotty groaned. 'Oh bugger, here comes Mary.'

They looked at each other for a few seconds before the corners of their mouths upturned and Jesse started to giggle. By the time Mary reached them, they were both lying on their backs on the sun loungers screaming with laughter, tears rolling down their faces, trying to talk but making no sense whatsoever.

Mary took in the scene before her with confusion. 'Christ! What happened to your legs?'

The girls just laughed louder. Jesse tried to explain by talking gibberish in between sobs of laughter, just about managing to point to the sea, while Dotty made a clawing action in the sand. Dotty lay on the sun bed with her pink shorts over her face trying to drown out the manic screams that were coming out of her mouth.

They managed to eat most of their ice creams between giggles and spurts of laughter and eventually gave Mary the entire story.

The next five hours of sunbathing went quietly. They read their books, occasionally slept and ate pizza and chocolate. If the girls got hot, they walked to the beach shower and pulled the chain that released freezing cold water over them. They each vowed never to so much as paddle in this sea again.

Mary arranged for a waiter to bring three Piña Coladas over to their loungers just as the sun began to set. By this time Jesse had a sun lounger of her own and the three girls dragged their beds so they were positioned side by side directly facing the setting sun. They drank in comfortable silence, watching the sky turn from turquoise to red. The breeze had turned cool and there were only a handful of people still sharing the beach with them.

Dotty raised her glass to the sky and made a toast. 'Here's to the most embarrassing day of my entire blooming life.' Jesse choked on her laughter and for the third time that day found herself covered in snot.

***

Jesse couldn't settle on what to wear. She had planned on wearing jeans but the material was too hard on her grazed knees. She tried her bootleg trousers but could only wear her knee-length boots with them, and the soles were too thin for her swollen feet. In the end she settled on baggy black linen trousers, top and white trainers. Not the most flattering of outfits but reasonably comfortable. Dotty had exactly the same problem. She settled on black velvet trousers, a black floaty smock and she also wore her white trainers. Mary looked exceptionally glamorous stood beside the two of them. She chose a long chiffon navy-and-cream dress which made her waist look tiny, and navy pumps which matched her navy clutch bag perfectly.

Early on in the day they had decided to go into the main town of Rethmynon. The plan was to try a few bars, have a nice meal and then find a club to boogie the night away in. The only problem was two of the three girls had painful feet - not ideal for dancing. Instead of ordering a taxi they took a leisurely stroll to the bus stop to save some cash. The bus stop was in sight when Dotty stopped in her tracks and said, 'Sod this.'

'Yeah, bollocks to it,' said Jesse, 'let's go back to the taverna and get hammered at the bar with Niko.'

'Sorry Mary, do you mind if we wait until tomorrow? My feet are really killing me. I don't want to stand, never mind dance,' Dotty said.

'No problem at all.' Mary's smile was huge. All afternoon she had been wondering how she could get the girls back to the pool bar so she could meet with Niko, and now they had offered it to her on a plate. 'Right,' said Jesse. 'Let's eat,' and the girls all linked arms and made their way back up the street. They were headed to the taverna next to the apartment complex when they walked past a Chinese restaurant. They stopped in their tracks and took in the rich smells of sweet and sour, did an about-face and walked into the restaurant. There were six tables outside set underneath a structure of ferns. Tacky red lanterns were hanging on the metal beams and oriental music was wafting out gently from within. The chairs looked strong and sturdy so the three girls settled happily outside. They decided on a bottle of cheap white wine and some prawn crackers to keep them busy until the main dishes arrived. Slowly they began to unwind and relax. As evening closed in, the red candles on the tables were lit, giving an air of romance.

It took nearly an hour for the food to arrive. Normally Mary would have created a fuss. She hated bad service, but not tonight. The portions were small but the girls had guessed they would be so had ordered six main dishes to share, not including the rice and noodles. Another bottle of wine later and the girls were happily people-watching from where they sat, waiting for their lychees and ice cream. They were all grateful for the evening shadows when Dotty spotted Carlos on the opposite side of the street.

As Dotty's head ducked under the table, instinctively the other two followed suit.

'Who've you seen?' Mary asked.

'Carlos!' whispered Dotty.

'Oh shit, did he spot us?' asked Jesse.

'I bloody hope not or we'd better find an excuse to be under this table,' Mary said.

'Excuse me, ladies.'

All three inwardly groaned as they slowly lifted their heads above the chequered table cloth.

'Lychees and ice cream?'

Their relief was palpable. They all smiled at the small Chinese waitress and gabbled, 'Oh thank you, thank you, lovely.' Dotty was in the best position, being nearest to the entrance, so she scanned the length and breadth of the street until satisfied that Carlos had not seen them and had moved on.

In between mouthfuls of dessert, Jesse asked,

'So Mary, what exactly do you intend to do about the Greek fuckwit?'

'Oh Jesse! Don't be so mean. There's nothing wrong with him.'

'Not much!'

'Cradle snatcher,' chimed in Dotty.

'Ha, ha! I'm sure he realises I've blown him out by not meeting him last night. He must've got the message.'

Dotty and Jesse dug into their ice cream.

'Anyway, so long as I don't bump into him tonight, he'll definitely have got the message then.'

'It's a shame', Dotty said, 'I really liked that taverna.'

'Ah well, we can go on our last night when there'll be no repercussions,' said Jesse.

'I suppose.'

Mary caught the waiter's eye and asked for the bill.

'I haven't even finished eating yet,' said Dotty.

'Oh, sorry.'

'In a hurry, by any chance?' Jesse winked at Dotty.

'No! I just fancied a drink, that's all.'

'Yeah, right,' Dotty said, 'You just want a drink and an ogle at Niko!'

'That's not true!' But Mary's cheeks were rosy and she knew she'd been caught out. 'Okay, okay. Give me a break, will you? You have to admit, he *is* gorgeous.'

'Yes, I have to admit he is very easy on the eye,' agreed Jesse.

'But let's not forget he is also married,' added Dotty.

'Yes, I haven't forgotten, Dotty. Anyway, I'm only window shopping. I have no intention of buying the goods.'

'Or renting them,' Jesse smirked.

'Or putting them on the layaway plan,' laughed Dotty.

Jesse signed her name on the bill and drained the last of her wine. 'Okay, let's get a move on,' and with that they were off, Dotty and Jesse holding onto each other for support as they hobbled down the quiet street towards the bar.

Mary was two paces in front as the bar was coming into view on the left. She stopped in her tracks and ducked her head. Instinctively, Dotty and Jesse did the same and snuck up quietly behind Mary so they could get a view of whatever had caused Mary to halt.

'Oh shit,' whispered Jesse, looking at Mary, 'what do you want to do?'

Sitting at the bar talking to Niko was not only

Carlos, who Mary had decided never to set eyes on again, but also Antonio, who she had been making eyes at two nights previously. The fact they were talking to Niko, with whom she fully intended to get off tonight, made her inwardly cringe.

Mary put her fingers on her lips and pointed behind Dotty to the side of the apartments. They tiptoed around the corner and put their backs against the cold concrete building. All three were laughing, quietly covering their mouths in case of an unexpected outburst. 'Oh shit, Mary, what the hell are you going to do?'

'I don't know, I don't know!'

'This is awful!' said Dotty as she covertly ducked her head around the wall to see if she could see the bar, but her view was obscured by climbing ferns. They were so close they could hear the low rumble of men's voices travelling over the soft Greek music Niko had on the CD player.

'You're going to have to brazen it out,' Jesse said. 'Just breeze over there, say hello to all of them and sit at the far right of the bar. I'll sit next to you with Dotty next to me. That way they have to get through both of us to get to you. They'll get the hint.'

'But what if they don't?' wailed Mary.

'Then I'll get pissed and tell the two of them to shag off.'

'Mm.' Mary raised her eyebrows and thought about it for a few seconds. 'Okay, how do I look?'

220

'Fine, except your lipstick's worn out.' Two minutes later, all three freshly powdered and preened, they casually strolled out from behind the apartment and approached the pool area.

The walk around the side of the pool to the bar felt like a long one, but they were thankful for the three bar stools over to the right just waiting to be claimed. 'Hi guys,' they all chimed.

'Hello, my lovely ladies!' cried Niko, waving his arms in the air and approaching them from the other side of the bar.

'Hello,' said Antonio in a deep raspy voice and nodded to the girls. Carlos sat back on his stool so he could see past Antonio, and just smiled broadly at Mary, who ignored both of them completely and focused on Niko. Niko arrived and kissed each girl's hand before pouring them all a tequila shot.

'Yamas!'

Not wanting to mix their drinks, the girls ordered a bottle of wine to share between them. All three pulled faces at the first sip. Mary was clearly very uncomfortable being under the eye of all three men. Carlos never took his eyes off her. Mary never would have known this as she wouldn't look at them, but Dotty relayed every movement or look from all three. Jesse was also uncomfortable. Not only was she trying to protect Mary but she'd noticed Dotty looking over her right shoulder into Antonio's bar, where Stavros was working. Jesse was getting tense and could feel her irritation growing.

Elton John was on his second verse of *Candle In The Wind* when Jesse exploded.

'Oh for pity's sake, Niko, change the bloody music! It's like a morgue in here. Put something lively on before I kill myself!'

Niko, visibly startled by her outburst, trotted swiftly over to the stereo system and started fumbling through his CDs. 'No problem, no problem. I'll find something you like.' Moments later Anastasia had replaced Elton and the volume was turned up. The change of music achieved what Jesse had hoped - a break in the romantic ambiance. Everyone had to raise their voices to reach above the heavy bass, and a lively energy was injected into the bar, making it much easier to pretend Carlos and Antonio didn't exist. Their cautious approach to alcohol was put aside and vodkas and martinis were soon flowing freely. For every long drink they ordered, a different-coloured shot was given by Niko. Jesse had just downed a B52, Baileys and Tia Maria when a hand rested on her back.

'Another one of those for everyone, please, Niko.' Jesse turned in her seat to find the face belonging to the hand on her back. She recognised the blue eyes but for the life of her couldn't remember where from.

'Hello ladies, enjoying yourself?'

'Yes thank you,' nodded Dotty.

'I didn't see any of you girls at the welcome

meeting yesterday. You missed your complimentary drink.'

The penny dropped. He was their rep. She vaguely remembered him from the coach journey. She recalled he had bored them silly and had encouraged a sing-song by starting everyone off with the theme tune from *The Flintstones*. Jesse sensed a different air about him out of his uniform. Seeing him in jeans and a white T-shirt gave him a laid-back look. He still looked nineteen years old, which he was, but his cocky persona from the day of their arrival was not with him now. He gave Jesse a warm smile.

'Here we are, Steve, four B52s! Yamas!' announced Niko.

Five other people around the bar, including Antonio and Carlos, raised their shot glasses to Steve and drank. Steve took this opportunity to introduce himself to the girls properly, pulling up a bar stool and squeezing between Jesse and Mary. Jesse paid no attention to Steve's introduction. She was far too amused watching Carlos and Antonio's body language as Steve now sat next to Mary. Antonio soon downed his drink, slowly lifted himself off his stool and sauntered off to the cocktail bar across the road, tilting his imaginary hat at Mary as he went.

Carlos stayed a few minutes longer, casting withering looks at Steve before accepting that Mary wasn't going to pay him any attention tonight. So he left his half a lager on the bar and stomped off around the pool and into the night. *Two down, only one to go*, thought Jesse and she couldn't help but smile at how the quietest girl in the bunch had managed to ensnare four males in so few days.

'What's that smile about?' enquired Steve quietly. She turned her head and realised he was so close that if she'd have spoken, he'd have felt her breath on his face. She had been so focused on the situation Mary had created with the men in the bar that she hadn't realised Mary was talking to Dotty and not Steve. She could sense rather than see that Steve also had his hand on the back of her stool, and the look he was giving her was amused and flirty.

'Mary was in an uncomfortable position with two locals and they've both gone now so I found that a little amusing, that's all,' Jesse answered flippantly.

'Ah, understood. So what about you? Have you got yourself in any sticky situations so far?' Steve enquired with a lopsided smile. Jesse didn't miss the double meaning and could smell the sweet alcohol on his breath; she decided he was probably drunk. 'No, actually, and I don't intend to either.'

'That's a bit disappointing. I was hoping you might consider spending some time and having a drink with me this evening.' Jesse decided honesty was the best policy this evening.

'Look, Steve, I don't mean to be rude but you're far too young for me and I don't like men who drink, and you've obviously had a few tonight. So let's just leave it at that, shall we?' She gave him a sweet but apologetic smile.

'I may be young but I'm not too young, and actually this is only my first drink of the evening. I only finished my shift thirty minutes ago and the Marias are my first stop. If I was drinking, I certainly wouldn't do it where I rep. I'd go into Rethmynon.' Steve took another sip of his drink and there was a long pause before he continued quietly, 'you and your friends have obviously had a few drinks. Why don't you like men to?' He was twisted in his chair now, one hand behind her stool, the other almost touching her hand, which was resting on the bar. His face was mere inches away from hers. Jesse's stomach did its first flip of the holiday.

'My ex-husband was a drinker and he turned nasty with it, so it makes me nervous to be around men who drink. Now if you'll excuse me, I need the loo.' Jesse left her seat and wandered casually around the pool, through reception, and let herself into the apartment.

Locking the toilet door she stood staring hard at her reflection in the bathroom mirror. She was holding tight to the basin and her features kept drifting from stern to laughing out loud.

'Don't be so fuckin' ridiculous, Jesse, he's a baby,' she told her reflection.

'He looks older than he is,' came the response, accompanied by a laugh.

'You haven't had sex in so long, you can't possibly break the spell with a kid!' and then laughter again. 'Get a grip, girlie. Just go and have a drink and get an early night.' As the bathroom door shut behind her she whispered,

'Yeah, right, like that's gonna happen.' She was still smirking wickedly when she turned the corner of the building and saw Steve's silhouette leaning against the wall.

Another stomach lurch.

In total silence he pushed himself away from the wall, walked the short distance between them and took Jesse's hand. He then turned and walked them both straight past the pool and out of the complex onto the street and turned right. Once they got out of sight of the apartments and the two girls at the bar, Jesse stopped in her tracks and said,

'Okay, enough. Where are we going?' Steve answered with a look that took her breath away. He put his hand under her chin and kissed her with such longing that Jesse became lightheaded and was transported from this world entirely to another. It was the most passionate kiss she had experienced in her life, coupled with a real gentleness, as if he knew she'd been hurt before and that what you saw wasn't actually exactly what you got when it came to Jesse. In silence they strolled hand in hand past tavernas and bars and closed supermarkets, until Steve took a left turn off the main stretch and led them into an alley where a few houses nestled close to one another. They stopped at the one with a faded blue door.

'Steve, look, I'm not sure about this.' Jesse felt she should protest to show she had at least some principles. He no longer looked like he was a naïve kid. He looked like he was going to do whatever he wanted to Jesse and she believed she was going to let him. This was beginning to frighten her. He simply opened the door, returned his keys to his pocket and, reaching his hand around her neck, he kissed her again. The house was dark and silent and he didn't turn any lights on to light their way.

'Hang on, Steve, I need to use the bathroom.'

'Okay, just here. Cross the hall when you've finished. My room is opposite.' With that, he let go of her hand and left her alone tracing her clammy hand up and down cold tiles searching for a light switch, hoping some illumination would break the spell she was under. It didn't. After using the toilet, Jesse removed the congealed eyeliner from inside her eyes, checked herself for any stray toilet roll and washed her privates with cold water. She was trying not to giggle out loud but was screaming with laughter inside her own head. What the hell she thought she was doing, she didn't know, but she did know she was going to do it, whatever it was. Feeling confident with her looks and thankful she had put on an exquisite lace all-in-one white body, she turned off the light and ventured across the hall. Jesse expected music to be playing but there was none.

A ripple of excitement fizzed through her as she entered the room to find Steve standing, lit only by moonlight cascading through a small open window which carried the breeze of the ocean through it. 'Jesse' was all he said and it was all that was needed. He went to her and undressed her slowly and carefully before positioning her on his bed. He then stood and undressed himself and when he was naked, he lay next to her on his side and started to lazily run his hand over her body. For a moment Jesse was embarrassed when he touched her most sensitive area, but he clamped his mouth on hers with such fervour that she didn't feel anything after that other than unadulterated pleasure.

Giving herself up to the moment, they rode high on a cloud together until morning, exploring each other as if they had all the time in the world. He was gentle with her and treated her as if she might break, which was a first for her and which she needed, although she would never have admitted that to anyone. Steve touched her in a way that healed her. She could feel it in every stroke that he gave, every caress and every time he said her name, breathless, over and over again. For the first time in her adult life, Jesse was unaware that she was overweight and Steve acted as if she was a goddess sent from heaven.

It was 7:30 am when Jesse finally left Steve's apartment. It had taken over an hour to say goodbye. Every time she went to leave he would pull her to him for a final kiss. She had left him lying on his bed wrapped in a sheet, which she could now tell was pale blue and not white as she had first thought. His blond hair was tousled and he had a sleepy grin on his face as he flopped back on his pillow with a contented sigh.

She could not wipe the smile off her face even when she came out of the alleyway and started down the main stretch back to the apartments. She received a few nods and waves from locals opening their shops and had to step into the road to keep from the wet pavements, where several were washing their front steps. She could hear only the sea as it climbed up the beach to her left, and her trainers slapping on the patchy tarmac. She felt wonderful. Truly happy.

She knew she would never see Steve again, but she knew she would never forget how he made her feel and she would be eternally grateful for the experience he had given her. She had been loved, beautifully, for just over six hours with a stranger in a way no other man had loved her. She had thought about sex for nearly the entire two years that she had been free from her husband, but she had never captured in her mind the real beauty she had just experienced. She felt like a whole woman and, until this morning, she hadn't realised there had been a space in part of her heart that was the residue from her failed marriage.

She crept into the apartment she shared with Mary and Dotty, grabbed her swimming costume from the floor and changed in silence out of her evening clothes into the black halter-neck costume. She could hear the drone of Dotty's snoring as she slid into her kaftan, tied her hair in a ponytail, grabbed her sunglasses and refilled her purse with cash and cigarettes. She left the apartment without the girls having ever known she had entered. Although it was very early, there were a couple of towels already claiming sun beds around the pool. But there was plenty of choice for Jesse as she chose a space near their balcony and moved three beds into position.

Lounging on the sun bed with her huge black Gucci glasses covering half her face she lit one cigarette after another as she watched the early morning quiet turn into the late morning rush and waited for her friends to emerge sleepily from the balcony. She didn't read her novel or pick up a magazine. She simply sat quietly and her mind was at peace for the first time in years. You would never know she had not slept the previous night. She looked positively radiant with her face turned towards the sun.

CHAPTER 18

Darren was six four, had lank brown hair, bad teeth and a six o'clock shadow, but something about him made Jesse wild from the moment she spotted his sweaty face cooking steaks behind the stove of her parents' Harvester restaurant.

Jesse was twenty-one years old and living with Gill and another three girls in a five-bedroomed house in Ilford just down the road from the Harvester. She'd met Gill at work six months previously and both spent lunchtimes moaning about living with their parents and how it afforded them no privacy. Gill had a vested interest in getting out of home as her relationship with her long-term boyfriend had just gone to 'the next level'. Although the girls hadn't known each other long, their friendship had been cemented when Gill asked Jesse just two months after she joined the company to go to lunch with her at Garfunkel's.

Jesse took it in her stride when Gill asked her to demonstrate with a banana split how to give a good blow job. Just what it was that Gill saw in Jesse that made her think she would have this kind of information didn't actually occur to Jesse to ask. Four months later and the girls were having a blast living together. They had encouraged a girl they knew, Kerry, to join them and then Leah and Helen had joined them within the month.

Jesse had spotted Darren one evening while sitting behind the bar chatting to Sam, one of the barmaids on duty.

'Who's the new guy?' Jesse enquired, trying to appear nonchalant.

'Oh that's Darren, he's been here for months actually but he's changed shifts as he's moved in upstairs with Eric. So he has to do evenings as well as days now.' Sam smiled at Jesse while she was drying a wine glass. 'He's nice, isn't he?'

'Not my cup of tea,' Jesse lied.

'Just as well, as he's screwing Dawn and Jane at the same time and Jane doesn't know about it, but that's between you and I, of course!' said Sam. Jesse was thankful it was Sam on duty as she loved nothing more than a good gossip. 'It's all going to end in tears when Jane finds out. She'll probably strangle Dawn and definitely beat the crap out of Darren. I can't believe everyone else knows but Jane doesn't. I feel sorry for her, myself.'

'Why don't you tell Jane, then?' Jesse asked.

'I don't think so, Jesse. Jane's the type to take it out on anyone in her path. No thanks, let her catch him red-handed in the act, then he'll not see it coming.

You'd never know it to look at him, would you? It's always the quiet ones.'

Although Jesse knew there was no way she was going to get involved with him, she found out as much as she could about Darren over the coming weeks. He was Irish, a gambler and a Leo. He'd been homeless for months due to an injury he sustained when cement poured onto his legs while he'd worked on a building site, and a vicar had taken him in off the streets, got him cleaned up and got him the job at the Harvester. He was exceptionally quiet, apparently, and very shy, which didn't quite tally with him screwing two women at the same time, but that just made Jesse all the more intrigued.

After some discreet enquiries to her sister, who worked in the bar, Jesse found out Darren's nights off and, whenever she could, she planted herself at the end of the bar in the hope that he would one day stop for a drink. She never managed to say more than hello as he made his way to the vending machines with his pint in hand, but just looking at him from afar kept her interested for longer than she'd ever have expected. Summer came and went and still Jesse had made no progress with Darren, although she'd learned he loved football, Manchester United being his favourite team and, as well as drinking, he loved playing pool. Unfortunately, the Harvester didn't have a pool table, or Jesse would have wowed him with her shooting skills - being the daughter of a publican had its advantages.

She could play darts and pool better than anyone she'd ever met.

Darren was to be found in the pub down the road, which was very rough and very male, and there was no way Jesse could find an excuse to walk in there.

She had never been consumed by someone like she had by Darren. She thought about him first thing in the morning until last thing at night. It hadn't occurred to her that it was just his looks she fancied. She simply assumed they would get on like a house on fire and be soul mates.

It was an unusual accident that finally got them together, and one that Jesse hadn't purposefully engineered. A month previously, Jesse had applied for a pay rise and it had been refused. Over the previous twelve months she'd taken on the roles of three people who had left the company and was managing the three jobs perfectly, so was furious when she didn't get the £1000 pay rise she felt justified in asking for. She'd resigned on the spot. She had applied for countless secretarial positions and been offered two, but just couldn't get excited about either of them. Not knowing which way to turn, she found herself four weeks later waking up on a Monday morning with no job to go to. Her parents owned a mobile home in Hastings so she decided to take a break, get healthy and hope that the change would help her make some hard decisions about where her future was going.

Once Jesse decided to do something, she threw

herself into it wholeheartedly. Her health kick was no exception. On the way to the caravan, she'd stocked up on bundles of fresh fruit and vegetables and bypassed the wine section of the supermarket, opting for water instead. By lunchtime she'd unpacked and settled in, changed into her new white tracksuit and headed out to the beach. On nearing the water's edge, she decided she'd start the jog which would take her one mile down the beach to the tourist shops, whereupon she'd then return and treat herself to a good book and an early night.

She had run for just over three minutes when her back gave in, which was just as well as she would never have made four minutes without a lung collapsing. It took over twenty minutes to hobble back to the caravan, where she took some Nurofen and put her feet up on the couch. An hour later, she couldn't move. Jesse eventually got herself to bed and awoke in the morning in pretty much the same condition. She got some help in loading up her car, and by the afternoon she'd managed the painful drive back to Ilford. She had lumbago, apparently, and the doctor said she needed seven days' rest. Rather than stay at the empty house she shared with the girls, she came to her mum and dad's pub to escape the boredom, which is where she found Darren sitting on his own having an afternoon drink.

Darren had noticed her hobbling into the bar and offered to get her a drink. She nearly peed her pants she was so excited, and ordered white wine without realising it hadn't yet turned noon. An hour later and they were slowly making their way to the grotty pub at the end of the road for a game of pool. Amazingly, Jesse's back wasn't anywhere near as bad as it had been earlier in the day. It only took two games of pool for the trouble to start.

Jesse appeared to be the only female in the pool area and had been oblivious to the stares she was receiving. Towards the end of their second game she was approached by a young guy, probably early twenties, with a cute face and blond hair, asking if she'd play the next game with him.

'She's with me, mate,' Darren growled.

'Sorry,' she said apologetically to the young guy, who shrugged and walked away. Once he was out of earshot, Jesse sidled up to Darren and asked, 'Am I with you?' with a coy smile.

'Yes,' he said, returning her smile and he leant down and kissed her full on the mouth. Ordinarily, Jesse would have been embarrassed at such a public display of affection but she was feeling pretty loaded on wine and so didn't think anything of snogging over the pool table for a good fifteen minutes. They left the pub to a cheer of 'Get a fucking room!' but just giggled and zigzagged back to the pub, where they spent the next hour fumbling around in the dark in Darren's dirty single bed before Jesse dashed from his room and snuck out before anyone saw.

It was a whirlwind romance. Two days after their first kiss, Darren had finished the relationships with Dawn and Julie. Dawn had cried and Julie gave him a black eye as a souvenir. Jesse got away scot-free and she told herself it wasn't just that she was the boss's daughter. They were in love, weren't they? People were happy for them, weren't they?

Whatever the truth was, no-one commented a month later when they returned from a trip to Darren's parents in Ireland and announced their engagement. It was going to take a few months for Darren to save enough money to buy her the ring she wanted, a beautiful solitaire, but she could wait. They had booked the function room in the Harvester which would easily accommodate the 150 guests they had planned on having between them for the following August.

Six weeks into their relationship and Jesse had her first doubts as to whether their relationship would work.

Darren had saved six weeks' worth of pay and was going to present her with the engagement ring that evening. It was a Friday and Jesse had come bounding into the pub desperate to try the ring on and show it to all her friends in the house later that night. When she approached Darren, though, he looked moody and wouldn't meet her eye. He kept saying, 'In a minute, in a minute,' until Jesse twigged there was a problem and asked, 'Where's the ring, Darren?'

He looked like he might cry when he whispered,

'I don't have it.'

After a moment of silence, Jesse asked calmly, 'Why not?'

'I blew the lot on a horse.'

They might never have walked down the aisle if they had stayed with the plan of waiting until August, but arguments with Jesse's mum over black-and-silver balloons and Cameo soap invitations sent Jesse in the other direction and, two months later, they were married on a beach in Saint Lucia.

She was in trouble just two months after their honeymoon. Darren came into their rented house and stormed into Jesse's makeshift office brandishing a pair of her knickers. His six foot four frame loomed over her from the doorway as she sat in her chair in her tiny office, wondering what on earth was going on. 'You had these on when I went to work this morning and now they're in the washing basket. They're damp... and they smell of sex. Who've you had here?' Darren's voice had risen and risen until he was red with exertion.

Jesse was dumbstruck, she was so shocked. Without realising it she had also gone a very deep shade of red.

'Tell me who the fuck he is and I'll kill him!' Darren screamed.

In a measured and quiet voice Jesse answered, 'I've been in those knickers since six am and took them off an hour ago. I've been burning up in here all day and my bra and knickers were damp and uncomfortable. If they smell of sex, it's only from last night where I didn't have a shower before getting dressed this morning, as I had so much to do today.' Jesse had gone from mortified to furious. 'Satisfied?' Darren looked sheepish but before he could respond, Jesse started to retaliate.

'When the fuck do you think this mystery guy may have had sex with me, by the way? I've been locked in this house for eight weeks trying to get this business off the ground. I am working from six am until midnight and I'm also cooking your fucking dinner so you can sit and watch Man United on the box while I continue to earn the bloody rent. I haven't left the house for nearly a month and the only person I get to speak to in the flesh is the postman. Now, if you can find some time in my day for me to meet someone and invite them over here for sex, please tell me. Or did you think I was running dial-a-fuck from here?'

'Jesse, I'm really sorry, I really love you. I can't stand the thought of anyone being anywhere near you. I didn't think it through. Sorry.'

It was only a few days later when Jesse began to wonder what had brought him to the laundry basket, or whether it was a daily routine for him.

***

Jesse worked tirelessly trying to get her business off the ground. She had received no support from anyone and that was just the way she liked it. She never went out and any weekends that weren't spent working were spent in front of the television with Darren, eating pizza washed down with white wine.

After a few months of marriage Jesse had paid for Darren to be retrained in London and got him a job working in an up-and-coming ad agency via her friend, Anne, who had pulled a few strings. He was to start off at the bottom but could soon progress if he worked hard, which he did. Darren was soon earning good money and had earned two promotions at work. He was in a position with responsibility by the time Darrens firm threw its first Christmas party which was for clients, staff and their partners.

Jesse had worked from home for so long that she didn't have a single outfit suitable for a fancy occasion and spent several shopping trips trying to find the perfect dress. Instead she settled for one that fitted. Without her paying much attention to it, her weight had soared and she was now in a size twenty four. Her wedding dress had been a size ten.

In the end, she opted for a turquoise silk two-piece skirt-and-blouse set from Evans which had large red abstract flowers dotted on it. She managed to buy a pair of cream strappy shoes and a handbag to match and wore her hair long and curly. Looking at her reflection in the mirror she refused to admit she didn't recognise who looked back at her. She had to be upbeat as this was Darren's evening and she was going to be the perfect wife on his arm, which is what he wanted.

Jesse felt underdressed when she arrived at Darren's workplace in Piccadilly. All the women were wearing black cocktail dresses. Jesse looked and felt much older than her years and was regretting wearing the skirt as, although she wore shorts underneath to stop her legs from chaffing, she felt frumpy. They were less than a month away from their first wedding anniversary, but Jesse had learned very quickly that Darren was a jealous and possessive man and had made it very clear that Jesse was his and his alone. There had been several occasions over the year where Darren had come to blows with complete strangers because he'd believed they were flirting with Jesse, even though only one, a bartender in a cocktail bar, had actually spoken to her. With this in mind, Jesse knew better than to talk to any of Darren's male work colleagues, and especially avoided a stunningly good-looking guy who was even taller than her husband, and who had held eye contact with her just a little too long. Over the course of the evening she had been asked to dance several times and had declined until asked by Darren's best friend, Stuart, to do the jive. Stuart was a strange man to look at. He was incredibly short, incredibly fat, he had a deep scar down the length of his face and had pockmarked skin. He was Darren's friend and was a happily married father of one, so Jesse thought it would be okay to accept his offer of a dance.

That was a mistake.

Halfway through the song, Darren grabbed

Stuart by the throat and threw him across the room. He grabbed Jesse by the arm and, screaming abuse at her, propelled her through the crowds of colleagues into the cold night air of London. He was drunk so the arguing was fierce, culminating with Jesse being slapped across the cheek and left crying in an alleyway in Soho just before midnight.

An hour later, Jesse climbed out of a black taxi, paid £100 for the privilege and entered the house they called home to find Darren sitting with his feet up on the sofa watching the Man United match he'd missed earlier.

Jesse should have left him there and then. She had imagined several times packing her bags and walking out. But the sad truth was that she didn't want to fail at her marriage and she was insecure with her business, and had isolated herself from all her friends. She had no support system and both she and Darren knew it. The main reason she stayed was she wanted a family, always had, and she wanted children with Darren. Darren would be a good dad. He would stop drinking if he had a child. He would stop being so jealous if they were a complete family. Jesse wrapped these thoughts around her like a warm blanket when he came to bed that night and lay on top of her with his stinking breath on her face.

***

The irony was not lost on Jesse that while reading *Parenting* magazine, she had come on. As had been the case for the last eighteen months, tears silently slipped down her cheeks and she felt another chink loosen within her chest. Every time she had a period, she felt like she had lost a child. She had never miscarried, but she had also never fallen pregnant and she had been clear of the pill for eighteen months. When she emerged from the bathroom and stood in the living room, visibly devastated, Darren took her in his strong arms and hugged her.

'Don't worry, honey, it will happen soon, I just know it, darling.'

'I want to be tested now. They said to wait two years. With my coming off the pill and waiting six months to be sure, it's been exactly two years and I want the tests. We have to know what is going on and why I'm not falling pregnant.' Jesse was wailing now and Darren just hugged her and shushed her gently.

Two months later and the tests were in. Darren had had mumps when he was younger and was completely sterile, information which Jesse was surprised he had never shared with her before, and Jesse didn't ovulate regularly. No treatment was available to allow for a natural pregnancy. The doctor suggested IVF and adoption.

Later that afternoon once the shock had started to subside, they sat holding hands across a wooden table, staring at their coffee cups. Jesse's business had taken off and they found themselves living in a four-bedroomed house in Staines near the riverfront, a perfect house for children.

That was why they were in a coffee shop and not their home.

'Okay,' Jesse eventually spoke. 'Our choices are IVF or adoption.'

'No, I can't do that.'

'What do you mean, you can't do that? Which one? Why not?' Jesse couldn't believe what she was hearing.

'If I can't have a kid of my own, I don't want one at all. I'd never be able to love a kid that wasn't mine, simple as that.'

'Even if it came from my body and half of it was genetically mine?'

'Nope. We'll just have to accept that we're not going to have children. It's just you and me from now on.' Jesse couldn't speak, as all she wanted to do was throw her scalding coffee in his face. Why, she didn't, she'd never know. She kept quiet, nodded her head like the dutiful wife with no heart, and sipped her coffee.

Jesse tried to love Darren for another three months before coming to the realisation quite unexpectedly while having a soak in the bath that she'd rather be alone than be in a lonely marriage with someone who wasn't prepared to at least attempt to give her children. She could have coped with the drinking and the shouting and the jealousy, but not even considering other options for a pregnancy hardened her to him and she couldn't love him again.

She might have stayed if it hadn't been for the events of the previous four weeks.

Only a month previously, they had both gone to a Psychic Fair. Jesse had wanted to go alone but Darren wouldn't hear of it. So they sat in front of a gentle man called Vincent in a busy room full of various mediums who ignored Darren entirely and focused only on Jesse, telling her that her life was singing, that she would reach the masses and that it was something she had to do and would succeed at it. He also said that she had three children available to her. But when she asked him to elaborate, he wouldn't, just repeating that they were *available* to her.

Afterwards Darren nonsensed everything that Vincent had said but a seed had been planted for Jesse. In her spare time between projects at work, she started to write songs, pathetic ones at first about lost love and disappointment, but they soon became structured and better. She formed melody lines for them and two weeks later she had four songs ready to be recorded.

Darren didn't understand why she would want to record the songs and why she had to go to a professional studio to do it, but he certainly wasn't prepared to let her go on her own. So he spent five hours at a studio in Windsor moaning and groaning about being bored and cold, while Jesse sang her soul out to two enthusiastic sound engineers. By the end of the session she had four songs recorded. In black marker pen she wrote the word *Justice* across the silver

CD and a fire in her belly was lit.

***

A week after cutting her CD she auditioned for a recording studio who were looking for a powerful singer for a new project they were embarking upon.

Jesse left it until the morning of the audition to tell Darren what she was doing. She knew he would never be able to get out of his work commitments at the drop of a hat, so she'd be able to go it alone. The journey was long and complicated with three changes of train, an hour in a rickety old bus, a taxi to the B&B she had booked and then a long walk from the B&B to the bottom of a steep hill in four-inch stiletto boots.

Jesse looked confident. She was not. She looked like she didn't care that she was fat. She did. But she did know she still had a pretty face and she also knew that she had a damn good voice, so she wasn't going to make a fool of herself. She was a successful businesswoman and treated the audition as she would a business meeting. She recorded three versions of the song they wanted, leaving Jesse to choose her favourite for the boss, David, to listen to.

The only thing that went against her that day was that the travelling and audition had lasted much longer than she had anticipated and the Diocalm tablets she had taken at eight am had worn off by the time she met with David. She had cut the meeting very short and asked for the toilet, which she knew made her come across as abrupt. He led her through an office, where five people were working quietly, through to a large bathroom, the door of which was within the office walls. She sat on the toilet and her insides howled as they left their home and fled into the toilet bowl. Nothing she could do would lessen the sound and she knew David was standing directly outside the door, listening to every loud note of shit spraying enamel. Jesse was horrified but all she could do was hold her head in her hands and let the lava of her insides make its journey to the cool water beneath her. She was on the toilet for what felt like hours and must have been at least seven or eight minutes.

David was good enough not to flinch as she opened the door of the bathroom. She walked with him through the office towards the front door of the building and couldn't help but notice two of the secretaries' faces were scarlet, so she guessed her bathroom music had carried through. Jesse, too, had colour burning her cheeks as she realised the smell of shit wafting behind her was not competing well with the Calvin Klein Obsession that she had sprayed liberally around the toilet. They said they would let her know in the morning how she had got on, so she went to the B&B to die in shame.

***

The following evening, Jesse was trying to sell an idea to Darren. She would work five days a week supporting a new girl band who were going on tour, and then on the weekend, whichever country she was in, he would come out and spend it with her. She had thought long and hard about how to make it work for them both, allowing for his jealousy but also knowing this was something she had to do.

After much discussion, Darren decided he would not join her at weekends but instead give up his job and become her bodyguard.

It was the word 'bodyguard' that sealed their fate.

Jesse left him two days later.

CHAPTER 19

It couldn't have been a late night, as Mary arrived on the balcony with her chocolate croissants and Nescafé before 10 am.

'Morning,' was all Mary said before tucking greedily into her breakfast on the balcony above where Jesse lay. Thirty minutes later, Mary handed Jesse a cup of coffee. After she settled into position on the sun bed beside her friend, Mary lit two menthol cigarettes, handed one to Jesse, took a sip of her second coffee of the day and said, 'Right, I want to hear all about it, every single detail. Leave nothing out.'

'Do you know what?' Jesse said with a smile. 'It was lovely and wonderful and truly fantastic, but I want to keep it all to myself. Is that okay?' Mary wanted to say of course it bloody wasn't okay. She had been wondering all morning what had happened the night before after she'd seen Jesse walk nonchalantly past them into the road out of sight. But she also saw something else within Jesse that made her stop probing. Jesse had an aura of calm about her and a glow that made Mary almost visibly flinch with jealousy. She understood her friend had experienced something that she wanted to keep secret, about which she was delighted but also incredibly envious. Mary just raised her eyebrows as if to say 'fair enough' and took a long drag on her cigarette.

'When are you seeing him again?'

'I'm not, actually.'

Mary looked puzzled. 'Why not? I thought you said it was lovely.'

'I did, and it really was. But it was enough. Any more and it would be spoiled. We could never beat last night and I'll never see him after the holiday, so I'm going to leave it at that.' Jesse was smiling.

'Blimey, Jesse, you're serious? You've been wanting sex since leaving Darren and now you've had it, and a lot of it, by the look on your face. I can't believe you wouldn't want that until you go back home. We still have a few nights left!'

'I know! Mad, isn't it? But I really feel no need now. I feel fab. It was fab. But it was a one-time-only deal. I won't be looking for more. I tell you something, though, I know nothing at all about him, nor him me. We didn't have a single conversation!'

'Whore!'

They both jumped when they heard Dotty's low remark from directly above them. She had been listening to their entire conversation from the balcony, hoping for a snippet of something juicy. Dotty was smiling broadly, 'Of course I'm madly jealous, you know, but I'm hungry and you can fill me in over breakfast.' Dotty disappeared out of view. They could hear her Jesus sandals clip-clopping over the marble floor as she headed towards the apartment door to leave and join the two girls.

Mary leaned over towards Jesse and whispered, 'Wait until you hear what happened last night with Stavros.'

'What?'

'I'll tell you later.'

'Hey, that's not fair!'

'Now you know how it feels,' said Mary quietly as she stood up and prepared to walk with Dotty and Jesse to the taverna next door for a second helping of breakfast. As Mary went to walk past her, Jesse linked her arm around Mary's and kissed her grumpy friend on the cheek.

'Love ya,' Jesse whispered. Instantly Mary was no longer annoyed or jealous of her. She squeezed her arm in hers and followed Dotty to breakfast.

***

The bar had been busy and Jesse wasn't there to recognise the signs that Dotty was getting drunk as she was already in the land of pleasure with Steve half a mile away. Mary was gushing over Niko and wasn't paying any attention to the fact that Dotty was steaming. Had Jesse seen her, she would have known trouble was brewing and got her out of there fast, but she hadn't. Mary was leaning over the bar getting a light from Niko when Dotty left her barstool. Mary didn't realise how light Dotty could be on her callused feet when she wanted to be, as only three seconds after Mary realised she was AWOL, the whole town of Rethymnon heard Dotty screech at the top of her opera-trained lungs.

'Stavros, get your arse over here now!' As if that wasn't mortifying enough, Dotty was standing in the middle of the road between the apartment bar and Stavros and Antonio's cocktail bar, one hand on her hip and the other viciously pointing from one bar to the other, with a face like a bulldog chewing a wasp.

'Come on, can't you hear me, Stavros?!'

'If he's in Greece, I guarantee he heard you,' came the voice of a patron of the bar. He was clever enough to ensure his comment never reached Dotty's ears. It did reach Mary's, who didn't know what on earth to do. She cursed Jesse under her breath. Jesse was the one who could deal with Dotty in these situations. She would know what to do. But she'd abandoned them for a quick shag with the rep and left her alone to sort out a rather demented Dotty. Mary was aware that Dotty could crush her like an ant if she said the wrong thing, and the image brought her out in a cold sweat but got her moving off the bar stool and into the street to try and talk Dotty down from her anger.

Dotty saw Mary coming in her peripheral vision and stopped waving her hands about, and placed them both on her hips, glaring at Mary. 'I don't think he can hear me, Mary!' she shouted, as if she were in an un-miked play at the Royal Albert Hall trying to reach the deaf person on the back row. 'Let's go and find him!' With that, Dotty took two purposeful strides and was off the road and on her way to the bar, the lights of which had strangely been turned off two minutes previously.

Mary couldn't see any light until Dotty moved to the right of the stairs, but could then see there were ten or so candles still burning in the bar. There was a metallic smell of smoke in the air so it was obvious to Mary that they had tried to blow out all the candles to throw Dotty off the scent and hide, but hadn't managed them all before she had headed into the bar.

Stavros stood within the confines of the serving area with Antonio. They both looked like rabbits caught in a headlight, although Antonio looked more like a rabbit that had been shot for Sunday dinner but was hanging on by his last breath.

The silence was deafening until Antonio flipped a switch and *YMCA* started to play loudly through the stereo speakers. He picked up a pack of cards and chortled.

'Dotty, you have come for more magic tricks. Let me get you girls a drink.' He was trying to sound jovial but he sounded terrified to Mary, and with good reason, she thought. Antonio started throwing the cards in an arc in the air with one hand and catching them with the other, but Dotty was oblivious and was looking directly at Stavros, although truth be told, she was looking at two Stavroses, one swirling around the other.

Being up close to her prey had calmed her somewhat and she said rather petulantly, 'You said you'd meet me for a drink tonight and you didn't come. I was looking forward to seeing you all day. Don't you like me? Is it because I'm fat?' Mary could have cried for her, but she was absorbed in her own world of trying to figure out how she could get out of this situation and get away from Antonio and back to Niko, who was primed at the apartment bar.

'Sorry my darlink but it's my wife, she watches me closely, she has friends to watch me.' Stavros's arms were held out and shoulders up as if to say 'what could I do, I know nothing.' He produced an old pink plastic rose from under the counter and handed it to Dotty meekly. 'I am sorry, my sweet, you are lovely. You don't deserve bastard like me.'

'Nor does your wife,' muttered Mary, just loud enough for Antonio to hear, and he gave her a wise nod.

'Bless you, my love,' Dotty said sweetly with tears in her eyes, accepting the rose as a token of his love. Before anyone saw it coming, Dotty's long arm had reached over the counter and around Stavros's neck and had him in a headlock while tonguing him passionately. One of Stavros's arms was on the counter trying to lift his weight to avoid strangulation, while the other was waving up and down mid-air around the back of his neck trying to grab Dotty's hand.

Mary and Antonio were visibly horrified. The scene reminded Mary of a lioness ripping the face off a deer it had just hunted and killed for its lunch. Dotty was relishing the moment, while Stavros was obviously being choked to death. Dotty let out a scream of pain when Stavros managed to grab a manicured finger and prise it backwards away from his neck. 'Ah, shitty death, that hurt!'

'Sorry, Dotty, my breath.' Stavros grabbed more oxygen while he could. 'You very strong. Took me by surprise -' another gulp of air - 'lovely lady.' The last comment had Mary laughing out loud.

'What are you finding so funny?' Dotty spat at Mary, simultaneously sucking her wounded finger and trying to hold the martini that Antonio had just handed her.

'Nothing. Sorry, Dotty, I must be a little drunk.' Mary prayed that Dotty wouldn't get angry with her. That was one thing she definitely wasn't equipped to deal with on her own.

Still pouting and sucking her finger, Dotty mumbled, 'Can we change the music, Antonio? This crap is giving me a headache.' Unfortunately for both Stavros and Mary, the soft tones of Norah Jones came on the stereo, which both Antonio and Dotty felt would be perfect for dancing in candlelight with their reluctant partners.

'Right, let's dance!' Dotty declared. She was slurring her words and managed to knock over a bar stool en route to the six-foot space that she considered her dance floor. She swayed patiently, waiting for Stavros to get himself together and open his arms to her.

Antonio had already made his way around the bar, taken Mary's hand and pressed his cracked lips to her knuckles in a leery kiss, leading her slowly to where Dotty was about to engulf Stavros.

Mary had to keep constantly moving Antonio's yellowed hands from her bottom back up to her waist, very aware that Niko might be able to see them dancing from across the street. Just the one dance and she was out of there, she promised herself. The realisation that she was leading Antonio on had happened the day before, but she didn't know what to do about it. Slow dancing with him to candlelight wasn't helping the situation. She was relieved to hear the song come to an end. She removed Antonio's hands from her body and stepped back to the bar, grabbed her handbag and turned to Dotty. 'I think we should leave, Dotty, I'm not feeling too good.'

Dotty did not hear her. She had her eyes closed and didn't break her circular stride when Norah Jones turned into Dido on the stereo system. Stavros looked catatonic, with the side of his face pressed hard into Dotty's full bosom. She had a firm grip of his bum and her other hand ran up and down his thick head of hair which was now extremely dishevelled, while his arms hung limp at his sides. All he needed was a trickle of drool in the corner of his mouth and he'd have looked like a cadaver.

Mary went to Dotty's side and impatiently started prodding her arm.

'Dotty! Dotty! Come on, we have to go now!' When Dotty opened her eyes, Mary felt a spike of panic rush through her chest as she saw Dotty's eyes couldn't find Mary's face. Dotty's eyes rolled around and around in a way Mary would never have believed possible. Dotty suddenly grabbed Mary's shoulder with her left arm. 'I don't feel too goo…' she slurred and magically pulled Stavros from her bosom by his hair with her right arm, just in time for her dinner to hit the sandstone tiles. The second round of vomit covered Dotty's shoes and had both Mary and Stavros gagging so loudly that Niko could hear it from across the street.

She had staggered to the top of the stairs for round three but Mary managed to find a way down on tippy toes without getting any chunks on her shoes. Mary was mortified to find herself still gagging as she tried to support Dotty on their escape back to the apartment. She knew there was nothing attractive about the sound she was making and the action forced her tongue to protrude and tonsils show every time she retched. The stench was dreadful. The martini Dotty had just finished smelled ten times more concentrated as it followed them past Niko's bar on Dotty's shoes.

Mary wasn't sure if her mind was playing tricks on her but she was sure she could hear Dotty's shoes squelch with each step and had a visual of Dotty's toes playing with the vomit as it seeped through the material of her once-white trainers. Mary would never be able to drink a turquoise shot again without recalling the stain on Dotty's trainers from that night.

Mary didn't care a damn that Dotty was now crying loudly, with snot running down to her lips. She was humiliated, gagging, exhausted from trying to guide Dotty around the pool and didn't have any patience left for her drunk friend. Mary couldn't understand much of what Dotty was wailing about but she did hear 'Stavros' several times and 'married' and 'why me?'

Mary had a pain in her chest with the dry heaving and a burning sensation in the back of her throat, but she managed to get Dotty into the apartment relatively unscathed. She sat the sobbing drunk on the edge of her bed, put a pair of clean socks on her hands to protect them, took a deep breath and then prised off Dotty's shoes and socks. Her top was covered in vomit so that had to come off, too. Although it had damp stains on it, Mary couldn't bring herself to remove Dotty's bra for her and she couldn't risk getting her to stand up to get her trousers off in case she toppled over. It took the longest time to get Dotty to lay down, but the minute she did, she was snoring.

Mary wasn't surprised to find the pool bar shut

by the time she stood on their balcony twenty minutes later with a green carrier bag filled with Dotty's soiled clothes and shoes. She tied a knot in the bag, placed it in the farthest corner of the balcony, sat on one of the white plastic chairs and lit a cigarette.

Mary was gutted. The night had seemed so promising and all she'd managed to achieve was humiliation in front of Niko and had managed to spend more time with Antonio than she'd ever wanted. She could hear the ocean in the distance, crickets singing and the buzz of flying insects she couldn't see. Dotty was snoring loudly as Mary sat with her bare feet resting on a chair, forming smoke rings in the dark. They were about to start day four of their holiday and, at that moment, Mary felt desperately lonely. The tear didn't fall down her cheek, but it wobbled in her vision for a few minutes before disappearing as quietly as it had arrived.

***

Jesse had to clamp her thighs together until they hurt to stop the pee trickling down her leg where she was literally wetting herself laughing at Mary's retelling of their escapades the previous night. Mary left out the truly sad bits for Dotty's benefit - she would fill Jesse in when they were alone, while Dotty had her siesta. But she retold the story so graphically that Jesse could completely visualise Mary carrying Dotty on her back through the swamp of vomit, all the while gagging on the stench of her friend's dinner as she glided past Niko at the bar.

It wasn't the story so much as Dotty's face that got Jesse roaring with laughter with the realisation that this had actually happened. She could see everything clicking into place in Dotty's mind as Mary told the story. Jesse howled louder when Dotty put her knife and fork down and pushed her full plate of belly-buster breakfast away from her in disgust. Thankfully, Jesse had the kind of bellowing roar that was infectious. Ripples of laughter were heard throughout the early-morning breakfast crew as the other two girls joined Jesse in a screaming chorus of hysterical laughter.

A few minutes later Jesse gently slid into the cool blue water to cleverly disguise the fact she had a developed a wet patch on the crotch of her swimsuit. As she glided along the length of the pool it occurred to her that it might not have been caused purely by her leaking due to excessive laughter.

By the time she slowly turned and swam back to the steps, her wonky smirk had been replaced by a thin line as the thought 'we didn't use a condom' played over and over in her mind.

***

While Dotty had her afternoon nap, Mary and Jesse took a stroll along the beach. The heat of the day could be felt through Jesse's baseball cap, but the breeze blew warm around her body and lifted the hem of her sarong. They walked in silence, enjoying the sand beneath their toes, the sound of the waves mingled with squeals of delight from children nearby. Jesse had two things on her mind, the lack of condoms the previous evening being one of them, but oddly not the priority. *What the hell am I doing with my life?* was the main thought that kept bashing against a brick wall in her mind.

'Let's sit for a while,' Jesse suggested, as she saw two abandoned sun beds near the edge of the surf. Both girls sat with the beds between their legs, feet in the sand, facing the sea with their handbags in front of their large stomachs.

'Are you okay, Jesse?' Mary asked between puffs of her newly-lit cigarette.

'Yeah, I'm okay,' Jesse mumbled.

'Okay, what's wrong?' Mary knew Jesse wanted to talk and she knew it must be serious as Jesse never sat for a chat unless she had something on her mind. If she had a problem she could never discuss it while walking or driving - it was just one of those things that were unique to Jesse.

'It's beautiful here, isn't it? I keep wondering if I could move here. If it wasn't for the bad winters, I think I really would consider it, you know?'

'I know, but unless you want to pick olives four months of the year, it's really not going to be for you, Jesse.'

'Is there really nothing else I could do?'

'Not really, not without learning the language.'

'Yeah and bollocks to trying to learn Greek. French was hard enough.'

'How's that going?' Jesse had told Mary months previously that she'd bought a home-study course to learn French but, as she hadn't mentioned it since, Mary assumed it was one of Jesse's fads and hadn't even opened the box. She was beginning to wonder if she'd been wrong.

'I'm on verbs and bloody hell, I really don't get them. Everything else I'm okay with and I was rocking along, but the verbs are really throwing me. I might actually go to lessons for a little while to see if someone can explain them more. I'm more than halfway through the course so I don't want to stop just because I can't figure out a poxy verb.'

'I didn't realise you'd been doing it. You never mentioned it.'

Jesse just shrugged her shoulders. 'I got sick of getting drunk every night, so when I feel in the mood I put a CD on and learn a little more. It's very good as you don't write anything down - just listen and repeat. It's okay. Still not sure why I'm doing it. I can't see me moving to France on my own somehow.'

'I'll come with you if you want me to,' Mary suggested, but they both knew that Mary was lying. Mary was so stuck in her ways that she wouldn't change anything unless she had absolutely no choice. She certainly wouldn't proactively move in the hope of getting a new life. She would have to be guaranteed a new one first.

'Thanks Mary, I may take you up on that,' Jesse

lied. 'I'd love a little farmhouse in a village, not too rural, though. Maybe near the coast.'

'Have you thought about where you might like to look?' Mary asked.

'Not really, I was going to stick a pin in the map, to be honest, and then check that out. You know, see where fate takes me and all that. So long as I put a Post-it note over Paris I'm sure I'll be fine!' Jesse tried to shake the awful memory of Paris from her mind and focus back on Mary. Mary and Jesse ordered a cocktail each from a beach waiter and settled into the white plastic sun beds facing the sea.

'My only fear is that if I move away to France I'll just be taking my problems with me. I mean really, what will change?' Jesse asked.

'Well, you'll have a new house, a smaller mortgage, more sun. You like a challenge and it'll certainly be that.'

'But you know what I'm like. I like to believe that I'll have lots of friends when I go, but we both know that I'm extremely antisocial so the chances are I'll still be spending Friday nights in on my own, just the wine'll be cheaper. Probably not just Friday nights either.'

'Well, perhaps you can get a different job and meet people that way?'

'You know I couldn't. My business keeps me. Without that I'd be stuffed and I don't trust anyone else to run it so that's not an option. I suppose I could always work in a bar or something, but I'd have to really know the language for that and it'll take years.'

'It sounds like you're already talking yourself out of it.'

'Maybe I am. But if I don't move then I need to sort my life out. I'm so bloody bored sometimes it's awful. I only have three friends in the world and two of them live on the other end of London, so they might as well live in Devon, and you're constantly travelling.' Jesse paused for a moment and sipped her Piña Colada. 'I just get really lonely sometimes. I'll end up talking to the walls like Shirley Valentine soon.'

'Weren't you going to join that band?'

'Yes, I'm still thinking about it. Apparently they've sent a CD over for me to learn for the next rehearsal so it'll be interesting to have a listen and see what the set list is. At least it'll get me out of the house twice a week.'

'Anyone there you fancy?'

Jesse laughed, 'Hardly! They're all a very odd bunch. The lead singer is a high-kicking Bay City Roller type. The drummer likes to think of himself as an Italian stallion but I think he's more of a Shetland pony. The trumpeter is like a mannequin and the keyboardist, well, let's just say I've never seen such bad skin in real life. The saxophone player looks okay, but sooo not my type - he spent the whole two hours I was there bouncing on his heels. He kept telling me to join in and sing. Actually how I didn't tell him to bugger off,

I'll never know.'

'Ah well, like you said, at least you'll get out of the house a few nights and you'll be gigging, too, won't you?'

'They don't seem to gig very often, but they're such a huge band, I'm not surprised. Apparently they're at some school fete in a month's time, not exactly high fliers, hey? Still, it'll be good to be singing again. Jesse's dream was to sit in the corner of a little bar with a guitar and perhaps one other guitarist, and just play and sing her own music. The problem was she couldn't play the guitar and didn't know another guitarist who would join her. When drunk, she entertained grand dreams of her CD landing in the right lap and getting a record contract and travelling the world, but she also knew this was highly unlikely. She knew her size would go against her. Her age wasn't helping. She had a pretty face, but her body let her down time and time again.

'Fancy going on the Slim-Fast diet when we get back?' Jesse asked.

'Oh I'm not sure about that one, Jesse, you know how the bars give me wind.'

'I think it's the only way I'm going to manage to get rid of some of this weight. It doesn't bother me so much in the winter but in the summer, I mean, look,' she said, grabbing one of her tummy layers, 'no disguising this in a bloody bikini, is there?'

'Jesse, you don't look anywhere near as bad as you think you do.' They both knew Mary was lying but it still helped to hear it.

'Thanks, Mary. Maybe Slimming World again, then. I liked that one.'

'But you didn't lose any weight on that one, did you?'

'Didn't I? I don't remember. I remember eating whole chickens of an evening and thinking it was great!'

'I'm sure you didn't lose on it, though. Rosemary Conley was better for you, wasn't it?'

'Yes, but it's always a drag to get out to the club and then do an exercise class, although I liked the kebab we had on the way home every week.' Jesse grinned and slurped the rest of her cocktail through the bendy straw. 'I guess I could always go back to counting calories. That always works but it's a bit depressing. It's always a toss-up between a Mars Bar or an evening meal, or a bottle of wine or lunch. Mmm, I'll have to think about it a bit more.' They sat in silence, enjoying the heat on their faces until the breeze cooled and the beach started to empty.

'Come on, Mary, let's go back. We can stop off at the shop on the corner and get a bar of Dairy Milk to go with our coffee when we get back.'

'Let's get a couple of choccie croissants as well for the morning,' Mary added, all thoughts of dieting put aside.

***

After a lazy afternoon at the pool, the girls had taken their time getting dressed into their evening clothes.

Moisturised, primped and preened, none of the three had ever looked better. Each had varying brown tones on their faces from the four days of sun worship, giving them a healthy glow. Jesse glowed all the more when she saw Steve approaching the apartment as she made her way to the pool-side bar. She was thankful for the heavy foundation she had applied to her face so her blushes couldn't be easily seen as she realised he was heading directly for her. She wasn't sure how to broach the subject of their not having used condoms the night before. However she ran the different scenarios through in her head, she didn't have the words to start the conversation she was desperate to have.

'Hello Steve, how are you?' smiled Jesse seductively.

'Not good. I need to speak to you.' Jesse was disappointed to hear his harsh tone. He grabbed her arm and leaned in close enough that she could feel his breath on her ear.

'I can't believe I didn't use a fuckin' condom and all I can think about now is you giving me AIDS. How much do I need to worry?' Steve turned his head from her ear to stare directly into Jesse's eyes. Jesse was speechless and just stared back.

'Well?' Steve hissed, 'How much do I need to worry about getting HIV or crabs or gonorrhoea off you?'

'You don't!' whispered Jesse, wounded. Steve continued ranting in his quiet-but-harsh tone.

'I can't believe I was so bloody stupid, taking your bloody word for it that you haven't slept with anyone since your husband. Christ, I know better than to sleep with any old slag without a condom.' Unfortunately for Steve a switch was now flicked and any chance he had of keeping his affairs quiet blew out of the window.

'What did you just say?!' Jesse bellowed, loud enough to make Niko jump in shock behind the bar and drop the shot glass he had been drying.

'Okay, keep your voice down, I didn't mean...' Steve's patronising tone was swallowed up by Jesse's booming shout.

'Who are you calling a fucking slag, you stupid little boy?' Lowering her voice to a low growl she continued. 'If anyone should be worried it's me, screwing a kid of your age, and a fucking rep no less. How low can you go? If I'd have been less drunk I wouldn't have insisted on a condom. I'd have sent you home to your mummy for hot milk and a cookie, you stupid wanker. How dare you call me a slag?!' She emphasised the final word with a hefty shove in his chest. Mary and Dotty were already halfway across the pool-side racing to help Jesse. They had both dropped everything and started to run the minute they heard Jesse shout. Steve shoved Jesse back, which was a mistake as Jesse shoved him again even harder.

'Who the hell do you think you are?' Another

shove. 'I've been married for seven bloody years, single for two. You're the first man I've been with since my husband. How dare you call me' - Jesse shoved again - 'a fucking' – shove - 'slag!' Jesse watched Steve's arms windmill twice before he lost his balance and fell backwards into the pool, hitting his head on the low diving board as he went. Mary and Dotty stood beside Jesse, hoping to form a protective barrier against any possible repercussions as Steve coughed and spluttered, holding a hand to his head and shouting 'stupid fuckin' bitch' several times. Niko rushed to help a sopping wet Steve out of the pool as the three girls retreated to the bar, never taking their eyes off Steve, who was purple with fury. Niko cooed softly, trying to placate Steve and remove him from the pool-side area with as little fuss as possible. Steve was having none of it.

'Oh shitty death,' Dotty muttered as Steve wrestled away from Niko and marched towards Jesse screaming and pointing at her. 'You're going to pay for that, you bitch.' Jesse braced herself and, as much as her instinct was to run as fast as she could, she got ready to defend herself.

A loud calm voice came from behind Jesse. 'I don't think so, mate.'

Before the three girls could turn fully to see who had come to their rescue, a large man stepped from beside Dotty and Mary and stood directly in front of Jesse.

'I don't know what your problem is, mate, but

you're not going to do a thing but go back to where you came from.' Steve had stopped dead in his tracks about a metre from where Jesse's knight in shining armour stood, and took in the scene. He recognised the man in front of Jesse and could see the three other figures he had travelled with standing behind Dotty and Mary. He would never have opened his mouth if he'd known anyone was going to get involved, let alone four large men whom, he realised, were significantly older and stronger than he was.

There was a long pause before Niko put his hand on Steve's shoulder and quietly said, 'Come on, Steve, I help you get dry, this not worth your job, no?' Steve let out a dramatic sigh, pleased to have Niko give him a way out.

'No, Niko, this is not worth losing my job.' He shook his head at Jesse in mock disappointment, turned on his heel and walked slowly around the pool and out of sight.

'Praise the Lord!' Dotty declared when he had turned the corner, 'I really thought he was going to wallop you one.'

'I have no doubt that's exactly what he was going to do,' replied a shaken Jesse. It had taken a beat for her to realise the man in front of her was Ben, one of the men with whom she'd danced drunkenly on their first night. She was touched, and very relieved, to see his three friends were all behind her too, each ready to wade in if there had been trouble.

270

'Are you okay?' Ben asked, while gently tucking a piece of her hair behind her ear where it was supposed to sit.

'Fine. Thanks for that. Guess it's my round!' Swiftly Jesse turned away so he wouldn't see her cheeks flush and walked back to her stool at the bar, plonking herself down and motioning the others to follow. Jesse let out a long silent breath.

Ben pulled up a stool next to Jesse and absent-mindedly rubbed his large hands up and down Jesse's back while he turned to have a quiet conversation with the tallest of his friends, Tom. Jesse was sure his gesture was meant to comfort her, but a heat sparked in her stomach that had her desperate for the oblivion of alcohol... or sex.

'Come on, Niko,' Jesse muttered, desperate for a drink of something alcoholic. Whisky would be good but even Metaxa would do at this stage.

'Not a bad idea, Tom,' Ben replied before turning to Jesse. Addressing all three girls, Ben suggested a night in the main town of Rethmynon. There was a nightclub Tom had spotted the previous evening and thought looked good to check out. The night was young so the boys had planned on hitting a few bars on the stretch by the beach, grabbing a pizza, and then heading out to the nightclub for a dance. Tom, Mike and Kevin confirmed they would be delighted if the three girls would join them for the night.

The entire time that the group chatted and waited for the two taxis, Ben's hands moved slowly up and down Jesse's back, causing blood to rush in her ears so loudly that she just nodded, smiled, tried to hide her feelings of excitement and look as if it was every day that a good-looking six-foot male with strong muscly arms, bright white teeth, gorgeous hazel eyes and a husky voice touched her. She was terrified of mistaking his gentle touch that got her feeling hot and flustered as just friendly.

As much as making love with Steve had been a truly wonderful experience at the time, it was now tainted and she had put the whole night in a mental box labelled 'do not open' and tried to ignore the fact she'd had sex just one day previously, and unprotected sex at that. While she had tuned out from the conversations around her, she had time to think about the awful scene between her and Steve and decided that the chances of her catching something from him were remote. He was so angry and worried about her history that his must have been relatively clean. She knew she probably couldn't fall pregnant so decided to chalk it up to experience and not worry about it, although she was mortified of thinking Ben and his friends might have known what started the fight. She'd hate for them to think she really was a slag, but then would Ben be stroking her back so gently if he believed that to be so? No, he wasn't the type. Quite why she hadn't realised he was the prince-on-a-charger type when she'd met him on the first evening, she didn't understand. If she was honest, she wouldn't have known if he was butt ugly or gorgeous on the first night due to the excessive amount of alcohol in her system, which caused everyone to be in soft focus anyway.

Prior to meeting her ex-husband, alcohol had often softened the edges of an ugly bug so she was quietly happy when she awoke with her head in the refrigerator on the first morning rather than in a stranger's bed. She hadn't really thought of the four men she'd met since then, which she was bitterly regretting now.

It was a good job the taxi driver didn't understand English very well as he may have thrown the girls out of his cab for their screaming obscenities. The four boys had jumped one cab and the girls followed them in another, giving all three a chance to scream and giggle at the possibilities of the night ahead and the repercussions of pushing Steve in the pool.

'Shitty death, Jesse! Ben is gorgeous, GORGEOUS! Can you believe the way he stood in front of you like that? I didn't even know he was near the apartment. Bloody hell! What are you going to do?'

'About what?'

'Ben and Steve, of course!' Dotty rolled her eyes.

'Nothing. What can I do? I'm certainly not going to tell Ben I slept with Steve, unless he openly asks, which I bloody well hope he doesn't. It's not as if

Steve is going to say a word to Ben after that standoff at the pool. I just hope he doesn't do anything to upset our holiday now. After all he is the rep and no doubt has ways to ruin a holiday if he wants to.'

'Don't worry about that,' said Mary with derision. 'He can't do a thing unless he wants us to reveal he's slept with a client - that'll get him fired and I get the feeling he likes his job. I really don't think we'll have a problem with him. It's not as if we need to see him again until we leave for the airport.'

'Mmm.'

'What's that supposed to mean, Dotty?' Both girls glared at their friend who was avoiding their stares by looking out of the window.

'I was meaning to tell you earlier but didn't have the time, what with Steve and everything...'

'What!'

'I've organised all of us to go to a Greek folk night tomorrow. I thought it would be fun and we've not been on an excursion yet and I really thought it'd be a nice surprise.' The heavy sighs that came from Mary and Jesse told Dotty all she needed to know. They were not amused. At all.

Both Mary and Jesse knew exactly what to expect at the Greek folk night. They'd been to their fair share and now they were in their thirties they knew they were far too old to find the night appealing. As their taxi screeched to a halt on the seafront, Ben approached Jesse's door to open it for her. She cast a quick eye over Dotty's worried face and said,

'We'll talk about this tomorrow. Let's just enjoy tonight. I need to blow off some steam. Agreed?'

'Agreed!' both girls chimed and scooted across the seat to follow Jesse.

As they walked the promenade, the sea breeze rustled Jesse's curls away from her face. The scent of seaweed coupled with the gentle crashing of the waves onto the sand helped her relax and she smiled gratefully up at Ben when he put his arm around her and gripped her shoulder possessively. No, she was fairly certain he wasn't just being friendly, but forward. He was letting her know he had claimed her, and she was just fine and dandy with that. They didn't speak as they strolled down the busy tourist stretch, taking in the sights and keeping their friends in view.

Up ahead they could hear Dotty laughing with Mike and Kevin as they pulled up to a caricaturist who was set up in the street.

'I don't think so, Mike!' laughed Dotty, as Jesse and Ben approached.

'Oh come on, Dotty, it'll be fun. We'll stand on either side of you! It won't take long.'

'Go on, I'll pay for it,' chimed Mary. She was fluttering her eyelashes and giggling, but only Jesse and Dotty knew Mary had taken a shine to Tom.

Fifteen minutes later the three girls were sat on high bar stools waiting for the men to bring them some drinks from the bar.

'I think it's a great likeness of you,' Mary said to Dotty, who was still looking intently at the caricature for which Mary had paid 5000 Drachmas. Faced with two skinny men and a very large woman, the artist had done a great job of giving Dotty a skinny body and massive head, and tiny heads on the men. The likeness was very good of their faces, even if the artist had risked painting Dotty's tongue hanging out in lust for the man on her right and her hand stroking the thigh of the man on her left.

'I look like a right man-eater,' Dotty said, only half-jokingly.

'The men look okay about it, especially Tom, the way he's painted his eyes rolling with a big grin on his face,' Mary commented on Tom solely, so she could legitimately continue to look at Tom as if comparing the caricature.

'So, I gather Tom's next?' asked Jesse rather nonchalantly. Mary tried to look puzzled.

'What do you mean?'

'You know what I mean, Mary! Is Tommy boy going to get into your knickers tonight?' Jesse had kept her voice very low but still Mary shushed her fiercely.

'No! He's not getting into my knickers, and keep your voice down, Jesse.'

'I hope you've got some nice silkies on,' Jesse egged her on, knowing Mary was going to get indignant, which would give the girls plenty of ammunition in the morning to rib Mary after she'd done exactly what she was saying she would never do.

'I have my waistie white Sloggis on, thank you very much, so no-one except us three will be seeing my knickers tonight… or for the rest of this holiday, for that matter.'

'Mmmm, hmmm,' chimed both Dotty and Jesse, watching the men at the bar intently.

'Anyway, it's not my knickers that we should be worrying about today. It's yours, Jesse. Ben is obviously a fast mover by the looks of it.'

'God, I hope so,' Jesse muttered with a smirk as she watched Ben approach her, carrying a large Piña Colada and two bottles of Beck's.

'Are you ladies okay?' asked Ben with a warm smile.

'Yes,' chimed all three girls.

'Fancy a dance?'

All three yelled 'yes!' and they headed towards the dance floor with Ben and Tom. Mike and Kevin stayed on the warm seats and watched the small group find their place and start dancing. They looked an odd bunch. Dotty had great moves but a face like thunder, almost daring anyone to laugh at her. Mary was so petite and serene that she created an illusion of floating softly rather than actually dancing. Jesse was the contrast, with her arms in the air, hair all over the place and eyes closed while singing the song lyrics. Tom was doing a kind of pogo, not quite in time with the music, and Ben managed to look quietly sexy, moving his feet from side to side while his shoulders swayed. His gaze never left Jesse's face.

Thirty minutes later, Jesse made her way to the toilets as she had beads of sweat dripping from her long hair into her face, so she figured she'd better powder her nose. Looking in the mirror in the grubby toilets made her cringe. Her face was soaked in sweat with a slight smudge of black mascara under each eye. Her lipstick had gone but the reddish brown lip liner was still prominent on her lips, which was not a good look at all. Her hair was plastered to her face where she'd exerted herself so much dancing that she'd perspired terribly. She couldn't find one thing to like about her face at that moment and it brought her mood down. What was she doing, thinking she could bag someone like Ben? He was totally gorgeous. Maybe he was drunker than she thought. She'd only seen him drink one beer but he might well have had plenty to drink before he came to her rescue at the apartment bar.

Lifting her chin so she couldn't see any flab under her neck, she proceeded to clean herself up using toilet tissue and hanging her head under the hand dryer until her hair fluffed a little. Jesse reapplied lipstick, blotted her face and put on a look of confidence that she only wished she could feel.

The heat of the club touched her skin as she threw open the toilet door and the disco strobe lights caused her to squint slightly as she started the walk to where her friends were. She didn't see Ben in the shadows leaning against the wall as she passed him, so was caught off guard when he grabbed her wrist and pulled her back to where he stood. She practically fell against his chest and it took a second to realise it was Ben and another to realise his mouth was on hers, searching for her tongue.

He tasted sweet, and he held her in a firm embrace. For a few moments his mouth crushed hers and then he gently softened his grip until he was brushing her lips with his and tenderly touching his tongue to hers. He held her jaw with his fingers as he explored her mouth and gently turned her face so he could kiss her neck. She felt a little dizzy when he gently pulled away, put his arm around her waist and led her towards their friends. She had so many thoughts whizzing through her head that she couldn't grab hold of one to make any sense of what she was feeling. So she simply walked and managed a wistful smile to Dotty, as Ben picked up Jesse's bag and said, 'See you later, guys' to their friends and walked slowly out of the club with Jesse tucked snugly under his arm.

The air was warm outside the club but still strong enough to lift Jesse's hair as Ben guided her towards the beach. She realised she was a little tipsy but was thankful she wasn't drunk. She knew she'd want to remember everything in the morning.

They didn't speak as they approached the sand and Ben crouched down to remove Jesse's boots and socks before removing his own. He took her hand and led her towards the water's edge and they continued to stroll along the shore, leaving the busy promenade behind them. They had walked for over five minutes before Jesse realised she could see only via the moonlight and the only sound was the gentle swoosh of the waves moving their way up the sand. She was tingling with anticipation.

Ben led Jesse slightly away from the water's edge before he put his mouth to hers again. This kiss felt different to the one in the club. He hardly touched her lips while he probed for her tongue. Jesse could feel her heart pounding in her chest as Ben took his time undressing her. As she stepped out of her trousers she was aware of the breeze licking her naked skin. She forgot to feel self-conscious about her body. She was so highly tuned to Ben and his caresses that she'd not even registered the fact she was about to have sex on a public beach.

While Ben took his time kissing, stroking and tasting her body, Jesse gazed at the night sky, shiny black with dots of diamond light. The salty breeze played over her body and ruffled her hair. Was she dreaming? Ben's hazel eyes came back into view and he looked intently into her eyes as he ever-so-gently took her. She lit up inside. There were no acrobatics, no performance. Just a gentle rhythm and tantalising kisses. This was love, not sex, Jesse marvelled. They rocked together for what felt like hours until Ben finally let himself climax. They lay together murmuring and gently kissing for a while, Ben propped up on his strong arms so as not to put his entire bodyweight on Jesse. Jesse could feel semen slowly making its way from her body to the sand but had no care about it other than wondering what kind of state her black clothes would be in by the time they got back to the apartment.

'You are so beautiful.'

'Am I?'

'Yes, you are. I wanted you from the very minute I first saw you at the bar.'

'Ah, yes, I don't remember an awful lot about that night I'm afraid.'

'I do. Watching you dance really turned me on. I was gutted when you called it a night - I was hoping I might have got you alone.'

'Mmm. Well, you did tonight.'

'Yes, I did, and I hope to spend many more nights with you.'

'That can be arranged.'

'Good, I'm banking on it.'

Ben slowly stood up and offered his hand to Jesse. In an instant she became aware of her body and its flaws and how droopy everything was. She prayed it looked better in the moonlight. She must have hid her embarrassment well as Ben ran her down the beach and into the water, seemingly oblivious to her bouncing tummy. Once she was up to her waist in cold seawater, she felt better about herself. Her nipples stood to attention and all her major flaws were now under water.

She tipped her head back into the sea and soaked her hair, hoping it would make her look sexy and carefree in the moonlight. Ben gave her a wicked smile before diving under the black water. A few seconds later he caught her ankles and allowed his hands to skim up her thighs until he found her core. Coming out of the water, one hand inside her, the other holding her back, his kiss was urgent, and deep and impassioned. The taste of salt was intense, their faces were soaked, the breeze bringing goose bumps out on their skin and the sea rocking them both. Jesse wasn't sure she could cope as each of her senses was heightened. When he entered her, it was urgent and brutal and Jesse held on for dear life, unsure of how much she could take without crying out loud. The weightlessness of the water enabled her to cling to his strong shoulders and wrap her legs around his hips as he plunged into her over and over. The pull of the waves bobbed them around but somehow Ben managed to keep them upright until he emptied himself into her with a low groan. Still inside her, Ben carried Jesse a few steps nearer the shore before dropping onto his knees and allowing the water to cover their bare shoulders. He kissed her tenderly and she rested her head on his shoulder, and there they stayed until the sky started streak with colour.

Jesse was a little mortified trying to put her clothes on over a soaking-wet body. It took longer than she'd planned to pull her trousers up and over her thighs, which she was sure were now turning blue with the cold. She chaffed her skin, turning her bra around after clasping it at the front, and she realised her hair was looking decidedly straggly now it had had time to air dry in the sea breeze. It didn't help that Ben had somehow managed to get dressed within seconds and was patiently standing watching her get herself straight. She was thankful daylight was a good hour away as her cheeks were burning with embarrassment.

Once dressed, they clasped sandy hands together and made their way back down the beach to the main town. She was surprised to get back to the promenade and still hear music playing from bars and found people staggering drunk around the streets laughing and joking. The atmosphere broke into their serene world, but the advantage was there were taxis everywhere and the last thing either of them wanted at daybreak was to try to walk back to the apartments.

Within five minutes they were back at the Marias. After a gentle kiss goodnight and a, 'See you in a few hours,' from Ben, Jesse tiptoed across the marble floor and dropped onto her bed fully dressed. *What an amazing night* was the last thought she managed before falling into a deep and happy sleep.

CHAPTER 20

Laughter rippling through the open apartment windows roused Jesse out of her slumber. She had no idea what time it was but when she rolled onto her back, the smile fell from her face as she realised how sore she was. Gingerly stepping out of her sandy trousers and knickers, she took small steps to the bathroom and had a hot shower. As she soaped herself it stung like antiseptic on an open wound but the smile soon returned to her face over the memory of how she got so sore in the first place. Sand, salt water and sleep were obviously not a great combination for a fanny. She had no idea what time it was. All she knew was she was hungry and sore. Opting for a black halter-neck swimsuit and black floaty skirt, she put on her large sunglasses and headed to the pool hoping to find Dotty and Mary... and Ben.

After a brief chat with Niko, she found the girls in the taverna next door having lunch. It was just past noon.

'Morning.' Jesse sang with a broad grin on her face.

'Afternoon, more like.' Dotty grinned back at her.

'Dirty stop-out,' Mary offered, while beckoning the waiter so Jesse could order lunch.

Jesse took her time sitting down and getting comfortable before lighting her cigarette and, after taking a dramatic drag, declaring,

'My fanny ain't half bloody sore', to which all three girls started shrieking and laughing. Many questions were asked and Jesse filled them in with as much detail as she could remember, between mouthfuls of chips and tzatziki.

'I'm going to need to stay in the pool a lot today I think to heal. I'm really bloody sore.'

'And it's just from the sand, yes?' asked Mary with a slight look of concern on her face.

'Of course it is. We were having sex for hours on the beach and then in the sea. I'm surprised I still have a fanny, to be honest.' It was just as well that Jesse hadn't noticed Mary's eyebrows twitch up and down or she'd have realised that Mary was alluding to Ben having given her something to worry about.

'Have you seen Ben at all today?' Jesse asked. She'd been disappointed not to find him around the pool when she'd been looking for the girls.

'No, I haven't seen any of them today. Have you, Dotty?'

'No, none of them. Maybe they're already on the beach, or still asleep.'

Mary knew that at least one of them wasn't still asleep as Tom had slipped silently out of their room only three hours previously. She'd been amazed that Jesse had strolled straight past Mary's bed and hadn't realized there were two people laying in it.

Mary had felt a spark of envy when Jesse had left the club with Ben and had decided to up the ante with Tom. He was much taller than her, but then again, most people were, so she'd used it to her advantage and played the china doll card. Mary had two flirting techniques. One was friendly-friendly where she was touchy-feely and overtly friendly without actually batting her eyes, which normally left men really confused as to whether she was coming onto them or just being friendly. Her favourite flirting game was china doll though, where she worked on her height deficit to bring out the protective nature of men, not quite managing to get on stools, fluttering her eyes from the floor to their eyes like a lost rabbit - this was her specialty and it rarely failed.

It hadn't taken Tom long to hold Mary close on the dance floor where she somehow kept getting bashed around by other dancers. He helped her onto the high stool and kept his hand firmly behind her just in case she came to any harm. Had Jesse been there, she would have enjoyed watching Mary lure Tom in without him having any idea she was flirting with him.

By the time Dotty decided she'd had enough and wanted to head back, Mary and Tom were discreetly holding hands under the table.

Mary and Dotty shared a taxi back and the boys went in another. During the five-minute journey, Dotty had ensured that Mary had condoms in her bag, which Mary insisted she'd never need, and Dotty instructed her that she would be going to bed immediately so she'd be dead to the world within thirty minutes, should Mary decide to entertain Tom. Mary was adamant that Dotty had the wrong end of the stick and she most certainly would not be entertaining anybody, and certainly never in their apartment.

Forty-five minutes later and Mary was lying in bed with Tom.

Mary always enjoyed the flirt and the thrill of having a man kiss her but after that, fear always spread in and regret soon followed. Her mother's disapproval came to mind as soon as she moved past kissing a man. Mary so wanted to be loved and cherished but to date, she had had absolutely no luck on that score. The odd thrill of kissing a stranger was about as much as she'd come to expect in her life. She'd pretty much resigned herself to being a spinster.

As she lay in bed with Tom, she realised it wasn't what she'd wanted at all. In fact, she couldn't keep her mind off Niko, who had seen Tom take her hand just before they turned the corner from the bar. She was feeling foolish and embarrassed but didn't have the first clue how to get out of her current situation.

'What's wrong, Mary?' Tom asked. He could

obviously sense the change in Mary as she'd stopped responding to him and had stopped moving entirely.

Mary just looked into Tom's eyes and had no words to express what she wanted. She bit her bottom lip and stared at Tom with her big brown eyes. For a moment Tom thought she was going to cry.

'What have I done? What's the matter? Tell me!' Tom rolled out of bed and stood up, running his hands through his hair, not sure what to do. He'd never been in this situation before. Had he read the signals wrong? He didn't think so, but he had had a few drinks.

'I'm really sorry, Tom, I don't know what's the matter with me but this doesn't feel right. I'm really sorry.' With that, Mary did start to cry, not for the situation she was in with Tom but for the realisation that she was never going to get what she wanted. She'd found herself in this situation time after time, normally with married men, when all she wanted was a man of her own. But time was not on her side to waste like this.

Tom was disturbed by Mary's change of demeanour and he sank beside her on the bed and held her hand while she cried silently. He could see the digital clock shining bright on the wall and a flutter of shame came over him as he realised he didn't have as much time as he'd hoped and needed to leave. Tom murmured platitudes to Mary in a quiet whisper, hoping he was making her feel better, even though he really had no idea what had gone wrong and why he wasn't enjoying sex right now instead of dealing with a weeping mess. He gave Mary ten more minutes until he started to yawn and said he really needed sleep and had to go. Mary didn't protest. She watched him gather his shirt and shoes and managed a slight smile as he opened the apartment door to leave. The light from the hallway reflected her face and even the soft glow did nothing to disguise the mascara that had made its way down to her chin. Tom raised his hand in goodbye and gently shut the apartment door. At the same time they both let out sighs of relief, for very different reasons.

***

Jesse noticed Mary wasn't listening to her and touched toes with her under the table to catch her attention.

'Everything okay, Mary?'

'Yes, sorry, fine!' Mary blushed.

'Good, so do you know what time we have to be ready for the excursion today? I want to make sure I have plenty of time to get dressed and put my full face on. I feel like dressing up. I'm thinking black trousers and my black silk shirt with hair up. No idea what shoes to wear, though. What about you, Dotty?'

'I was thinking of my dress with the big sunflowers on it with my yellow flip-flops. Bagsy first in the shower today, though. It's my turn for some hot water. My hair is looking really fluffy, too, so I'm thinking of putting a treatment on it and sitting on the veranda for half an hour or so to see if it makes it any easier. Maybe you could jump in while I'm waiting on my treatment to work.'

'Good idea. Mary, fancy painting each other's nails before we go out? Mine are a bit faded after walking in the sand.' Everyone looked at Jesse's scratched nail colour and came to the same conclusion - that it was unlikely to be the walking on the sand that had caused the problem, but perhaps the skinny-dipping with Ben that was more to blame.

Jesse indicated to the waiter for the bill. 'Once we've finished here, shall we go to the beach? It's a bit hot today and the breeze makes it more bearable.'

'I thought you needed to soak your privates,' Mary piped up.

'I do! But maybe the sea salt will do it good.' Jesse winked at Dotty before paying the bill and leaving a generous tip.

***

Jesse spent the afternoon drifting in and out of sleep under a coconut-wood umbrella. Although her face was shaded, she chose to keep a sunhat lying over her face to darken her vision enough that she could visualise the previous evening with Ben. She replayed the sex scene on the beach over and over in her head, embellishing slightly and adding to the scene long beautiful curled hair, slimmer thighs, flawless make-up, and totally omitting the embarrassment of getting dressed under Ben's watchful gaze. She had enjoyed lying all day on the sun bed, a warm breeze languidly lifting the hem of her sarong, interrupted only by the occasional trip to the beach toilets and an hourly cigarette. Lunch had been light as they were expecting a feast at the Greek night that evening. They'd all grazed throughout the afternoon on slices of pizza, chocolate doughnuts and chips washed down with Piña Coladas from the beach shack bar.

Jesse had played out many scenes in her head of how the next meeting with Ben was going to pan out. She was hoping that they'd bump into each other at the Greek night, although as she hadn't mentioned it to him, she had no idea if the boys were going or not. They weren't expecting to arrive back at the apartments until gone midnight, but in Greece that was still early. If they didn't see the boys on the trip, she was sure they'd be at the hotel pool bar drinking when they arrived back. As this was the more likely scenario, most of her imaginings had been of her stepping off the coach as the wind caught the chiffon of her long flowing black dress, the moon lighting her delicate cheekbones, scarlet lips shimmering. Ben would be sitting at the candlelit bar watching for her, standing to greet her with a look of adoration on his face as she headed towards him, a smile playing across her lips. He would take her by the hand, tell her how gorgeous she looked and devour her there and then. Of course in the imaginings no-one was around the pool bar, which was secluded in her dream, and they made slow soft-focus love until dawn, when he told her he loved her. She realised she'd better bring herself out of her dreamland once the fantasy had moved past their wedding and onto children, as she really had no intention of ever having any, so the dream became annoying.

It was five o'clock by the time all three girls had gathered their belongings from the beach and trudged up the sloping path to the hotel. The hotel pool was empty and no-one was at the bar. The girls hoped not everyone was going to the Greek night; if everyone was getting ready, they'd all be having cold showers. To Jesse's relief, by the time her friends had taken their turn in the shower there was still plenty of hot water for her. She took the time to ensure there was no sand left on her body before rinsing off her hair treatment. This was desperately needed as the sun was ruining her blonde hair.

Mary was playing *Mama Mia* through her iPod speakerphone while the girls sat around in their underwear applying their various creams and make-up, humming to the dance tracks and getting in the mood for a good boogie. Dotty was dunking her Cadbury Whole Nut into her mug of Nescafé, while Mary and Jesse shared a bottle of red wine. All the girls had made an extra effort tonight and each one practically shone from head to foot. Certainly they had all applied bronzing dust to most parts of their lightly-tanned skin and wore more make-up than usual.

'I'm really looking forward to tonight!' Dotty yelled to her friends in the bedroom while applying her mascara in the small bathroom, 'I think it's going to be a real laugh!'

Mary and Jesse looked at each other and rolled their eyes. 'Mmm, hmmm,' they chimed.

An excursion was not normally on their itinerary on holiday as Jesse suffered terrible travel sickness and hated swallowing pills before an evening. She had to take travel pills and Imodium as, even though she didn't get physically sick on the pills, the nerves always set her stomach off. How stressed she got herself depended on whether the pills were strong enough to keep her nervous system in check.

Two years previously they'd decided on Tunisia as a quick winter break and Dotty had booked a two-night stay in the Sahara desert as a surprise birthday present for Jesse. Dotty thought it sounded amazing, travelling around the Sahara in a four-by-four, sleeping in tents, riding on camels, eating a banquet under the stars… but she hadn't taken on board the five-hour coach travel to the desert and then the various trips to and from the desert to the tents and back again. Jesse tried to look pleased when Dotty proudly announced her surprise, even though they all knew there was nothing Jesse hated more than a surprise, except for travelling.

The one saving grace of this particular holiday was that a fourth friend had joined the girls, Anne-

Marie, who loved the idea of the Sahara trip. She was pretty much up for anything, even daring to go to the markets and haggle with the local stallholders, which everyone knew was just asking for trouble, but not Anne-Marie. She was six foot and large and extremely hard-faced so she was fearless about most things, as far as the girls could tell.

The morning of the trip arrived and Jesse had swallowed all the pills, washed down with a can of Coke, and felt ready for the weekend. It turned out that there would be several pick-ups along the way from different hotels before they headed out to the motorway, which was a good job as each time the coach stopped, Jesse ran to the hotel toilets and emptied her bowels at every single stop. After the fifth hotel, Jesse realised she was never going to make the journey if she couldn't stop going to the toilet for more than fifteen minutes at a time. The Imodium had definitely not worked. Just before they headed out, much to the tour operator's annoyance, Jesse retrieved her bags from the coach and said her goodbyes to Dotty and Anne-Marie, assuring them she'd be fine and to take lots of pictures to show her. Although Jesse didn't ask for it, Mary also gave up the trip to keep Jesse company on her birthday.

The two girls decided to treat themselves to a full day at the hotel spa getting pampered and preened as recompense for missing the birthday weekend in the desert. Although Dotty and Anne-Marie came back with exciting tales of the weekend, including attempting to get on a camel and not actually managing it as the camel took one look at Dotty and pretended to die, Jesse was delighted not to have been a part of it. As much as eating out under the stars sounded interesting, being pummelled by an aggressive Greek masseuse and then enjoying a luxurious delicate facial was far more Jesse's idea of fun.

Tonight's Greek night excursion was within the realms of cope-ability for Jesse. The holiday rep had assured her that the journey would only take thirty minutes and there was a toilet on the coach if she needed to use one. Jesse knew just having a toilet available would ensure she didn't need to use it.

Still in the small bathroom, Dotty hollered,

'I spoke to the rep and she showed me some photos of the night and it looks really good! Lots of Greek dancing and plate smashing, and the way you ask for another drink is by putting your empty bottle or glass on your head!'

'And the hits just keep on coming,' Jesse muttered.

'So long as you don't have to sit with a bottle on your head for twenty minutes before they bring you a new one!' Mary added, nudging Jesse away from the bedroom mirror so she could apply her eyeliner.

Jesse retreated from the cloud of perfume and deodorant to the balcony, where she lit a cigarette and sipped from her mug of wine. She sighed heavily and wished she could muster up the energy to believe she might enjoy the night. From the balcony she could see the pool bar and Niko's wife behind it polishing shot glasses. There was no-one else to be seen.

'It's very quiet tonight!' Jesse called through the balcony doors.

'Maybe it's changeover day,' Mary suggested.

'Maybe.' Jesse took a long pull on her cigarette and contemplated how she was feeling. Normally changeover day would mean the excitement of new blood arriving for the girls to party with, but Jesse had no interest in anyone other than Ben. She ached for him tonight. In fact, she'd ached for him her entire life, the possibility of him, at any rate. She knew she had to watch herself as her emotions were heightened very quickly and she was known to fall in love in a heartbeat, but this felt different. This felt right. He was gorgeous-looking, brave, chivalrous and an amazing lover. The way he kissed her told a thousand secrets to her heart about how he felt about her. She gave a wistful sigh as she realised that changeover day was of no consequence to her at all.

***

The journey to the Greek night went as expected. Dreadfully. There were several pick-ups from different hotels before the driver was able to put his foot down fully on the accelerator to ensure he had breakneck speed around the hairpin bends balanced on the tops of the mountains. Jesse's eyes had remained closed for the final thirty minutes of the drive to avoid screaming out loud, but her nerves were shot to pieces and she was in a foul mood by the time they arrived.

'Thirty minutes' drive my arse,' Jesse blared at the rep by the door of the coach. Gesturing towards the driver, she added 'he's a fucking lunatic. It's a bloody miracle we survived the trip.' She turned on her heel and stormed off to form part of the queue before the rep could give her any kind of explanation or platitudes, either of which would have fallen on deaf ears.

Jesse outwardly groaned when she saw the venue properly. Walking through the dusty courtyard she could see what looked like plastic stadium seating built around a large square, where a grubby fountain splurted bubbling water from a concrete Greek goddess. There were strings of coloured lights everywhere which at night might well make the place look a little magical, but at six o'clock it just looked pitiful in Jesse's eyes. She could see trestle tables with white paper cloths and plastic cutlery. She was not amused.

'So Dotty, exactly how much did this evening cost us?'

'I can't remember exactly.'

'You sure about that?'

'I think it was around £75,' Dotty admitted sheepishly, and they all knew if Dotty admitted to £75 then it was probably quite a bit more than that.

'Bloody hell, what a rip-off.'

'You've only just got here. How can you say that?' Dotty protested.

'Really? Really, Dotty? Look at the place! If we don't end up with dicky tummies tomorrow I'll eat my hat. I can't see a bar, which makes me think it's going to be bloody jugs of wine and cheap bottles of beer, and if we have to hold them on our head to get a refill, what are the bets we get no more than two drinks all bloody night?'

'You'll be fine once you've got a drink and a seat,' Mary chipped in.

Jesse just raised an eyebrow and glared into the distance, not daring to speak in case she exploded.

Three hours later Jesse was proven to be right. It had taken over an hour for everyone to arrive and get to their seats only to watch one dance of eight people in traditional dress before being told to come for food, of which there was not enough. There were a few hundred people taking turns queuing for dips, chips, curry and moussaka. It wasn't worth trying to get past everyone already eating on the stadium seating so the girls huddled together, each trying to eat standing up with a plastic spoon. Dotty had remained fairly upbeat until that point.

She'd assumed Greek banquet meant exactly that, and was looking forward to more than filling her stomach with a whole host of imagined Greek delicacies. What she had on her plate was the equivalent of a starter, and a lukewarm one at that. She was not amused. It was obvious the food wasn't going to stretch very far so she was too embarrassed to go back for seconds - not that the taste would send you back. The food was flavourless and greasy. But Dotty was hungry and she needed more food - now. Although Jesse was hungry too, she gave Dotty her plate of food and just ate a bit of pitta bread dunked in tzatziki, while Mary offered up her pitta bread. She wanted to help Dotty out as she knew Dotty would find it hard to enjoy the night if she was hungry, but she knew if she didn't eat something herself, she'd end up drunk and that would spoil the plans she had for later that evening, which involved Niko. This concept didn't even flutter across Jesse's mind. She simply saw her friend suffering and did what was needed to keep her happy.

***

Mary lay her head against the glass of the coach window and closed her eyes, trying to block out the noise of the loud off-key singing. It seemed the entire coach was behind Jesse's rendition of Beyonce's *Single Ladies* song, even though they were on the fourth repeat of it. In Jesse's drunken state it appeared she had no other repertoire to bring to mind and as there was no-one else on the coach coming forward with requests it was repeated over and over. Jesse was in the front seat waving her arms around to the audience while singing loudly into the rep's microphone. To her credit, the rep had tried to get the microphone away but realised quickly that the glint in Jesse's eye turned dangerously fierce for a second when she was told no, so she decided to cut her losses and let her have it. The rep was a good judge of character, Mary mused.

All in all the night wasn't as disastrous as it could have been. After all, there could have been a mud slide or tsunami or other natural disaster, but instead Jesse was drunk, and happily so at the moment. Given the way the evening had started, Mary thought it was a miracle that Jesse's mood had improved at all, especially since the entertainment got worse as the evening wore on.

Jesse was right in that they were indeed served cheap jugs of wine and bottles of beer, and Dotty was also right that they had to put their empties on their head to get a refill - what they couldn't have imagined though was Jesse fluttering her eye-lids to the young waiter, who must have just turned seventeen, and persuading him to leave her the entire jug of wine. Mary could only imagine that Jesse had decided that drinking was the only way she was going to get through the terrible evening, as she went for it on an empty stomach, something Mary was always careful to never do.

Jesse was the first to make her way down to the traditional dancers when they asked for volunteers and she gave a stellar performance with the Greek dancing, right up until the moment she fell on her arse. Mary was sitting low in her seat, hands over her eyes mortified, Dotty was pointing and laughing, shouting 'Someone help the poor girl up,' and Jesse had tears falling down her face from laughing so much. It took two male dancers to heave her back up to her feet, where she took all of two seconds to compose herself before joining in with them again.

When it was time to head back to the coach Jesse was well and truly hammered and looked a wreck where she had sweated so much with her frantic dancing. But she was laughing and happy, and as far as Mary was concerned, that was great news. All they had to do was survive the coach journey to the hotel pool bar and the evening Mary had planned in her head would begin.

She'd been grateful for the quiet afternoon of sunbathing so she could get her head around what had happened with Tom and what she was going to do about Niko. Why oh why had she even taken Tom to their apartment? Was it jealousy as Jesse had found Ben? Was it to ease her loneliness, knowing Tom was keen on her? She really hadn't wanted to have sex with him, she rarely had one night stands, but she knew inviting him in would lead to that, and yet still she had. Very quickly she'd realised it wasn't Tom she wanted at all, it was Niko. And of course, he was married. Normally this would be a bonus for Mary as she didn't like to get involved and she knew from experience that married men very rarely actually wanted to leave their wives, so it suited her emotionally as no-one ever got really hurt when it was over. But this was different. Niko's wife was very much in the picture. It was her home turf, not Mary's, so Mary had no idea how to play the situation.

She wanted Niko badly, not for sex, but for affection and he made her feel good. His kisses were strong and passionate and made her feel like a bud coming into flower. She knew she would have to let him go in two days, but the *idea* of him she would be able to take with her and her dreams would keep her company for many nights after the plane hit the tarmac at Gatwick. She needed to be in his arms again. She yearned for his lips on her neck. She wasn't sure how she was going to rein herself in if his wife was at the bar when they returned tonight, but she'd worry about that when she was faced with it.

They were the last drop on the coach and as they pulled up Mary could see an older couple sitting at the pool bar, no boys to be seen and no Niko. Dotty leaned over her to get a view of the bar.

'Bummer, looks dead in there. Mind you, it's not midnight yet so hardly surprising. Oi, Jesse! Fancy going to Antonio's bar?' and to Mary's dismay Jesse shouted back,

'Fuckin' A!' and literally fell into the rep on the way down the two steps to the pavement.

Jesse and Dotty took a few minutes to reach the bar, as they were trying to perfect the dance to *Single Ladies*, which they both did perfectly but looked hysterical performing due to their size.

Antonio's bar was lit with candles and smelt fabulous. The girls went straight to their usual chairs which overlooked their hotel bar. Although there were plenty of chairs available, Jesse chose not to sit. Once she'd glanced at the bar and not seen Ben, she went straight to the dance floor and danced, on her own, evidently enjoying the music, not caring that she was the first on the floor.

Mary felt small in the big wicker chair but enjoyed the soft breeze floating in, lifting her fringe and catching the back of her neck. She ordered a virgin Piña Colada, a Diet Coke for Jesse and Dotty a Martini. After fifteen minutes Dotty had visibly relaxed, obviously happy that Stavros wasn't in the bar. She had scanned the place for anyone of interest, and realising there was no one worth bothering with, decided she had nothing to lose by joining Jesse on the dance floor.

To Mary's mortification *Pour Some Sugar On Me* by Def Leppard came over the speakers and Jesse and Dotty threw any inhibitions they may have carried up until that point right out of the window. Jesse was head banging. Mary hadn't seen anything like it since she was a teenager but Jesse had remembered all the moves, the stance, and had the best hair to whizz in circles around the dance-floor; droplets of sweat flying off the ends on each full-circle. Dotty performed two full head rotations before stopping and staggering backwards. Once she could see again she went back to Jesse and started thrashing her hips wildly instead while moving her tongue visibly around her mouth. Mary was horrified to be associated with either of them.

Sipping her drink and trying to ignore her friends' antics, Mary gazed over her glass to the hotel bar. She could see Niko's wife sitting on a stool behind the bar, chatting to the older couple they had spotted earlier. Even from this distance Mary could see she was beautiful. She envied her long blonde hair and shapely arms. Mary tried to think mean things and paint her in a bad light but she couldn't manage it. She knew she was beautiful and she was Niko's wife and she was totally innocent. It was her and Niko who were not. Mary really wanted to feel bad that she couldn't stop herself thinking about Niko but no matter how much she watched the slender beauty from afar, drumming it into her head that she was Niko's wife, she couldn't quite bring herself to let go of the idea of him.

Mary's back straightened when she saw a small white car pull up beside the bar. She couldn't see the driver who got out but she was fairly certain it was Niko. A few minutes later she was downing her drink as she realised that not only had Niko arrived but his wife had finished her shift and driven off in the white car. Finally! Her night could begin.

***

Mary's plans did not involve heavy music and dancing with Jesse and Dotty so she simply tapped Jesse on the shoulder and indicated she was going to the hotel and before Jesse could protest she smiled and headed for the stairs. Crossing the road between the two bars Mary was trying to figure out what she would say. She hadn't been with Niko for two days now and she wasn't sure if that was enough for him to lose interest, or whether instead it would pique his interest. She was about to find out. She shrugged any guilt about the situation off in Antonio's bar and strode into the Maria bar as if she had not a care in the world.

'Hi, Niko.'

'Kalispera Mary. 'Tis good to see you.'

'You too.' Mary pulled a stool to the furthest edge of the bar where she couldn't be seen from Antonio's, sat on it and leaned over the bar, offering her cheek to Niko.

Smiling, Niko gently kissed her cheek and stroked her hand briefly before reaching for a long glass.

'Black Russian?' Niko asked while confidently adding ice to the glass, not really waiting for Mary's gentle nod. She'd watched her alcohol carefully all night so she knew she could have one or two drinks and not get too drunk. Remembering tonight was top of her list if it went to plan; looking back at it through the haze of a hangover was not on her To Do list.

'Why have you not been to see me, Mary? I was expecting you.' Niko kept his hand on the glass long enough for their fingers to brush as Mary took it from him, very much aware that the older couple were within their view.

'I really did want to see you Niko, but after what happened with Stavros and Dotty I just felt so terrible. And then seeing your wife and how upset she was over Stavros made me realise how awful it'd be if she found out about us. I guess I just felt too guilty.' Mary sipped her drink, looking both apologetic and sultry over the rim of the glass.

'Ah darling, Stavros and me are not the same. He is not careful who he sees. I am very careful with you. I want to see you.' Their faces were very close, she could feel his breath on her lips and actually moved forward an inch before Niko pulled sharply away and picked up a glass to polish. He gave her a cheeky grin with a gentle shake of his head so Mary sat back and relaxed on her stool, happy to watch him. She had a fascination with veins, and Niko had some beauties on his forearms standing proud under his tanned skin. His white shirt billowed gently and Mary envisioned gently undoing every single button, very slowly, until reaching his leather belt. She could feel her cheeks burning so she hoped Niko would take charge of the rest so she didn't have to think past removing his shirt while she was watching him.

Mary discreetly watched Niko leaning over the bar casually talking to the other couple and tried to tune out the heavy rock music that was floating across from Antonio's bar. The last thing Mary wanted was Jesse and Dotty showing up drunk trying to drag her around the pool for a dance. Mary felt cool and fresh and wanted to be seen as delicate in Niko's eyes. She had made a real effort tonight and knew she still looked good. She'd used every toilet break to ensure her nose was powdered and lipstick in place, hair smooth and eyes smudge-free. She did have a feeling she'd forgotten something though but couldn't put her finger on it. She checked her purse again and in the small zip sat two condoms. She was almost certain she wouldn't get to use them as she didn't plan on having actual sex with Niko, but she was never going to be without just in case she changed her mind. Knowing Jesse for so long had drummed into Mary that being almost certain you weren't going to have sex wasn't as good as being absolutely certain so, if in doubt, you picked up a condom.

With a jerk Mary realised what had been bothering her. What it was that had been hiding just outside of her memory. She grabbed her bag, tucked in the stool and casually strode to the hotel toilets to remove her panty liner from her lacy knickers. Disaster averted.

***

Dotty was watching the scene play out in the hotel bar, sipping cold water out of a bottle with a straw. She'd thrown up in the toilets and was feeling much better now she'd had a packet of crisps and a cold drink. Everything had stopped spinning and although she couldn't trust herself to get out of the chair without falling over, she felt she was slightly sobering up. She heard Jesse returning from the toilets before she turned to watch her. She'd grabbed some poor sod off his stool for a ten second dance before twirling and leaving him standing bemused as she sauntered back in Dotty's direction, laughing loudly.

Jesse plonked herself down heavily and crashed her two legs onto the small wicker table. Scooping up a can of Diet Coke she took a big lug and burped quietly before smiling at Dotty. Nodding towards the hotel bar across the road, she asked,

'Any gossip yet?'

'Not yet. I can just about see them. They're just sending each other gushy looks but nothing else. Mary's just gone into the hotel by the looks of it.'

'Mmm. Wonder what she's playing at. She's playing with fire.'

'Yeah. It's a bloody shame. Why does she only like the married ones?'

'Tell you what, I'm pissed and can't be arsed to figure that one out! Uh oh, don't look now but here come Stavros!'

Jesse took her feet off the table and was ready

to pounce when she saw that coming up behind Stavros on the stairs was his wife. Both girls silently studied the couple as they approached the bar and ordered drinks. Stavros evidently hadn't seen either of them and was playing happy families, being attentive to his attractive wife. He pulled a stool out from the bar for her and stood next to her, a hand on the naked skin of her spine. A barman Jesse had yet to know shook his hand and got them some drinks, what looked like a brandy for him and a wine for his wife. He seemed relaxed as he scanned the bar area until he spotted the girls, drink poised an inch from his mouth for a moment before his gaze slid from Dotty's and returned to his wife's.

Uh oh, was all Jesse could think. Swivelling in her chair to give Dotty a pep talk, she was surprised to see Dotty wasn't paying any attention to the couple and was in fact looking back at the hotel bar, spying on Mary returning to her place at the bar.

Jesse whispered, 'Did you see Stavros arrive?'

'Mmm.'

'Are you okay?'

'Yeah, don't worry about me. So over him. I can't stand the prick.'

Jesse had no idea how to respond so just nodded her head and joined Dotty in watching Mary and Niko play cat and mouse together across the street.

'It's ever so quiet at the bar tonight, don't you think? Wonder where everyone is?' Jesse said loudly, still very pissed.

'Do you know what, I'm really tired now and there's chocolate back at the room. I'm heading back. Coming?'

'Not to the apartment but I'll walk across with you and ask Niko if he's seen the boys.'

'Help me up then!'

'Bloody hell, okay. Grab hold.' Jesse took Dotty's hand and somehow managed to help her up without crashing over the table herself.

For some reason known only to Jesse, she left the bar loudly singing the theme tune to the Wizard of Oz and tried to skip across the road, narrowly avoiding ending up in a hedge when the inevitable curb trip happened.

***

'Mary! Niko!' Jesse shouted. 'Lovely to see you!' Waving her arms above her head in welcome, she paid no notice to Mary's look of anguish and threw an arm around her friend's shoulders. Dotty couldn't squeeze into the space next to Mary so she leant on her back, causing Mary to give a little yelp of pain when her ribcage met the wooden bar top with force.

'Oops, sorry darling. Didn't mean to crush you. I only came over to say goodnight as I'm whacked now. Heading to bed. You okay here?'

Wincing from the fresh smell of vomit on Dotty's breath, Mary nodded.

'I'm fine Dotty, you go ahead. But don't walk around the pool yeah, go the other way.'

'Good idea, wouldn't want me falling in, would we? Night Jesse. Night Niko. See you in the morning.'

Dotty walked slowly following the path to their apartments avoiding the pool area entirely. Every few steps she paused, swayed, and carried on. She only tripped once and never actually fell, which in itself proved God was looking down on her that night.

'Right, Niko! I have no idea what I want, so surprise me!' Jesse pulled up a seat close enough to Mary that their thighs touched, and waited on her drink. She whispered to Mary,

'Any sign of Ben at all?'

'No. I wonder if they went into Rethmynon.'

'Bit surprised if so, he said he'd see me tonight here. What about you and Tom? Did Tom say where he'd meet you?'

'Ssshh Jesse, I don't want Niko to know I was with Tom.'

'Sorry!' Jesse lowered her voice and moved her lips even closer to Mary's ear. 'But did you arrange to meet him?'

'No, I didn't see him after we all got back to the apartment.'

'Mmmm.'

'The Maria Special,' announced Niko delivering her drink with a flourish. Bumping the ice cubes around her cocktail with a striped straw Jesse tried to sound nonchalant when she asked,

'Don't suppose you've seen Ben and the boys tonight have you, Niko? Thought we'd have seen them around by now.'

Niko laughed loudly and slapped his palm on the bar. 'Jesse, you sweet thing! You must be really drunk to not remember the boys went back just this morning!' He found this so funny that he didn't see the horrified look on either of the girls' faces.

'Niko, are you sure?' Mary asked quietly.

'Of course I'm sure! I waved them off this morning, very early flight, I didn't think Tom was going to make the coach in time, you should have seen him running with his case!'

'I assumed they arrived when we did and weren't heading home for a few days,' said Mary.

'They did arrive on same day but it was only a few days for their stag party.'

Jesse really didn't want to hear the answer but heard herself ask,

'Whose stag party, Niko?'

'Ben's! He marrying lovely girl. They've been together many years. He's very much in love I think.' Niko beamed at them, obviously thinking this was tremendous news but the smile rapidly slipped when he saw Jesse's face crumple.

***

Mary turned the key in the latch to ensure she closed the apartment door behind her quietly, fearful of waking either Jesse or Dotty. It had taken what felt like hours for Jesse to cry herself to sleep and as much as Mary felt for her she was mindful of the time and wanted to get back to the bar to see Niko. She was living in the moment, sneaking silently across the marble hotel corridor in bare feet, holding her shoes against her chest.

Relieved to find Niko still behind the bar as she turned the corner, Mary slipped quietly into her shoes and slowly made her way to the bar. Niko was alone. The bar completely empty. Niko caught her eye and his expression clicked straight to smouldering. Mary felt her insides jump. She enjoyed the walk around the pool, taking her time, locking her eyes on Niko's face, watching his move over her as she made her way towards him.

Her stomach leapt with excitement as the lights illuminating the bar snapped off and she could see just a shadow that was Niko.

Although darkness covered him, Niko knew shadows could be seen if you were close enough so when Mary came to him he didn't move in to kiss her, but slowly slid his hand up her dress, gathering the silky material as he went. Mary's breath hitched in her throat and she gave an involuntary gasp as his warm hands moved first around the top and then dipped inside her panties. She thought for a moment about whether she should protest but his fingers found her and all thoughts of protest evaporated, only sensations remained. And they engulfed her.

Niko took her wrist and gently guided her hand towards him, she jolted slightly when she found his hard flesh, his jeans and boxers already at his ankles. A low groan escaped his throat as Mary gingerly moved her hands around him and found a slow rhythm. Within moments Niko grabbed Mary by the waist and lowered her to the ground behind the bar where they couldn't be seen.

As his mouth ravaged hers he slid inside her for a fraction of a second before Mary hissed,

'Get out, get out, what are you doing?!'

Still slowly rocking inside her Niko whispered, 'What do you mean what am I doing? We are making love, come on baby, relax.'

With a shove and a buck of her hips she dislodged him. Crying now with rage she raised her voice slightly above a whisper.

'How dare you! You didn't use a condom! What if I got pregnant? I didn't want to have sex with you!'

'What do you mean you didn't want to have sex with me? Of course you did. You've wanted me all week! What are you saying? You are here just to tease me?'

'No! Of course not. I wanted to be with you, but not like this, not full sex. I don't just sleep around and I certainly don't have unprotected sex... behind a bloody bar for Heaven's sake.'

The sense of shame that was creeping over her skin was familiar and she hated it. Scraping her knees on the floor she scrambled to find her underwear and shoes among the shadows of empty bottles and beer kegs.

'Darling, do not do this. Come on. Why don't we go down to my apartment and have a drink and talk about this?'

'No way! I can't believe it Niko, I'm going to have to get tested for everything now. I can't believe you'd just do that!' Mary was close to wailing now and Niko was getting worried they'd draw attention from Antonio's bar across the road and he really didn't want to have to bribe Antonio to keep quiet again; last time he was caught it cost him a season of free drinks.

Trying to pacify her Niko attempted to help her straighten her clothes and put her shoes on.

'Come on darling. I'm sorry. It will all be okay, I promise.' As he leaned forward to kiss her, Mary inadvertently head butted his nose as she swooped down to grab her bag.

'Ow, crap, that really hurt!' Rubbing her head in the dark she allowed a slight turn upwards of her mouth as she watched Niko jumping around holding his nose, trying not to make the noise of his yell slip out from under the hand he held over his mouth.

Hot tears still sliding down her cheeks, Mary raced from behind the bar, head down in case any late night revellers were around to witness her life falling to pieces. She paused long enough to remove her shoes so as not to make any unwelcome noise in the corridor as she scurried to their apartment. She wasn't sure how long she stood with her head resting against the cool wood door of their room, hand on the handle waiting for the tears to subside, before she simply turned and slid to the floor and allowed herself to sob with remorse.

CHAPTER 21

Opening her eyes, Jesse groaned as she felt her head thump and stomach cramp. Rolling onto her side to get the pressure off her stomach she took a few seconds before remembering the night before. A cold blanket of dread draped itself over her as she lay staring at the whitewashed wall of the apartment. Jesse wished she was in her own home, in her own bed, looking back on this morning rather than experiencing the sense of loss that was smothering her insides. She didn't want to cry, she really didn't, but she felt so bereft she couldn't help the tears silently making their mark on her pillow. She had so many complex feelings she found it difficult to focus on just one. Foolishness was the most prominent. What a fool she had been. Why oh why had she yet again slept with someone almost instantly upon meeting them? Not only that, but why did she then take that one moment and run with it to create a future in her head that wasn't ever likely to exist? She was dealing with the loss of a future she had carved out for her and Ben that she hadn't actually lived, but it felt like it had almost happened.

The promise of Ben and the future she'd

created was so strong she had believed it completely. She hadn't looked at her actions over the past few days and thought for a second that she was being foolish, although she had wondered what Ben might feel for her once he found out about Steve, but she thought he'd understand when she explained exactly how it had happened and her frame of mind at the time. *You didn't use a condom* fluttered across her mind but she squashed that chain of thought immediately - she had enough to cope with without worrying about something that would be very unlikely to have happened. She was struggling enough to cope with the basic facts of her current situation.

Slowly she eased herself into a sitting position, placing her feet on the cold marble floor, and waited for the thumping in her head to ease enough to let her focus. Tears were still drifting slowly down her face when she reached for her drawer which housed her various tablets. Pulling out Nurofen and paracetamol, a blue-packaged condom dropped onto the floor and with it came a hitch in her breathing and a sob broke the quiet. Dotty murmured in the other room and then her snoring recommenced. Jesse looked over her shoulder to check if she'd woke Mary and was relieved to see she wasn't in her bed. She was alone in her misery, just the way she wanted it. As soon as the girls knew what had happened she'd receive pity and she had no intention of embarrassing herself by showing her true feelings to them, so she allowed the rush of tears to tumble over now with more speed.

She swallowed four of the painkillers and drank half a litre of warm water which she'd kept at the side of her bed, with a prayer that they would kick in quickly. She rested her elbows on her thighs and covered her wet face with her hands. What a bloody fool she'd been. She could almost taste her misery, thick and black like the cloak of regret hanging on her shoulders. She felt heartbroken, which she knew was ridiculous but regardless of what her mind told her not to feel, her chest hurt and her heart was squeezed. She felt loss. A part of her had died, she could feel its loss, a section in the middle of her stomach didn't exist any more, just a space filled with nothing.

She knew she could never explain this to her friends, they wouldn't understand, *she* didn't understand, but she felt like she was grieving. Shame came next. Hot, boiling shame. She was mortified that someone had hoodwinked her the way Ben had and she'd had no inkling at all of the betrayal to come. How on earth could he behave the way he had knowing he was about to get married? What a monster! The poor woman waiting for him at home doubtless trusted Ben implicitly and had no concerns about his fidelity whatsoever. Would he stray once he was married? Yes, of course he would. He was such a good liar that he would get away with it forever most likely, and probably had never been faithful to his fiancé. Of course Jesse knew this was just conjecture, but Ben was now the enemy, and rage was far easier to handle than shame. If he'd been practising for years how to lure women to his bed then she could give herself a bit more of a break about falling for it, rather than for being such a fool to not realise a man's one last night of freedom before marriage.

She had to physically shake her head when the image of her lying naked on the beach came to her mind, the horror of what she'd gotten involved in on this holiday was starting to sink in and she wasn't prepared for it at all.

Jesse had never considered herself promiscuous; in fact she felt practically nun-like as she'd not had sex for well over two years, and yet given the opportunity she'd happily given herself to two men in as many days.

Feeling slightly sick, she quietly opened the sliding door to the balcony and stepped out into the mild morning breeze. Jesse's brows knitted together in concern when she saw Mary sitting alone on a sunbed, head in hands. It was early, very early, the sun had only just risen and the pool area was barren. Jesse dressed quickly in a long sundress that had been lying on the floor and padded barefoot out of the apartment and headed towards the pool, leaving Dotty's loud snoring behind.

Jesse could tell by Mary's posture that something was wrong and she instinctively lit two cigarettes before reaching her friend. 'What's the matter?' Jesse asked, handing out one of the menthols.

Jesse sat on the edge of a facing sunbed watching Mary's tears drop from her chin to her knees. After a few moments Jesse touched her friend's hand and sat alongside her, remaining silent. The two women sat together in silence, smoking, waiting for Mary's tears to subside.

'Is it Niko?' Jesse asked breaking the quiet.

'Mmm,' was all Mary managed.

'Can you tell me what happened?'

Taking a long pull on her cigarette Mary answered. 'Yet again I've made a complete fool of myself, but this time I've really stuffed up.'

'In what way?'

'I had sex with Niko last night.'

'Really? That's a surprise.'

'I know. Believe me it wasn't planned. He was inside me before I knew what was happening. Literally, one second he was kissing me and the next he was inside me... and without a condom.'

'Shit! Did he cum?'

'No, didn't have time. I practically threw him off me, but that's not the point. I can still get pregnant. And, more importantly, I could catch something off him regardless. He could've given me a disease or infection. I feel sick to my stomach.' Jesse watched as the tears began to drip in rhythm onto Mary's knees again.

'Okay. Let's think about this calmly for a moment. What are the chances of him giving you anything? No disrespect or anything Mary, but he's a married man with a kid, I imagine he's unlikely to often sleep around and risk giving something to his wife, is he? He probably thought the chances of you sleeping around were remote.'

'What makes you say that?' Mary took her sunglasses off and Jesse could see the sorrow etched on her friends face.

'Because you look like a good girl. You *are* a good girl, Mary.'

Mary snorted. 'Oh yeah, really good. Just had unprotected sex with a married man on the floor behind a bloody bar on holiday. Really good, yeah.'

'Actually Mary, you *are* a good girl. You know you are. You very rarely actually have sex with anyone and never normally unprotected. I think you're being a bit hard on yourself.'

'Do you really think so? Come off it Jesse, we both know that's not true. If I really was a good girl I'd be married with kids by now, not playing around with other women's husbands.'

'Bloody hell Mary, I don't know what to say.' At a loss for comforting words Jesse gently rubbed her friends back as they sat beside each other looking into the distance.

'What about you? How are you doing?'

'Not great to be honest. I feel sick to tell the truth. I genuinely can't believe Ben would just up and leave like that. I feel such a fool. I'm not sure who I'm more annoyed with, him or myself. Obviously he suckered me like a good 'un but I was the one who allowed him to have sex with me after only one bloody drink.' Lighting another cigarette from the butt she was still smoking, Jesse continued. 'Seriously Mary, I've had sex with two complete bloody strangers, two days in a row, completely unprotected. And guess what?' Jesse didn't actually wait for a response from Mary. 'Yup, you guessed it. I could be pregnant from either one.'

'It's unlikely that you'd be pregnant Jesse, isn't it?'

'Yes, it's unlikely, but not impossible. Wouldn't it be ironic that after years of trying to have a child with Darren that I fall pregnant on a holiday in Greece and wouldn't know who the father is? Really how fuckin' tragic.' Jesses sarcastic tone was laced with bitterness. 'Seriously Mary, I really can't believe my behaviour the last few days. I've gone years with no sex and now I'm sleeping around with anyone that looks my way.'

'That's not exactly true, either, is it? Ben and Steve both did more than just look your way. Steve was utterly charming and young and gorgeous and you really deserved to feel wanted after being alone for so long.'

'True, but he's also a complete asshole. Didn't see that coming, did I?'

'No, but that's not your fault either. And Ben, well, let's face it, he's bloody gorgeous and he charged in like a knight in shining armour to save you in your hour of need... anyone would've fallen for that.'

As Mary spoke, Jesse felt another kick to her stomach and groaned aloud. 'God, I really did think he was the one. How absolutely moronic am I? I mean really, what was I thinking? I'd practically named our kids after just one night.'

It was Mary's turn to console Jesse. 'I'm sorry, Jesse. I didn't realise you felt that strongly about him.'

'That's another thing, I shouldn't have, should I? Just one night and I'm planning marriage! Even if he hadn't had a fiancé waiting for him at home, he would have smelled desperation on me. Quite how I thought it was going to work I have no idea. He didn't even know me. Knew nothing about me, in fact. Yet here I am planning our future together. I'm such a bloody idiot, Mary.'

'You and me both hun, you and me both'.

The girls watched in silence as Niko's wife arrived to set up the bar. Several minutes later and Jesse carried over two coffees to where Mary sat. Dropping sweetener into their coffees Jesse said,

'Mary, I don't know about you but I'm going to take a walk into town and see if I can find a pharmacist that speaks English and get the morning after pill.'

Mary's mouth fell open. 'Really? Bloody hell, I hadn't even thought about that as being an option.'

'Well, I know it's most effective after twenty four hours and I'm forty eight hours since Steve, but I think it's definitely worth it and it'll certainly work against what happened last night with Ben. My friend

Annabel took it a year or so ago and she had no effects from it so I'm thinking it'll be okay. Not sure if it stuffs up your hormones or anything like that, but I think it's worth the risk. I know I shouldn't be able to fall pregnant, but I really don't want to take the risk at this stage. What about you?'

'What do you mean, what about me?'

'Well, you had sex with Niko last night, are you going to take the pill or see how it pans out next month?'

'Oh my goodness, I really don't know. I've not thought about it until you just said. Wouldn't it be abortion?'

'I don't think so. Although I'm not entirely sure. Surely if it's only twenty four hours later it would only be a cell if you were pregnant, isn't that still okay? And of course you may not even be pregnant so you wouldn't be getting rid of anything.'

'But how would you know that?'

'I don't know, I guess you wouldn't. I think I'd just be happy to not be pregnant by a stranger and as it's unlikely I could ever fall pregnant it's just an insurance policy really. I think it'd give me peace of mind rather than having to wait a month to know if I've fallen pregnant with a child I don't want from an unknown father.'

'But how does it work? Does it kill anything or stop it happening?'

'I don't know Mary. Why don't we get the

Blackberry out and see if we can find any info about how it works and then we can also look it up Google translate to see how to ask for it. The way our luck's going, it wouldn't surprise me if we were given a cold remedy!'

***

'Are you sure you want to take it, Mary?' Dotty asked

'Yes, I've had all morning to think about it and it makes sense. It won't stop me from getting a bloody infection but it'll probably stop me falling pregnant.'

'But what if you *are* pregnant, Mary? You know as well as I do that a child is a gift from God and shouldn't be killed.'

Mary visibly winced at Dotty's words. 'I know what you're saying Dotty but it was only twenty four hours ago, I really don't think there's much chance of it. I'll take the risk and I'll never know if I was pregnant or not. I can't bear the idea of being pregnant by a married man at my age. Anyway, it's just a form of contraception.'

Dotty raised her eyebrows and her lips were pursed thin but she didn't say anything as she watched her friend swallow the morning after pill. Dotty prayed to God that Mary wasn't pregnant and that she wasn't ending a life, and asked God to forgive her friend if she was. Dotty had strong beliefs and was very much pro-life, but was careful to not make her friend feel worse by voicing her feelings.

'Feel better?' Dotty asked.

'No, actually. But let's go and see where Jesse is and try to enjoy the last two days of our holiday.'

'Okay, you go ahead, I haven't seen her come out of the apartment so she must be changing or something. I'll go and get myself a coffee. See you in a bit.' As Mary headed towards the apartment Dotty put on her sunhat, threw her bag around her shoulder and headed out of the complex. She was in need of some space and a walk would help her clear her head. She felt saddened that Mary and Jesse were both taking pills that could possibly end a life. Dotty had realised many years previous that she would probably never have children naturally and as she was getting older she might also be losing the possibility to even adopt. She certainly didn't want to trade places with her friends, but they had the opportunities to fall pregnant. Dotty was losing hope of ever finding someone who could love her. She was never far away from a reminder that she was huge. Just minutes into her impromptu stroll her thighs were starting to blister where they were rubbing together. She stepped into a shop and bought a bag of chocolate, pouring the contents into her pockets so no one would know she was eating as she continued to walk.

It wasn't as if she'd never tried to do anything about her weight, just nothing had worked for her. She had tried everything from the cabbage diet to health farms but nothing stuck. The cabbage diet lasted all of two days as the stench of her farts were unbearable even to her, never mind her poor flatmate who refused to sit in the lounge with her after more than ten minutes of uncontrollable stinky flatulence.

The health farm trip was filled with promise. In the brochure Jesse had brought over one evening, Henlow Grange Health Spa seemed like the perfect place to lose vast amounts of weight in a short period of time. It was expensive but all the meals were calorie controlled, and loads of exercises were thrown in, along with facials and something called G5 treatments, which they were later to realise hurt like hell.

They had a deal on a four day break and were excited to arrive and see the grand house among acres of woodland. Tennis courts sat behind the house, along with inside and outdoor swimming pools. There were organised walks and group activities and both girls signed up for nearly everything, wanting to get the best out of their stay.

By 8pm on the first evening Dotty had paired up with three ladies from London who had come more for the break rather than to lose weight, so it took no time at all for Dotty to join them in heading out to the local pub. Jesse was exhausted from her day of exercise and fell asleep waiting for her friend to return before 9pm. It wasn't until breakfast the next day that Dotty admitted to Jesse that not only had she had two glasses of wine at the local pub but she'd also had two Mars bars. Apparently the pub did a great trade in chocolate, being so close to Henlow Grange. Every night they had a variety of ladies sneaking down the long drive from the spa to guzzle wine and chocolate or crisps.

Dotty remembered with a pang of guilt how upset Jesse had been at the end of their retreat when they got weighed and she had lost only one pound, when Dotty had lost five pounds, even though she'd got into a nightly routine of drinking wine and chocolate with her London buddies.

Even eating two bars of chocolate per night Dotty had managed to lose weight, and a lot of it by all accounts, but she just couldn't bring herself to do what was needed to continue losing weight, which was basically to deprive herself of exactly what she wanted to eat. Why shouldn't she be able to eat whatever she wanted? She knew she was kidding herself when she told herself that skinny people ate more than she did and didn't gain weight, that it was just unfair and part of her body make-up. The reality was that it was just too big a task to get hold of. Every time Dotty started a diet she'd set herself a goal to lose one pound per week, knowing that she would only lose fifty two in a year if she stuck to it, which wouldn't make any kind of dent in the amount of weight she actually needed to lose.

Her ankles had swollen and her thighs were beginning to get very sore, so she turned around and headed back towards the apartment. She was sick and tired of having to do what her body asked of her, rather than what her mind wanted. She wanted to dance the night away, take part in a triathlon and have at least four children, all of which were impossible in the body she now shuffled along the dusty road.

She struggled to keep her sadness at bay - longing to wear feminine shoes rather than the size nine men's shoes she had no choice but to buy. She fantasised about walking into a restaurant without having to wonder if the chairs would support her or whether there was enough room in the toilets for her to wipe herself or even get in the door.

She pushed back the memory of making her way up the stairs to the toilet in Bar 163 one Friday evening only to realise to her horror that she couldn't close the door behind her. There was no way she could get inside the tiny toilet cubicle and close the door and the two women who had come in behind her looked at their feet when she gave up and had to leave the toilet, having not relieved herself. She couldn't forget the pitying look on the waitress's face when she had to ask if they had disabled facilities. None of these experiences drove her towards trying to do anything about her weight, they simply added to the sense of hopelessness she lived with daily.

She tried to cover her mounting sense of dread with a few more pieces of chocolate. What on earth were these girls up to? This holiday had definitely brought out the worst in all three of them. She couldn't believe both Jesse and Mary were in the situations they were in having had unprotected sex. She automatically said a prayer of thanks that she wasn't in their situations. She was thankful that she'd found out about Stavros being married. She would have been horrified if that had gone any further and then found out she'd been cavorting with a married man. Dotty took her faith seriously and adultery and coveting someone else's husband was definitely not something she would ever knowingly do. She was thankful that she wouldn't ever get herself in the kind of situations in which Mary and Jesse had just found themselves. Even though Dotty did not want to be alone, she would rather be alone than break a commandment from the Bible. She trusted God to give her a husband, but she was tired of waiting on His time and not on hers. She couldn't understand why she had to wait so long for Mr Right. She was sure there must be some lessons she was learning, but she still hadn't figured them out.

The one thing she had realised by dating 'Les' was that she had lowered her expectations a bit too dramatically and needed to get some self-respect back. Maybe she could expect more than just a pulse. Maybe she could expect to find Mr Right attractive, even. What was the point of being on holiday if you couldn't relax on a beach with the sun beating on your skin, dreaming of a handsome gent coming to your rescue? In her daydreams she was thin and didn't have three chins. She was graceful and could be carried easily.

Dotty was sure that all women who fell in love and married at some point in their lives had been picked up and carried by their husbands. She had watched *Dirty Dancing* so many times she could see herself in nearly any situation running towards a handsome dreamboat, muscles rippling, tossing her into the air and spinning her around as if she weighed nothing at all.

Dotty was delighted to find the pool area empty as she arrived back at the Marias. Her mood lifted and after polishing off the last of the melting chocolate she enjoyed sliding into the pool, allowing the cool water to soothe her inner thighs and ankles. There were only two days left of the holiday; she could either cry herself through them or enjoy them, and if Jesse and Mary were able, she was going to choose the latter.

***

London could be a lonely place when you were single but it was a desperate place to be if you were both fat and single. Everywhere you went there was hustle and bustle and people having what seemed like a great time, and you were excluded.

It was unknown for Dotty to feel anything other than vulnerable and on display when out for a night and she never got used to the stares cast her way. Some people were subtle in their glances and others were deliberate in their glares. If she could see think bubbles above their heads she believed they would read 'disgusting slob'. She had suffered many abusive shouts from cars, mainly young men hanging out of white vans, and had even been followed home by three teenage girls in the street shouting abuse at her. She suffered pitying looks in Boots when she stood on the digital scales in the Oxford Street branch, the only set strong enough to hold her weight. Worse were the daily groans she encountered on the commute home when passengers realised she was going to cram herself into their car on the tube. There were not many places she felt comfortable visiting, but finding Planet Big Girl in Leicester Square was a Godsend.

After their experience in Big Ladies Paradise there was no way Jesse would ever come to a place aimed at 'fatties' as she referred to them, ever again. Dotty was slowly working her way through her friends, taking them to Planet Big Girl whenever she could, without actually explaining fully where they were going.

Dotty had taken her unsuspecting work colleague Debbie with her last month, a skinny size ten beauty. At first she didn't really notice what was different about the environment. The music was current and loud, the lights were dark and inviting. The bar was busy and there was a lively atmosphere. When the girls found some seats near the dance floor Debbie spotted the bowls of Quality Street on each table and thought it was a nice touch. It took a few minutes of sipping her drink and looking around to realise she was the odd one out in this club.

Debbie had said that she didn't really mind the

club, that the atmosphere was okay, but she didn't appreciate being knocked around quite as much as she had been on the dance floor. She was very obviously in the minority and some of the bigger girls made her feel unwelcome by bumping into her. Dotty though was in her element, enjoying every minute of the attention she received from many men. The fact that all the men who had approached her were French-Algerian didn't put her off or concern her. Dotty was asked many times to dance and yet the skinny beauty she had brought along wasn't asked even once. Dotty knew it wasn't right for her to feel smug but there was a small part of her that was happy she was receiving so much attention for a change.

Dotty longed now for that feeling of inclusion as she bobbed about in the pool water in Greece. She was able to relax as it was an adult-only hotel but still, she would feel happier if she were surrounded by bigger women. Jesse and Mary were both very obviously overweight, but they didn't compare to Dotty's huge frame. Dotty knew they shared some of the same problems, not being able to fit on fairground rides or ride horses being just two, but they didn't understand the horror of friends asking if they could sit in the middle of the back seat so as to even the car out as the axle might snap under their weight. All three girls had difficulty fitting into and getting out of a standard bath but only Dotty had the humiliation of not being able to fit into women's shoes.

All three girls had endured well-meaning conversations with friends who were of a normal weight. They all handled with grace comments such as 'couldn't you just eat less?', 'maybe if you did more exercise …?', 'have you thought about a gastric band?' Well, all except Jesse who had just recently responded loudly at a dinner party 'Oh my God, I never thought of that! Just eat less? Fuck me, what a great idea, I must get onto that straight away! You're a fuckin' genius!'

Dotty smiled as she glided through the water on her back, eyes closed, enjoying the sun on her face. She loved Jesse. Jesse often said what Dotty felt but would never dare say for fear of causing a scene or worse - crying, which is what made spending time with her friend special. They had two days left. Dotty prayed they would all enjoy them.

***

'What time is it Jesse?' asked Mary.

'No idea, sorry. Why?'

'Just wondered if it was too early for a drink, I fancy a cocktail.'

Jesse got up off her sun bed and grabbed her purse.

'You're breathing and we are on holiday, so I reckon that makes it time enough for a drink! Come on. What do you fancy, Dotty?'

'Mmmm, I'm thinking Tequila Sunrise sounds

like a good idea. Can you see if they've got any chocolate in the fridge too?'

'Will do.' Jesse linked arms with Mary and headed towards the bar, where Niko's wife was writing on a blackboard.

'Hiya, can we have a Tequila Sunrise, a Piña Colada, and... is it a Black Russian, Mary?'

'No, actually a Mojhito sounds good,' Mary replied, watching closely the blonde behind the bar.

Jesse's interest was piqued when she saw the blackboard read 'Maria BBQ Tonight, home-made food and Karaoke'. Jesse knew Mary would be inwardly groaning at the thought of them all singing around the pool and this alone lifted Jesse's mood.

'I reckon that's our evening sorted, don't you, Mary?' Jesse asked, smirking at her friend.

'I'm not going to have any say in it am I, once Dotty knows about it?'

'Nope!' Jesse beamed at her friend and put her arms around her shoulders. 'Hunny, if ever we needed a sing song and a drink it's tonight, don't ya think?'

Mary nodded her agreement. 'You do know you're a pain in the arse, don't you Jesse?'

'Yes darling, I know. I love you too. Let's go and give Dotty the good news.'

***

Dotty spent half an hour warming her voice up singing

scales in the bathroom. She knew it was only karaoke but she still had an amazing voice and had never gotten out of the habit of looking after it properly. Jesse spent the same half an hour humming loudly while applying her make-up and fixing her hair. Her voice wasn't as spectacular as Dotty's but she did have a good voice, and she knew she would shine at the karaoke night if she warmed up properly. Mary sat on the balcony smoking, secure in the knowledge that she was not going to be anywhere near a microphone.

Mary knew she was taking a risk sharing Jesse's bottle of red wine as she'd already had two cocktails by the pool, but she was fairly sure she could get away with at least another mug in the apartment and then possibly one more cocktail at the bar before switching to water. She didn't like the sensation of being out of control, which was why she very rarely heavily drank but today she was appreciating how alcohol could deaden the creeping feeling of regret that had been crawling around her stomach since last night. She was enjoying the light buzz and the soft focus of the pool bar. She blew smoke rings while sipping her wine from the mug and watched through her slightly drunken haze as people busied themselves preparing for the BBQ which was due to start in half an hour.

The fairy lights had started to twinkle and the pool looked a mysterious turquoise shade where lights had started to glow beneath the surface. The air was thick with the smell of coals burning and although the apartment was filled with the sound of two singers warming up their voices, she felt lonely. Her stomach lurched every time she looked back on the evening before. How could she have been so stupid? What was it with her and Greek men? Not just Greek men, but *married* Greek men. One had broken her heart many years before and one might well be responsible for her hormones starting to fly off the wall as she'd been forced to take the morning after pill. How could he do it? But then, how did she not know it was going to happen? Hindsight was a wonderful thing, but so was denial. Deep down Mary knew sex would be on the agenda, how could it not? She had kissed him, egged him on, even worn her best underwear and why would she do that if she hadn't intended on taking it off? Okay, so maybe she had planned on having a moment with Niko, but what she had planned had involved a bed and candles and soft music, and a condom. It did not include the stench of beer and four thrusts of an unprotected penis. Nope, she was not amused at all.

Mary was vaguely aware that she was simmering, but also was maintaining a sense of calm. She could feel anger bubbling but it was almost like peripheral vision, she couldn't quite grasp it and when she tried to grab a hold of it, it slid away. She supposed it was the effects of the alcohol on the morning after pill so she didn't worry about it and finished her mug of wine with a large gulp, then reached for the bottle for a top up.

***

Jesse had never seen Mary fully drunk before but she was sure that's what Mary was. Dotty had insisted that she and Jesse had got to the pool bar early so Dotty could ensure she got a seat that wouldn't collapse underneath her but that was also close enough to not have to walk far to the karaoke microphone. They were sitting a little close to the pool for Jesse's liking but surprisingly a lot of the chairs were already taken when they arrived so once Dotty had chosen her seat, they had settled in. Mary had asked Jesse to get her a Black Russian. Never had she known Mary to mix her drinks, never mind to mix cocktails with wine, but she wasn't going to argue, she'd been waiting for years to see Mary fully drunk. Many a time Jesse had had to endure lectures from Mary the day after she'd done something or other to humiliate herself on a night on the raz and she was hoping to do the same for Mary in the morning.

It was only three weeks ago that Jesse had endured an hour of Mary's lecturing about her alcohol intake.

As Jesse worked for herself she rarely got the chance to meet ex-colleagues in London, so she'd jumped at the chance when her old work friend Annie invited her to dinner. Jesse needed someone to accompany her on the train as she didn't like to travel on public transport alone. She had suffered ridicule from youths on trains and had been groped more than once on a tube. She had become acutely aware of her personal safety so she asked Dotty to come with her. Jesse remembered the early part of the evening very clearly. She remembered getting into London via train and heading to the West End in a taxi. She remembered drinking a couple of vodkas in the Pitcher & Piano while waiting for Annie to arrive. She also remembered heading towards the restaurant on Frifth Street when she saw the most attractive black man she'd ever seen. She was always the first to give someone a compliment if she felt it was warranted. This one was warranted. She spotted him on the other side of the road - very tall, beautiful features, expensive suit, she had to tell him just in case he didn't know, it was her duty. So she had crossed the road and started to approach him. He saw her coming and stopped walking just before she reached him. He smiled broadly at her as she had purposely stopped him in his tracks.

'Hi!' he smiled.

'Hi!' Jesse replied, smiling back. 'I know this may sound odd but I really wanted to let you know how beautiful you look. I think you may well be the most attractive black man I've ever seen, and I just wanted to let you know that!'

'Oh! Well, I don't know what to say about that!' he said, although he didn't look particularly surprised so Jesse guessed maybe he was told often of his good looks.

'No need to say anything, I just wanted to let you know. I think it's important to tell people something that might make them feel good, you never know what people are thinking and sometimes a genuine compliment can make people's day! Anyway, just thought I'd say.' And without thinking Jesse stood on her tip toes and kissed the complete stranger on the lips before moving swiftly past him and heading towards her friends, who were waiting for her outside the Rasa Sayang restaurant.

Without looking back she marched into the restaurant and found the table she would later actually dance on.

Jesse used the term 'dancing on tables' a lot but had never actually done it until this particular evening. They mixed Long Island Iced Tea with Piña Colada and Jamieson and lemonade and were all smashed. The food had no chance of absorbing the amount of drink they were consuming and within two hours Jesse had started a party. There was a DJ in the far corner of the restaurant who had been playing some gentle tunes and as the evening had progressed and the noise level had risen, the music beats got louder and faster. Jesse had decided there wasn't enough room to dance so she got a few tables of like-minded people to push some tables together to clear some space for a makeshift dance floor and a group of twelve people started to boogie.

Annie liked to dance but particularly enjoyed the jive and grabbed hold of Jesse when a suitable tune played and the constant twisting and twirling had the expected result on her. She was legless. She didn't actually remember getting onto the table. Allegedly it was Beyonce's *Single Ladies* that had caused the table dancing, confidently showing the busy restaurant exactly how to do the dance. She'd managed a few uh, uh, ohs before tipping the table forward and careening into the back of a waiter.

'I can't believe you can't remember it,' Dotty laughed, 'honestly I nearly wet myself. The waiter was horrified, all those drinks went flying and smashed on the floor while you just turned around and carried on dancing as if you had nothing to do with it'.

'Well, I only wish I could remember it. No doubt I'll remember it in a few days when I get my Visa bill if what you say is right. If I paid for the entire bloody tray of drinks he dropped I'll be down quite a few quid.'

'We thought that and Annie started to argue with the waiter but you just said, "don't worry about it mate, just charge it," and carried on dancing! It was so funny, Jesse. You were so cool!'

That may have been so but she didn't feel at all cool when they told her how she had swooned over a bulldog in the street when they finally left the restaurant.

'I can't believe you don't remember the dog! The bulldog! You don't remember it? With the diamante collar? Oh Jesse, it was so funny!' Dotty could hardly breathe for laughing by the looks of her.

'You saw it coming up the street on this long lead and started with the usual "ah look at the doggie, is the doggie going for a little walk, can I stroke the doggie" and as the dog got to you, you leant down to stroke it but something went wrong with your jeans and you literally fell on it and rolled into the gutter!'

'Ah,' Jesse groaned, 'that will be why my jeans are in such a state and I have cuts on my knees.' And then the lecture had started from Mary. She had tutted and shook her head in disappointment at Jesse.

'You really shouldn't lose control like that Jesse, seriously, you drink far too much. Doesn't it worry you that you can't remember what you've done?'

'Not really, I've always got Dotty or you to tell me how much I need to be mortified in the morning,' Jesse retorted. The lecture had gone on for a good five minutes but Jesse had tuned out after the first sentence, wondering if her friends hadn't been with her if she actually would have managed to get home. She felt sure she would and if she had needed to get home she probably wouldn't have drunk as much – probably.

Watching Mary now walk in a slow zigzag around the pool towards their table filled Jesse with glee. Oh, she was going to make the most out of this if she could.

'Dotty!' Jesse hissed as quietly as she could. 'Look behind you and see Mary!'

Dotty's brows furrowed as she watched their

friend make her way towards them with a slightly curved smile playing on her lips.

'What's wrong with her?'

'She's pissed!'

Dotty gasped. 'No way! I don't believe it.' They watched a few moments longer in fascination and Dotty turned to Jesse. 'She bloody well is pissed, this is going to be fun!' Dotty picked up Mary's drink and handed it to her as she reached their table. 'Bottoms up, Mary!'

'Yamas Dotty, Yamas Jesse!' Mary drank her Black Russian as if it were milk.

Jesse spent the next few hours enjoying herself. That was a surprise; she'd thought she'd have to pretend for the rest of the holiday. She had thought it would take a miracle for her to forget the trauma of the night before, but her miracle had appeared in the shape of an increasingly drunk Mary.

Mary was always charming, but tipsy she was actually loud and quite forward, not at all like her sober self. She had become friends with the older ladies on the table closest to them and was enjoying handing out the folders for the karaoke presenter and suggesting, rather loudly, songs she'd like sung. Whenever she stood up she seemed to dance to a tune no-one else could hear. Jesse had to cover her mouth with her hand when she realised Mary had put her name down to sing *Red, Red Wine*. Mary could not sing - at all - and Jesse knew she'd be mortified in the morning to know she'd sung in public.

Mary swung her hips in tune to the singing, even though she couldn't stay in beat vocally. Jesse could hardly hear the song through her own laughter. She wished she could control herself so she could enjoy the bum notes more, but once she'd heard the first two she laughed so hard her stomach hurt. All but one of the pictures Jesse took were blurred but she managed to post the clear one to Facebook before the song had even finished. She decided she wouldn't tell Mary about the Facebook picture until the morning - she'd use it to help with the lecture she planned on giving her.

Mary had started a clapping taunt when Jesse said she didn't want to sing after all, so in the end Jesse stood to the microphone and sang *Summer of 69*, much to the delight of her friends. The evening was buzzing along nicely until someone suggested Dotty sing. Dotty being an opera singer couldn't sing karaoke for the life of her, which she tried to explain, but also explained she could sing an aria if they wanted *a capella*. All the older ladies who were now firm friends had demanded that everyone be quiet so Dotty could sing something. Groaning could be heard throughout but still Dotty stepped to the space where the karaoke machine was set up. She didn't touch the microphone other than to introduce her song.

'This song is about a girl whose lover dies as he kisses her'.

'Great,' muttered someone sarcastically.

Dotty handed the microphone to the presenter, took a breath, put on a devastated facial expression and started to sing. The entire area fell to silence. Dotty's powerful voice drifted on the air to Antonio's bar and within moments people were standing on the grass bank where the bar sat so they could see Dotty perform.

Everyone who could hear Dotty knew they were hearing something outstanding. Even those who didn't like the music could appreciate the perfect tone and pitch of her voice. As Dotty hung her head to indicate the end of the song, the place erupted in cheers. There were many faces with tears on their cheeks, but Jesse knew they were in trouble when she glanced at Mary and found her to be one of them.

Uh oh was all Jesse could think as she watched tears fall silently down Mary's face. Once the commotion was over and Dotty had made it clear she didn't want to sing any more, the next singer made their way to the bar area. Dotty returned to the table.

'Ah Mary, did you like it?'

Jesse looked at her incredulously. Did she not realise Mary wasn't crying about her singing? The girl was very obviously broken hearted and extremely drunk.

'Mary, shall we go back to the apartment?' Jesse wondered if Mary had heard her as she didn't acknowledge her. 'Mary?'

'What?!' Mary exploded. 'What do you want? Can't you leave me alone?'

Jesse gently touched Mary's knee and leant in so she could talk quietly to her. 'Mary, let's go back to the apartment and have a chat.'

'I don't want to go back to the apartment, why should I? I'm not the one in the wrong here!' Then she shouted 'Niko is!' Jesse hauled her by her arms to her feet and forcibly led her out into the street. Trying to drag a drunk into the apartments via the pool was not going to work so she found herself marching Mary down the main drag. Jesse knew that Mary would be bruised by the morning but she had to get her away from the bar as Niko's wife was already shouting, 'What was she talking about? Bring her back here!'

Jesse had tried physically shaking Mary to stop her endless shouts of 'Niko is a bastard!' She spotted a passageway down the side of the Chinese restaurant and pulled Mary down it until they came out the other side and were blasted with a warm sea breeze.

'Wait for me, wait for me, Jesse!' Dotty shouted a little way behind them. Jesse ignored Dotty and continued to walk Mary at speed towards where she hoped the beach was, thinking the crashing waves would drown out Mary's rants, so that at least only her friends could hear her and not any locals who might know Niko – or his wife. Eventually, Jesse stopped and waited for Dotty to reach them.

'For fuck's sake, let go of me Jesse!' Mary

demanded.

'If you're going to calm down and stop shouting then I will!' Jesse shouted back.

Mary glared at Jesse in silent defiance.

Jesse loosened her grip on her friend's arm and instead started to gently rub her hand up and down it, trying to comfort her. The move did not have the desired effect.

'Oh fuck off Jesse, it's all your fault!'

Both Dotty and Jesse gasped loudly and stood motionless as Mary started off towards the beach.

'What did she mean by that, Jesse?'

'Ignore her Dotty, she's drunk. This may well end up being a very long night.' Jesse sighed, not taking her eyes off Mary, who was now struggling to take her shoes off so she could walk onto the sand without ruining them. Even when completely drunk some parts of the personality are so ingrained that they won't be overcome by alcohol. Jesse mused that Mary would indeed be horrified to find her shoes ruined in the morning, and she wondered which would be more difficult for her to bear, the ruined shoes or the outburst at the bar.

The girls stood two metres behind Mary watching her struggle when Dotty whispered,

'It was all bloody kicking off in the bar Jesse, regardless of Mary I don't think we should show our faces there until the barbecue's finished. Niko's wife was being held back from coming after Mary.'

Jesse rolled her eyes and inwardly groaned. She had been thinking what a blast it would be to see Mary drunk and was now realising that not only was it a massive pain in her arse but that it could actually jeopardise their accommodation for the last night in Greece.

'Shit. How much did she hear?'

Dotty's eyes were wide and incredulous. 'All of it of course'.

'I was hoping my shouting at Mary might drown out her words.'

'Nope, you could hear Mary screaming "Niko is a bastard rapist" over anything you were shouting. Seriously Jesse, I can't believe she was shouting he's a rapist, we could get in some serious trouble for this.'

'Yeah, and so could Niko.' Jesse muttered.

'He didn't actually rape her, did he?'

'No, of course not.' Mary stepped onto the sand and strode purposefully towards the surf.

'Keep your wits about you Dotty, don't get too near the edge and whatever happens do not get into that water unless I say to. I can't afford to have both of you in the sea at the same time.' Jesse didn't have time to think about Dotty's feelings but in the morning she would remember the look of hurt that flicked across her friend's face.

Jesse caught up with Mary in just a few strides. 'Mary, what're you doing?'

'Going for a swim!'

'Really, in that outfit? Wasn't that the one you got from Phase Eight?'

Mary looked down at her navy chiffon skirt as if seeing it for the first time.

'Oh, bummer.' It appeared as if Mary couldn't keep her eyes straight when she looked back up to Jesse. 'I'll take it off then.'

'But where are you going to put it? You'll just cover it in sand Mary, and you know how much sand can rip that kind of material. Is it really worth it, hunny?' Jesse was hoping to play on the side of Mary that most irked her, the clean-freak side.

Mary's brows furrowed and she staggered back slightly.

'Bollocks,' she mumbled before making her way back up the beach and sitting down heavily on a plastic sunbed that hadn't been stacked away.

Jesse lit two cigarettes and handed one to Mary. Dotty wished she had something similar to act as a kind of pause, so instead of smoking she rifled through her handbag and pulled out four chunks of Dairy Milk and popped two in her mouth.

Nobody spoke for a long while. The waves gently crashed on the shore, the breeze lifted the hems of their skirts, moonlight lit the girls' faces so much so that Mary's mascara was clearly seen still wet on her cheeks and neck.

Dotty managed to get herself into a seated position in the sand, one that would take a while to get out of unaided. She was the first one to break the silence.

'Bloody hell, Mary.'

'What?' Mary slurred.

'I can't believe you were shouting Niko was a rapist.'

'Well, he was!' she blurted spitefully.

'Whoa, hang on a minute Mary!' Jesse interrupted. 'That's not true. You never said anything about rape to me this morning when you told me about last night. You've got to be careful with stuff like this, even if you are drunk. You could get into a lot of trouble, Mary.'

'Me get into trouble! Me! How dare you? I'm the one who was raped, it's not me who should be getting into trouble.'

'Mary, seriously, stop it. I'm getting really annoyed now. You didn't say he raped you, this is just the drink speaking.'

'No it's not! He put it in me and didn't take it out when I said stop, that's rape!' Mary was shrieking and trying to get off the sunbed.

'Mary, you told me he was only in you for a matter of seconds, so he couldn't have carried on when you said no! Seriously Mary, this is a serious allegation and you're drunk. If you feel the same in the morning we'll do something about it, but right now, I think we should just all calm down a little bit'.

'Well, I think we should go to the police.'

'Not on your life Mary, never gonna happen. Not tonight. Let's just think about the whole situation. If you went to the police, what would they say?'

'They'd arrest Niko, that's what they'd say.'

'No Mary, they wouldn't. They'd ask you what you were doing leading up to the rape and they would ask what your relationship was with him prior to last night. Then they'd realise that you'd been destined to get it on since you landed in Greece and they'd probably arrest you for falsely accusing someone of rape!'

'It's not falsely accusing if it happened!' Mary spat.

'But Mary,' Dotty chipped in, 'you knew you were going to have sex with him, didn't you? You've fancied him since we landed and you'd already had a snog with him. Okay, I'm sure you didn't want to have sex the way you did, I know you didn't want to have sex without a condom, but come on Mary, you were wanting sex, I can't believe for a second you can class it as rape. Don't you think you're blowing this a little out of proportion because you're annoyed with having to take the morning after pill?'

If Jesse had said what Dotty had, Mary would have started a rant, Jesse was sure, but instead she looked squarely at Dotty and said sheepishly,

'He didn't use a condom. He just shoved it in.'

'Ah, I know hunny, that must have been rubbish.'

'It was. I mean seriously, who did he think I was? He just got me on the floor and that was that.' Mary had started to wail again. Dotty scooted up to Mary on her knees and gave her friend a big hug. Jesse couldn't see Mary's face squashed between Dotty's heavy breasts but she could tell that the anger had left her friend and pity was starting to kick in.

Jesse checked her watch. 'Okay girls, it's just gone midnight. I don't know about you but I've had enough for one night, shall we try to get back into the apartments unnoticed?'

'How do you think we're going to do that, Jesse?' Dotty started the long process of trying to get off her knees.

'Well, we can stick to the left hand side of the road so no-one from Maria Apartments can see us and then I'll check out the apartments when we get near and see if we can sneak past. I'm thinking with all the drama of the night the evening might have ended earlier than usual and it may already have closed for the night.'

'I bloody hope so Jesse, Niko's wife was doing her tank when I left and even Antonio had come across to help calm the situation down. I don't think we're going to be very welcome back there somehow.'

'Well, thank heavens tonight's our last night so we only have to kill time tomorrow before coach pick up at lunch-time. I'm sure we can lay low until then. We'll stay on the beach in the morning and head out early. Nicola has only been at the apartments once in the morning so hopefully she won't be around tomorrow anyway. We'll have to play it by ear, but let's just take one thing at a time and get to the apartments tonight without getting into any more trouble.'

Dotty helped Mary brush off her skirt after she'd brushed her knees of sand and they all linked arms and slowly made their way back to the road. The Chinese restaurant was closed but from where they were they could see the lights were still on at Antonio's bar.

'Shitty death,' Dotty breathed, 'the bar's still open. How're we going to get past?'

'Don't worry about Antonio's, it's the Marias we're worried about, let's just see if we can sneak in the back way to our apartments.'

They walked single file, with Mary in the middle, on the left-hand side of the road, trying to stay in the shadows of the various shops that were closed until the morning.

Leaving the girls behind her, Jesse sneaked up to where she could see the apartment bar and was surprised to see the evening still in full swing. There were at least fifteen people around the bar, some of them dancing, most of them laughing and drinking with their backs to Jesse. Taking in the situation, trying to see which would be the quickest way to get Mary into the apartment, she locked eyes with Carlos, who was making his way towards her.

'Shit,' Jesse muttered. Ducking back into the

shadows she hissed 'you won't bloody believe this. Carlos is on his way over here.'

'What, the waiter from the other night?'

'Yup.'

'Bloody hell, talk about timing!' Dotty kept running her hands through her hair, obviously contemplating whether to run or not. Mary was leaning against a shop wall half asleep, not at all concerned about the situation unfolding before them.

Carlos's skinny frame came into view and even though Dotty and Jesse were expecting him, they were still startled by him.

'Mary! What is going on?' He was gesticulating with his hands trying to make himself understood, talking in fast Greek and Jesse thought he basically said: Niko's wife mad, Niko in trouble, Mary is slut, Carlos is upset and he thought she would kiss only him. Everyone upset with Mary. Again, Mary is slut. At which point Jesse said 'Okay Carlos, we get the picture, Mary's a slut, now fuck off.'

Mary seemed unaware of Carlos's presence, never mind any understanding that he might actually be upset with her or indeed calling her a slut. She pushed herself away from the wall and muttered 'Bollocks to this.' And bumped into Carlos's shoulder on her way out of the shadows and into full view of the Maria apartments.

***

'Thank you, Jesus,' Dotty muttered as Jesse opened the door to the apartments, having managed to somehow walk straight past the bar without anyone noticing.

'Keep the lights off, Dotty,' Jesse commanded, 'we don't want to draw attention to ourselves being back here. I don't know about you but I'd like a good night's sleep tonight, and I'm fairly sure Mary will need the same.'

Dotty looked down at Mary with pity in her eyes. 'Bless her, do you think we should undress her?' Mary lay fully clothed gently snoring diagonally on her belly across her bed.

'Maybe take her shoes off but leave her. Not being funny Dotty but if you move her now she's fallen asleep, she's likely to wake up and puke all over the place.'

'Good point, maybe we'll leave her just as she is then.'

Jesse smiled, knowing that Dotty had a strong aversion to puke, bordering on a phobia. 'Don't worry, I'll take her shoes off, just be careful going to the toilet in the dark...make sure your toilet roll goes into the bin and not the floor please.'

'Huh, as if,' Dotty snorted, but they both knew Dotty had been guilty of this on more than one occasion, even with the lights on.

Lying in the dark listening to the music and rumbles of laughter drifting on the breeze outside, Jesse felt lonely. She could hear Mary's gentle snoring in between the rhythm of Dotty's very throaty grunts, and yet she felt isolated. She could see a slice of sky from her position, shiny black with brilliant diamonds scattered through, some of which constellations she felt she should know the name of but didn't. Why didn't she know such things? Why wasn't she educated to the same degree as other people? If she'd finished school would things be different? She'd never know the answers to those questions, and she wouldn't normally care, but the events of the last few evenings had left her questioning more than one of her life choices.

She had been looking forward to seeing Mary drunk but the reality had been a depressing experience. Was she like that when she was drunk? Quite probably far more annoying as Jesse knew she was a loud drunk, albeit it amusing to be with. She wondered if Mary's switch from happy to angry and then sad was purely down to the hormones flying through her body, or whether the drink had brought to the surface a deep unhappiness which was normally suppressed by her facade of being in control. Jesse loved Mary but she didn't really understand her, and the feeling was mutual, she was sure.

Jesse couldn't understand why Mary always went for married men, whereas Mary probably couldn't understand why Jesse had given herself so easily to men in such a short period of time. No doubt they both had self-esteem issues, Jesse mused as she gazed at the stars, willing one of them to streak so she could make a wish.

Perhaps out of all of them Dotty was the one to be admired. Dotty had no inhibitions and felt sure that she would find the right man for her, given time. She was confident that there was a plan for her and it was a good one. She had told Jesse on many occasions that all she needed was faith and patience and she'd get all of her hopes and dreams. Jesse wondered if it was this way of thinking that had enabled Dotty to become so large. Since Jesse had known Dotty she had gained nearly a stone for every year that had gone by. Dotty thought nothing of buying a size thirty two top but when Jesse first met her she was in a size twenty six. It didn't seem to make much difference to Dotty's sense of well-being, other than she didn't have to be quite so picky over the kind of chairs she could sit in. And flying had become a nightmare.

Jesse inwardly groaned with the realisation that in just a few hours' time she'd be sitting on a plane next to Dotty, with her arm on her friend's shoulder as Dotty took up so much of her space, Jesse's own arm cut off the blood flow to her boob if she kept it by her side.

Goodness, she knew what it was like to try not to eat what you wanted, it was a daily battle for Jesse, and Jesse knew it wouldn't be more than another inch gained before she'd be asking for a belt extension on the planes too, but that knowledge seemed to be the main reason Jesse had stayed at least stable in her weight for a few months... nothing dramatic up or down, although when Jesse ever did see the scales register a one or two pound loss she knew what joy felt like, albeit it very briefly.

Running her hands over her bare belly never failed to give Jesse a vivid sense of hopelessness, and now was no exception. She guessed it was some sort of self-punishment that while she was feeling so lonely she also felt the need to remind herself of her failings and to reiterate how fat she had become. She recognised it was awful that she'd had sex with two people in as many days but also quite amazing when she considered how fat she was. Okay, she knew she was pretty, had striking eyes and a killer smile with a great mane of hair, but none of these things hid the fact she was obese and, in her opinion, therefore, gross and had saggy skin with enough stretch marks to be mistaken for the London tube network.

She was sick of tormenting herself like this. It was a daily routine. Wake up, feel awful about self, eat. She considered herself an intelligent woman but when it came to food there was no off button, in fact there was no button at all when it came to food intake. Mary could eat Nutella straight from the jar but eventually feel sick and stop. Jesse didn't have that. Jesse normally only stopped when the chocolate had run out. She didn't understand how her friend Gill could leave chocolate in her fridge for weeks on end without eating it. Jesse was lucky for her chocolate to actually get cool, it was in the fridge for such a short period of time. She longed to be one of those women who could offer friends biscuits when they popped over for a cup of tea, but not only did friends not pop over, she couldn't offer them biscuits as anything sweet in the cupboards would have been eaten within an hour of its arrival.

If ever friends did come to her house, which was a rarity, she would know in advance and head to the shops and buy a variety of biscuits. More often than not there would be one type left by the time the friend arrived for tea as all the other biscuits that made it a 'variety' had been eaten.

Jesse hated herself when she thought like this. She knew the cycle. She would feel bad about herself, roll her fingers around her flab to completely desolate her soul, then go on the hunt for chocolate to try and medicate the pain. With a sigh of resignation she slipped from under the sheet and padded quietly across the floor to Dotty's bedside dresser where she broke two rows of Dairy Milk from her friend's stash and then padded back to bed. Sitting on the side of the bed sucking each square in turn she gazed up at the trillions of stars again, willing just one of them to fall so she could make a wish that would make this destructive routine stop.

CHAPTER 22

As morning broke over the island Mary sat on the toilet holding a bucket in her lap.

My goodness, how on earth Jesse manages to do this every single weekend I'll never know.

Her insides were cramping and she was losing the previous evening's dinner very quickly. Her tongue was so dry she had awoken with it stuck to the roof of her mouth. She hadn't dared to look at her reflection yet as she had an awful feeling she wasn't going to like what she saw. She was annoyed enough to find her clothes from the previous evening still on her body, her best chiffon skirt was possibly never going to recover. She hadn't time to remove the skirt yet. When she woke up, she'd only just managed to run to the toilet in time; it was enough to lift the skirt out of the way of the bowl, never mind have time to remove it. The waves of nausea were something she'd never experienced in her lifetime and promised herself that she'd never feel again due to alcohol. She knew better. Much better. Well, at least she now knew that as much as alcohol might well dull the pain, its effectiveness was only short-lived.

She couldn't remember any of last night. Not a

moment of it. She tried to back track and work her way forward from getting her make up on, but couldn't even manage that. The entire evening was a blank void. She had a sensation of something crawling up her spine but she couldn't link it to anything so figured it was another side-effect of the alcohol.

After brushing her teeth with her finger (the electric toothbrush was too loud for her throbbing head), combing her hair and changing into a loose track suit Mary ventured out to the pool bar hopeful for a coffee. She knew someone was normally around at this time in the morning who would make her a cappuccino, which was exactly what she felt she needed. She'd decided it only fair to leave the two girls sleeping as they must have all had a late night. She had no idea what time they had called it a night but the fact she was still dressed showed it must have been in the early hours.

Mary sat on one of the bar stools, pulled an ash tray towards her and lit her first cigarette of the day. What a mistake. No sooner had she inhaled that her lungs protested and she started to cough and intermittently gag. Stubbing out the cigarette while clutching her stomach she didn't have time to register the shape moving towards her.

The hard slap across her face was shocking and exceptionally painful. She didn't have time to react before contact was made with her other cheek, catching her off balance and tipping her off the stool. Laying on the floor with her cheeks burning, trying to catch her breath, she was bewildered and had no comprehension of what was going on. She could hear someone shouting but couldn't understand the words. She was fairly certain she was going to vomit but didn't want to move from her foetal position in case she was kicked. She ventured a glance up to see who had hit her and it took her a few moments to recognise the wild-eyed wife of Niko spitting at her.

'Get away from her, you bitch.' The booming voice of Jesse felt like a warm balm being poured over her, she knew she wasn't alone now and soon the pain would stop. Mary watched in detached awe as Jesse leapt from their balcony and ran towards where Mary lay crumpled on the floor. Jesse's choice of words coupled with her lack of clothing would make for a great dinner story for years to come, but right now nobody was amused.

Nicola stopped shouting in Greek and switched to English as soon as Jesse got near.

'She screwed my husband! Little English bitch screwed my husband! She knew he was married and still she screwed him!' Spittle flew out of her mouth as she raged while Jesse ignored her and helped Mary to her feet.

No sooner was Mary up than Nicola tried to grab past Jesse to hit her again.

Jesse's fist connected with her right cheek without any sound. Later Jesse would marvel at how in the movies' fist fights were always loud and you could hear the punch, but in reality, Jesse heard no such sound when she punched Nicola hard in the face. Although she didn't hear it, she sure as hell felt it afterwards. Jesse hadn't actually meant to punch the woman, it was an instinctive reaction. She hadn't realised she'd hit her until pain started to break through her shock and her hand started to throb.

The three women looked at each other in shock. No more words were spoken as Jesse and Mary slowly turned and made their way back to their room, other than from a stranger on the second balcony up who muttered 'Put some clothes on love, you're putting me off my breakfast'. A weary 'Fuck off' was the reply from both girls, neither of whom had any fight left in them.

***

Dotty stuck her fingers in her ears and sang scales while Mary loudly puked up what was left of her insides. Jesse had managed to find a clean-ish pair of knickers, drenched them in cold water and then wrapped them around her knuckles to try to calm the swelling. Sitting on the balcony nursing her wounds Jesse felt the atmosphere around the pool was eerie. She hadn't seen anyone, not even the cleaners since settling onto the balcony over twenty minutes ago. Was this the calm before the storm or was the storm over?

Although she was in some considerable pain

she found herself smiling broadly. She giggled at the scene playing out in the apartment with Dotty and Mary; Dotty trying to dress in between Mary's retches, and when they began again, shouting and having to stop what she was doing to reinsert her fingers and begin her scales all over again.

She'd never known anything like it. Sure, she'd got herself into situations before, some of which were worse than what was playing out now, but so many dramas in so few days! It must be a record.

'What are you smirking about?' Dotty poked her head around the balcony doors, her naked body wrapped around the curtain to keep it out of view.

'Are you kidding Dotty? This whole bloody situation is outrageous!'

Dotty scanned the pool area and glanced down at the polka dot knickers wrapped around Jesse's right hand. Dotty lifted her eyebrows to the sky and stepped back into the apartment. Jesse chuckled when she heard Dotty mutter 'Outrageous, hey. Bloody outrageous? Listening to Mary puke her guts up is bloody outrageous, is it? Mmmm…' followed loudly by 'Hey hey, we're the Monkees,' as the retching from the bathroom notched up a gear.

***

Mary gingerly nursed her coffee as Jesse and Dotty tucked into their final breakfast at the taverna. It may have been their imaginations but they all felt the waiters weren't quite as attentive today as they had been during the rest of the holiday and the reception from the waitress was decidedly frosty.

Mary was now realising that the sensation crawling up her spine earlier had been one of dread, her subconscious had tried to break through to warn her but she'd not heeded the signs. She couldn't believe her own actions and was horrified to realise she'd accused Niko of rape, and at the top of her voice.

'I wonder what's going to happen with Niko and his wife now?' Dotty murmured.

'Mmm,' was all Jesse could manage.

'God I feel awful, really awful. I can't believe I just basically outed him in front of everyone. Why on earth would I do that?'

'Because you were pissed off and sick of the same routine of being the other woman.'

'Wow, that was a bit harsh, Jesse.'

'Sorry, I wasn't having a go. It's just that I was thinking last night about this holiday and how we've managed to cram in so many dramas and mistakes. The only one who's managed to scrape through with any dignity is Dotty.'

'Well, I felt I might have lost a bit when I puked on my own shoes, but if you say not...'

Mary spluttered on her coffee and it came out of her nose.

'Oh, gross! Mary! Seriously you can't keep anything in today!' Dotty laughed.

'Blimey Dotty, I wish I'd been there to see it.' Jesse laughed. 'I can see it so clearly.'

'Not as clearly as I did,' said Mary, cleaning the coffee from her face with a napkin. 'I can see it now, the way she removed Stavros from her just in time to chuck up on the floor! Honestly Jesse, you'd have wet yourself!' All three girls were laughing loudly now, oblivious to the onlookers' disapproving glares.

'Do you know, I think we'll look back on this holiday and laugh.'

'What?' Mary looked incredulous.

'I do. I think when we look back we'll all laugh at some of the outrageous things we've gotten up to.'

'I can't see that at the moment Jesse, you're on your own there,' Mary moaned.

'Come on. I know this morning has been a disaster, but even this we'll find funny in a few days' time.'

'How?' Dotty asked.

'Come off it girls. I jumped over a bloody balcony stark bollock naked and punched a fully-grown woman in the face!' To accentuate the point, Jesse waved her fist, still cradling the damp polka dot knickers.

'Actually,' Mary giggled, 'I can see you now so clearly sprinting past the pool with your boobs flying everywhere.' Dotty was laughing again. 'Honestly Dotty, she looked like Spiderman the way she flew over the balcony! It was like slow motion watching her run towards me. I'm amazed Nicola stood her ground and didn't run away!' Now they were all laughing and Jesse knew they would all heal from the day's events, even if some wounds would take a little longer to scab over.

***

'Hi Gill, it's me, how is everything?'

'Hiya, all good here, nothing major going on. No deadlines missed, so all good. What about you? Enjoyed yourself?'

'It's been... *interesting*, let's put it that way. All being well I'll see you by eleven tonight, provided there aren't any delays with the flights.'

'Did you get me anything nice?'

'Nice? In Greece? No. I'll buy you some vodka on the way back.'

'Ah boo. I wanted one of those ugly magnet things like the ones you've got in your downstairs toilet!'

'Har har. Okey doke hun, I'll see you later tonight.'

'Okay. Oh before I forget, that Henry Crud sent another email about the band.'

'Oh yeah, what did it say?'

'Well, apparently he isn't Justin. He's not the lead singer, he's the saxophone player and his real name is David.'

'Oh for Heaven's sake, what tossers to give themselves stupid bloody names. So what did he have to say?'

'Hang on, I'm getting the email now.'

Jesse was watching the clock impatiently, knowing the call was costing her a fortune.

'Okay, here we go. "Hi Jesse, so sorry to have confused you with the whole Henry Crud thing. I stupidly thought you'd remember me above all others when we met. I'm the saxophone player you were standing next to all night at the audition. Sorry I didn't make more of an impact as I was hoping you'd be open to spending some time getting to know each other. I hope to work on that once you get back from your holidays. Hope you are having a great time and look forward to sharing a Garibaldi biscuit or two with you on your return. Here's hoping – David, aka Henry Crud."'

There was a lengthy pause. 'Well, that was a bit weird wasn't it? Did it sound like he was trying to ask me out for a date or did I imagine that, Gill?'

'That's exactly what it sounded like to me. I liked his forwardness. What does he look like?'

Jesse tried to conjure up an image but couldn't. 'I have no idea. I have a vague recollection of someone with brown hair on a saxophone bobbing up and down the entire time. In fact I think he might have been a bit annoying. Can't remember, I could be mistaking him for the pleb with the trumpet though. I'll deal with it when I get back. That bit about the Garibaldi biscuit was a bit odd though, wasn't it?'

'Yes, I thought that, made him sound like a bit of a dickhead, but he could have been trying too hard?'

'Maybe. Who cares? He's shit out of luck if he thinks I'm going to share a biccie with him any time soon, I'm so off men after this holiday. I seriously mean it.'

'Really? Bloody hell, can't wait to hear all about it. I'll have a bottle of red open and ready for you when you get back tonight and you can tell me all about it.'

'That sounds like a good plan. Thanks for looking after things for me, Gill. I'm assuming the dog is still alive?'

'Yes, of course she is. We may have taken a while to get to know each other but we know who's boss now.'

'Chloe, right?'

Jesse could hear Gill smile by the tone of her voice. 'You got it girlie! See you tonight, and don't forget to buy me some Greek toot!'

'All right, see you later Gill.'

***

Dotty and Jesse were sitting on the balcony sipping bottled water, keeping a look-out for the coach to transfer them to the airport. The cases were packed. Greek toot bought. Cigarettes loaded and Mary was doing a spring clean of the apartment. It was her way of not adding to the awful situation she'd got herself in with Niko. Somehow by polishing the apartment she felt less guilt.

Twenty minutes later, Mary joined the girls on the balcony.

'Mary, for someone who drank the amount you did last night, and got into a bitch fight this morning, you look bloody brilliant,' said Jesse.

'Thanks hun. Feeling a lot better now I've taken some tablets. Think I'll skip on eating though, just in case it goes through me.'

'Good idea,' agreed Dotty, nodding. 'Don't want you chucking up at the airport.'

'How long until the coach gets here?'

'Should have been here five minutes ago. You know what they're like, they'll be here in time.'

'We'll probably be the last pick up as we were first on. How's your hand, Jesse?'

Jesse lifted her visibly swollen knuckles. 'Bit sore, glad my case has wheels; wouldn't be wanting to pick much up at the moment.'

All three girls were watching the pool bar where Niko and Nicola were serving three of the women they had made friends with the night before. Nicola and Niko were at opposite ends of the bar but Jesse marvelled that they were even in the same space as one another.

Maybe their marriage would make it through this. *Perhaps they've made it through this kind of situation before*, Jesse mused.

'Have you thought about how we're going to

play this, getting to the coach, I mean?' Jesse asked Mary.

'Not really. I think we should just go quietly and not even attempt to say goodbye to anyone. The sooner we get out of this place, the better.'

***

They had managed to get onto the coach with no fanfare or drama. The driver took the cases from each of them and they made their way onto the coach. Dotty was the last to get her cases on, ensuring that the driver locked the doors properly before she'd get onto the coach.

Mary and Jesse watched from their window as Antonio, Stavros and Carlos came into view and each took a seat on a stool at the bar.

Jesse's stomach lurched as Steve came onto the coach and turned on the microphone.

'Well, good afternoon everyone! Hope you've had a great holiday here in Rethmynon. This is the last pick up now for the airport, so I'll hand you over to Kosta, who is your driver. When you get to the airport you'll go to check in gate 33. I've been informed that there are no delays, so happy days. Thank you for choosing Sky Tours Holidays, hope to see you again soon.' Steve glanced at Jesse just once as he left the coach to a round of applause from six or seven passengers.

Mary leaned in close to Jesse's left ear. 'Can't

believe that, can you?'

'No, but look, he's gone to the bar to sit with the rest of them. God, I just want to puke.' Jesse felt immensely sad that they were leaving on such a low note.

Nicola and Niko were behind the bar, Carlos, Antonio, Stavros and now Steve were all sitting on bar stools watching the girls with contempt.

Normally Jesse would have found something funny to say to lighten the mood, but she didn't have it in her, so Dotty stepped up to the plate by standing in the doorway and shouting 'Later tossers!' She gave them all the finger while simultaneously blowing a very loud raspberry.

CHAPTER 23

Dotty had been willing the seat belt sign to go off for ten full minutes. There was more turbulence than they had come to expect on these flights and she knew that Jesse must have been in a lot of discomfort with her arm up the way it was. This was the worst part about going on holiday for Dotty. No matter how much fun she had on holiday the return trip was always looming like a black cloud ready to spew its load over her.

Every single year she promised herself that she'd lose weight, and every single year she gained it. Tears were pricking as disappointment threatened to overwhelm her. She was filled with shame that her friend was so uncomfortable. If anyone wanted to get past her in the aisle they had to literally squeeze past her while she held onto her thigh to try to give them some room. She was probably at the stage of buying two seats but couldn't yet actually bring herself to do it. Every time they booked a holiday she would tell herself that it really wasn't that bad, that it was only a few hours of discomfort and it wasn't worth the extra trouble and expense of booking another seat. Sitting here with her friend squashed by her side, that decision now seemed unforgivably selfish.

Unbeknown to her friends Dotty had been thoroughly researching gastric bands and bypass surgery. She rolled the possible pros and cons around in her mind for what must have been the hundredth time. Four weeks previous to the holiday she had attended an appointment with a surgeon just to see what the possibilities and outcomes might be for someone as heavy as her. He had seemed confident that he could achieve what she had dreamed of for twenty years, but had also made it quite clear that a number of people did die on the operating table.

Death didn't seem such an outrageous risk right now. If she had to experience another ten minutes in this position she might well will it upon herself, she thought sadly.

Two things had been holding her back from making a decision - fear of death and fear of being thin.

She'd had this conversation with Jesse once but she hadn't really got her point across properly, as Jesse failed to understand how she could be fearful of being thin, the one thing they both wanted so dearly.

Up until five days ago Dotty had worried that being thin would cause her to be seen as a threat to all women, including her friends' married husbands. She wasn't exactly sure where this thought had come from but she definitely had a sense that she'd be considered a threat by some of her close friends if she lost her weight. She had tried to explain to Jesse how she was worried about standing out if she lost her weight and becoming noticeable to the opposite sex. Jesse had pointed out rather bluntly that Dotty was already very much standing out because of her weight and was hardly unnoticeable as she was. Her current weight drew negative attention and Dotty worried that it might draw even more attention if she didn't have a weight issue as she'd then be deemed attractive. This argument had been shot down by Stavros though, as he had gone for Dotty in spite of her weight, and in spite of his being married. She was going to have to take some time to contemplate the repercussions of this experience as at the moment she wasn't at all sure how she felt.

She let out an involuntary derisory snort. Who was she kidding? She'd risk dying on a cold slab of metal before putting herself and her friends through this situation again. The seatbelt lights blinked off just as the first tear fell onto her cheek. Unbuckling herself, she hefted herself out of her seat, muttered 'sorry' to Jesse and headed to the front of the plane where the stewards were making drinks. Dotty stood in what had become an all too familiar place, watching the wings slice through the clouds, waiting for the sensation of the seatbelt digging into her skin to wear off.

She envied the slender air stewardess who was busying herself just a metre away and she saw pity in her eyes when she smiled at Dotty. Wiping another tear that had fallen from her lashes Dotty decided that she would make another appointment to see a surgeon as soon as she got home.

I'd rather die on an operating table than suffer this slow death of misery for another day.

***

Mary had disguised her delight when it was announced that the three girls couldn't sit together. The best they could do was put Mary two rows back in an aisle seat. Jesse had suggested Mary pull her travel agent card but Mary said she wasn't bothered and she didn't mind being on her own. In fact, Mary was relieved that she wouldn't have to watch the usual drama of flying with Dotty and Jesse unfold.

Mary couldn't understand how Jesse always made such a fuss about the prospect of sitting next to Dotty but in the end always did, and never complained during the flights. Jesse had admitted that she'd rather experience the pain than have some stranger sit next to Dotty and make Dotty feel even worse. Mary supposed Jesse had a better understanding of how Dotty felt than she did.

For once she wasn't returning home wishing she'd lost weight for the holiday, as she'd felt fat throughout. She was left contemplating a much more depressing scenario.

Although she could feel no physical pain she gently touched her cheek, and shame blazed through her. The horror of what she'd done with Niko, and her subsequent behaviour when drunk slammed into her. What on earth had she been thinking? She'd never in her life felt that she'd actually risked someone's marriage. To her knowledge all the men she'd slept with kept her a secret and their wives were none the wiser. But not this time. Was she responsible for the end of someone's marriage?

God, I hope not. For just a few nights of excitement she had risked a lifetime of upset for Nicola.

Antonio, Carlos and Niko had watched her pull away in the coach. What on earth had they thought of her, she wondered. Then an image of Tom came to mind. Bloody hell, four men in one holiday, and she'd been naked with two of them. How on earth was that even possible? This wasn't like her at all. She didn't get herself into these situations, she was always in control.

Control? What control? Control's an illusion. There is no control.

She was aware she was going to need to keep convincing herself that the decision to take the pill was the right one too. She had taken up praying again over the past few days. Praying for her period to arrive early and for her not to have an STD. .

She had given Dotty long enough to compose herself, so she unbuckled her belt and made her way to her friend. Jesse was right. Eventually they would all look back on this holiday and laugh. Once the sting was taken out of it and the memory had been softened by time.

Eventually.

***

Jesse struggled to keep her face blank while the blood drained back into her left arm. The pins and needles were awful but she didn't want Dotty to see any pain etched on her face. As much as Jesse was frustrated with Dotty and her lack of determination to do anything about her increasing weight, she also cherished her friend and knew her heart was hurting. As soon as Dotty was positioned at the door with her back facing her, she vigorously rubbed her arms and flexed her shoulder joints.

She closed her eyes and relished the luxury of empty space for a moment. She knew that unless the seatbelt lights flashed again Dotty wouldn't sit down until the descent, until Jesse traded places with her, which she would soon enough. It was no surprise to see Mary join Dotty a little while later. Their body language looked solemn, which was exactly how Jesse now felt.

She had slept with two men, and had failed to take any action to prevent pregnancy. She had held the morning after pill for half an hour before throwing it down the sink, deciding she wouldn't take it after all. The doctors had told her years previously that she couldn't fall pregnant with Darren. And yet her stomach fluttered every time she wondered about it. Could they be wrong? They said she didn't ovulate regularly, but that didn't mean she didn't ovulate at all did it? Could this be some strange plan playing out before her? Had she come to a crossroads in her life without realising it until she'd chosen a road and stepped on its path?

Looking out of the window, knowing there was ocean beneath them but not seeing it due to the cloud cover, she wasn't sure about anything any more. Jesse had always believed there was a consequence for every action taken, that she made her own destiny, but chance had a lot to play in the cards you were dealt in life. Well, she had certainly not had any control the last seven days and she was fairly sure there were going to be repercussions.

She was ashamed of her behaviour and yet she couldn't regret that she had been made love to in a way that she'd never known possible. Putting everything that had happened after that night with Steve to one side, she'd felt real peace about that and had a genuine sense of being cherished. She had felt desired and her body hadn't once spoiled the experience. That was a first for Jesse and she felt sure it was a big step in getting back a sense of self-worth.

Of course that all fell to the wayside when she considered Ben and how she'd been duped by him. But trying to pull the positive out of the situation, she had shared a moment in time with someone who had promise. He was easily the most handsome man she had ever slept with and for a brief moment she had entertained sharing her life with another person. She hadn't been sure after her divorce from Darren that she would ever want to give her heart to someone again, but the experience with Ben, however painful it still was, had given her hope. Maybe she would even share a Garibaldi biscuit after all with the saxophonist when she returned home.

She could feel the smile playing around her lips and closed her eyes as the sun's rays suddenly broke over the wing of the plane and shone warmth onto her skin. What was that sensation in her stomach? Was it hope? She wasn't sure but in spite of her stomach bubbling she felt a peace within.

Was she really entertaining the idea of being pregnant? And if so, how come she was happy about that? It didn't sit with everything she'd been telling herself for the past few years. She couldn't stand kids - could she? Certainly she'd never held one in her life and couldn't bear other people's kids, but something in her spirit rose up and she knew – she just quietly knew - that she'd make a good mother. Her chest heaved with a single ragged sob. Her hand flew to her mouth in case more came, but they didn't. No-one seemed to have heard her and she smiled behind her hand.

She might not know the first thing about motherhood but she knew she would do a better job than her own mother had done with her. Better than that, she was determined to be a *great* mother.

The days of dancing on tables were probably

over, but maybe a day was ahead of her where she would twirl with a child that she could call her own.

She felt no embarrassment when tears welled up and over-spilled. She had no idea what these feelings meant, she'd never experienced anything like them before. She thought it might be hope as the sense of peace moving through her felt tangible. Was she expecting or expectant? She decided she would take time to analyse her feelings properly and over time, she wouldn't rush to understand this. She had no idea what the next few months would bring, but she knew that she would take one step at a time, one foot in front of the other, and keep moving forward.

Her cheeks glistened as she approached her two friends. Standing on tip toes she kissed Dotty's cheek tenderly and gave her a gentle squeeze. She took Mary's face in her hands and kissed both cheeks in turn before hugging her tightly.

After a long pause, Jesse raised her voice to be heard over the turbine engines and shouted with glee,

'So, hands up those who want to go back to Greece!'

The End.

ABOUT THE AUTHOR

J M Bartholomew is 43 and lives with her husband David and daughter Faith in Surrey.

For more information visit: www.JMBartholomew.co.uk

Three Fat Singletons is a work of fiction and any resemblance to real people is purely coincidental. Businesses, locations, and organizations while real are used in a way that is purely fictional

44914117R00231

Made in the USA
Charleston, SC
08 August 2015